THE STRANGER ON THE STAIRS

RUTH MANCINI

Also by Ruth Mancini

The Woman on the Ledge

The Day I Lost You

THE STRANGER ON THE STAIRS

RUTH MANCINI

CENTURY

CENTURY

UK | USA | Canada | Ireland | Australia
India | New Zealand | South Africa

Century is part of the Penguin Random House group of companies
whose addresses can be found at global.penguinrandomhouse.com

Penguin Random House UK,
One Embassy Gardens, 8 Viaduct Gardens, London SW11 7BW

penguin.co.uk

First published 2026
001

Copyright © Ruth Mancini, 2026

The moral right of the author has been asserted

Penguin Random House values and supports copyright. Copyright fuels creativity, encourages diverse voices, promotes freedom of expression and supports a vibrant culture. Thank you for purchasing an authorised edition of this book and for respecting intellectual property laws by not reproducing, scanning or distributing any part of it by any means without permission. You are supporting authors and enabling Penguin Random House to continue to publish books for everyone. No part of this book may be used or reproduced in any manner for the purpose of training artificial intelligence technologies or systems. In accordance with Article 4(3) of the DSM Directive 2019/790, Penguin Random House expressly reserves this work from the text and data mining exception.

Set in 11.75/16.63pt Times New Roman
Typeset by Six Red Marbles UK, Thetford, Norfolk

Printed and bound in Great Britain by Clays Ltd, Elcograf S.p.A.

The authorised representative in the EEA is Penguin Random House Ireland,
Morrison Chambers, 32 Nassau Street, Dublin D02 YH68

A CIP catalogue record for this book is available from the British Library

ISBN: 978–1–529–96854–5 (hardback)
ISBN: 978–1–529–96855–2 (trade paperback)

Penguin Random House is committed to a sustainable future
for our business, our readers and our planet. This book is made
from Forest Stewardship Council® certified paper.

For Andy

Prologue

Christy Nicholls knew instantly what was going to happen. She knew the second she opened the back door to him; she knew before he had locked it and pocketed the key, before he had grabbed her round the waist and begun to kiss her, and straight away, she decided she would do nothing. She wouldn't fight.

She turned her head towards the living room in a barely discernible movement, missed by him – she hoped. *Go*, her eyes said to her seven-year-old daughter, who was hovering there behind the door, out of sight. It was late – well after nine – and Bella was normally in bed at this time, but she had been off school with an upset stomach and had been asleep all day, so Christy had allowed her to stay downstairs for a while. He wouldn't have expected that.

As his fingers groped her buttocks, pulling her phone from her jeans pocket and flinging it across the kitchen, Christy threw a second warning glance at Bella and jerked her head. *Go. Leave.* Christy wasn't quite sure what Bella would do. Would she leave through the front door and run to a neighbour?

Or would she run upstairs and hide? *Go upstairs and don't come down until I tell you*, Christy said with her eyes, and Bella – who had always been an obedient little thing who could read her mother's expressions almost as well as she could read the Jacqueline Wilson books she adored – turned and ran.

It was because of her daughter that Christy had decided not to scream out or fight him. She wanted to spare her the trauma. She figured that if she just gave in and accepted it, he would be satisfied and leave. Later, she would tell Bella that everything was fine, that she had wanted him to kiss her, even though the very thought made her feel sick. But she knew he wasn't going to give up and go away until he'd got what he wanted, so she allowed him to push her to the kitchen floor.

As it turned out, Christy didn't know everything that was about to happen, not all of it. She had seen the raw lust in his eyes the last time he came. She recognised the belligerence that can take hold in a man like him upon being rejected. But she had underestimated the hatred he felt towards her, had misunderstood the person he really was. Had Bella not been in the house that evening, would it have made any difference? Would she have fought for her life sooner? Or would she have been blindsided, just the same? After all, he was always going to get away with what he was about to do because she couldn't tell anyone; she just wanted it to be over with. And so she simply wasn't prepared for what would happen next.

PART ONE

1

Twenty years later

Eve turned out of the southwest exit of the University Parks towards Broad Street, the smell of hot chocolate from the crêperie on the corner lingering in her nostrils, making her stomach growl. She hadn't eaten since breakfast – she'd been too nervous – and now she was starving. She'd messed this up already, she reflected. By the time she reached Caffè Nero in Blackwell's – the designated meeting place – she would be too light-headed to concentrate on the man sitting across the table from her, and too self-conscious to eat. Besides, at her own suggestion, this was meant to be a quick after-work cup of coffee. If she told him she was thinking of ordering a sandwich, he might interpret this as an invitation to dinner, which would be fine if she liked him, but what if she didn't?

As she passed the Pitt Rivers Museum and waited at the crossing, she came to a decision. She turned, walked quickly back towards the entrance to the Parks and joined the short queue at the crêpe van. She was terrible when her blood sugar was low. It gave her the worst kind of brain fog; she couldn't think, or talk, and if the café was busy, she wouldn't be able to filter out any background chatter or music. It would be better to arrive late and to feel well and coherent – and ready.

She ordered a chocolate crêpe and sat down at one of the outside tables. It was February but warm enough, and a nice setting, too, she thought, as she looked at a spread of snowdrops blanketing the grass beyond the path. Maybe she should have suggested meeting here instead? She'd have an easier escape, that's for sure. She imagined her date – Chris; his name was Chris – sitting opposite her, a snatch of bewilderment on his face as she jumped up without warning and broke into a run towards the safety of the trees that backed on to Norham Gardens. The thought made her laugh.

Seriously, though, she felt ridiculous. What was she even thinking about, joining a dating app at her age? This was her sister's doing – Sascha, who had met Graham, her husband, online twenty-two years ago and was quite evangelistic about it. 'You're not going to meet anyone in a bookshop, Evie,' she'd said. 'If you leave it to chance, you'll be waiting forever. You have to take charge of your life.'

Eve had been dismissive. What about Rich, she'd argued, her soon-to-be ex-husband? He'd met someone by chance, hadn't he? But by the time her divorce came through at Christmas, she had started to concede that her sister might be right. After all, what did she know about modern-world dating? She'd met Rich in the mid-1990s. The internet had barely existed and mobile phones were only just coming in. They'd married young and had grown together for a few years before slowly, over the next two decades, growing apart. When Rich had initiated their separation two years ago, after twenty-five years of marriage, Eve had agreed it was for the best. But it had felt momentous, all the same. Mackenzie, their only daughter, was all grown up and living with her boyfriend. Rich had quickly moved on, and here he was getting married again. He and his fiancée had already started a new family. Eve didn't resent either of them their happiness, but she couldn't help feeling left behind.

Now, she folded a napkin and dabbed at her lips, hoping that her make-up hadn't smudged. The crêpe had done the trick, though; she felt loads better. She brushed the crumbs away, pulled out her phone and fired off a quick message. *Sorry, running a little late. On my way.* She got up and walked briskly towards Blackwell's. She'd be fifteen minutes late, at most. Her date had described himself as easy-going, and if this was true, he wouldn't mind.

As she walked, Eve couldn't deny that along with the apprehension, she felt a quiver of excitement – euphoria even – at what could be waiting for her just around the corner. Sure, she'd need to keep her wits about her, but they'd spent the past three weeks chatting, her and this Chris, so he wasn't a *complete* stranger. He was nice enough looking, seemed smart and had a good job, and they did really seem to get on.

And they *would* be meeting in a bookshop, wouldn't they, even if it wasn't an entirely organic meeting.

As she turned the corner into Broad Street and saw Blackwell's up ahead, Eve was even able to begin imagining the story she might tell about this in the future. *We met in a bookshop.*

She took a deep breath as she pushed open the door.

2

It was beginning to get dark outside as Eve headed through the New Fiction department and up the stairs. Caffè Nero was on her right. Thankfully, it didn't look too busy. She glanced at the smaller section in front of the counter – all young people on laptops – and then walked through the main seating area by the windows, where they'd agreed the first one to arrive would find a table. There were, in fact, two empty tables beside the windows. She looked left and right, scanning the remaining ones before taking in the rest of the room, but none of the other tables was occupied by a man on his own, or by anyone who bore any resemblance to the profile photo of the guy she'd been talking to online.

She took her phone out of her pocket and pulled down the status bar to check her notifications. He still hadn't replied to the message she'd sent from the park. There were three bars on her 4G, so the signal strength in here must be decent enough, in which case – if he hadn't been able to reply – then maybe he'd been held up, too?

Eve hovered near the counter for a moment to see if anyone might look up and wave her over, but she already knew he wasn't there. She ordered a decaf oat latte and sat down at one of the spare tables by the window, picking up her phone again and inspecting the messages they'd both sent. There were two grey ticks next to her most recent one, indicating that her message had been delivered but not read. He was now over twenty minutes late, which was a little too long to have gone without letting her know, but she didn't want to jump to any conclusions. *I'm here*, she typed. *By the window. Am wearing a light green cardigan, jeans and there's a stupid fake fur coat draped over my chair.* She pressed SEND and two more grey ticks appeared.

She sipped at her coffee, eyes on the door, glancing down at her phone again intermittently, but still there was no answer. Anticipation soon gave way to disappointment as the realisation settled inside her: he wasn't coming. He'd changed his mind. But . . . what if something unexpected had happened to delay him, something awful even – a family emergency, perhaps – which had justifiably pushed her to the back of his mind?

She opened her Kindle reading app, thinking she'd wait ten more minutes. As she did so, her phone bleeped, making her jump. But it was just her sister, asking how it was going. Eve felt a small stab of irritation. Couldn't Sascha have at least waited until the date was meant to be over? She sighed, knowing deep down that she was annoyed with the wrong person, but sometimes Sascha could be just a little too . . . self-referential. She had a heart of gold and loved Eve to bits,

Eve knew that, but she also knew it wouldn't have occurred to Sascha – whose very first online date had gone immaculately and ended in marriage – that her younger sibling might have been stood up.

Eve decided not to respond to Sascha, then saw that the grey ticks on her message to Chris had turned blue. She eagerly opened the log to see if he was typing, but there was nothing, so she opened the dating app to see if he had perhaps messaged her there instead, but he hadn't, and he wasn't online. She waited another five minutes, then five minutes more, but the light had completely faded outside the window by now. Taking a last sip of her latte, she slid back her chair and pulled on her coat. She took one last look around the café, which was even emptier now, and headed towards the stairs.

She felt deflated. Logic told her she shouldn't take this personally, that it was silly to feel rejected by a person who barely knew you – who hadn't even met you – but she couldn't help but wonder what had gone wrong. After all, he'd been the one to suggest they meet up, and he'd liked her profile photo – at least that's what he'd told her. Eve had deliberately uploaded a recent one, one where she looked nice but which wasn't intended to disguise the fact that she was almost fifty. Mackenzie had suggested she could look nearer forty with a few filters, but Eve didn't see the point in pretending, and anyway, she had already mentioned that she had a twenty-six-year-old daughter, which would be a pretty good clue to her true age, albeit not an entirely accurate one.

The thought brought with it the usual reminder of Rich's new baby and of her own failure in this department. Mackenzie was adopted, and Eve couldn't deny that she'd felt quite upset when Rich and his fiancée had announced their pregnancy a few weeks ago, highlighting for the world that the fertility issues she and Rich had gone through were down to her and not him. And yes, she had mentioned this to Chris in their most recent conversation, but he had been really nice about it – in fact, she was pretty sure it was after she'd told him this that he'd suggested they meet. But she hadn't said *that* much about Rich and his new family, had she? She didn't think she had seemed bitter or obsessive because, truly, she wasn't. She wasn't upset with Rich. He was a good person. He had told her his news in a careful, tactful way, and although it had hurt – even though it still hurt when she thought about it – she was also genuinely happy for him.

So why hadn't Chris shown up?

She cast her mind back. They'd talked about their jobs: Chris was a property developer; she was a law lecturer at one of the colleges – the same one she and Rich had gone to. Yes, her job was the more academic of the two of them, but it wasn't like she taught at *the* university, the one everyone thought of when they thought of Oxford, and he'd seemed interested in her work, not fazed by it.

Well, if it *was* her age, she was glad he hadn't showed up. Chris was already fifty – he'd told her that – but if his preference was for a younger woman with no baggage, there were plenty of those to choose from on the dating sites, although did anyone really come with zero baggage? She doubted it.

Eve reached the bottom of the stairs and exited the lobby, then stopped abruptly, briefly disoriented as she realised she wasn't on the ground floor that led to the exit, but had instead gone down an extra flight and was now in the basement of Blackwell's, which housed the legendary Norrington Room. She hadn't been down here for years, and as she took in the incredible sight in front of her, all thoughts of her online dating fiasco were pushed from her mind. She had forgotten quite how awesome this room was. It was the biggest display of books she'd ever seen in her life, stretching almost as far as the eye could see. Looking out into this vast ocean of knowledge was, she thought, like looking up at the night sky and realising you were a part of something incredible, something so much bigger than you and your minuscule problems.

She began to walk around the perimeter, taking in the hundreds, even thousands of books in each section, before going down some steps and then down again into the lower terrace, where she knew there was a law section. There was a big law library at college, of course, but she was interested to see what was new here. She found the law books to her left and began browsing the shelves. As she did so, she became aware of a man standing behind her. Feeling a little uneasy, she turned to catch a glimpse of him. The bookshop was quiet at this time of the evening, and she had thought this section of the room would be empty.

'Sorry,' the man murmured, pushing a pale blue paperback back into its place on the shelf and stepping away from her.

She smiled warmly, feeling for him. She, too, was prone to over-apologising, and as far as she could tell, he hadn't done anything wrong. Or had he? For a split second, she wondered if this could be Chris, her date, but she quickly dismissed the idea as stupid and desperate. Chris had stood her up. Chris was an arsehole. Why did she want this man to be Chris?

She cast her eyes over his face, his hair, his clothes. He wasn't Chris, but he looked a similar age, give or take. He was dressed in jeans and an Oxford motorcycle jacket that had clearly seen better days but which she liked. It reminded her of a boy she once used to date before she met Rich, which was comforting somehow. There *had* been life before Rich.

Could he be Chris? After all, she'd only seen the one photo of him and it was worth asking, surely? What if he wasn't an arsehole? What if he was just shy? She hesitated, studying the man in front of her. He had greying brown hair which was nicely cut and he was wearing reading glasses – she could tell by the way he pulled them down his nose to look at her. Behind them, he had steely blue eyes.

She cleared her throat. 'Is your name Chris, by any chance?'

The man smiled, just a hint of a smile, as if he found this amusing but was trying not to show it. 'No,' he said. 'It's not.'

Eve felt herself flush. 'Sorry. It's just I was supposed to be meeting someone and—'

He raised a hand. 'It's fine. Really. You don't need to explain.' He smiled again. He had a nice smile.

'Are you a law student?' Eve asked.

He shook his head. 'I'm not really here to buy anything.'

'Me neither. And that's OK,' she told him. 'Or so says the placard on the wall over there.' She pointed.

The man eyed her. 'Does it?'

She nodded. 'It dates back to the nineteenth century. It says something along the lines of Mr Blackwell – the original Mr

Blackwell – wanting those coming in from the noisy cobbled streets to find a warm and friendly vibe, and that we should feel we can pick up and handle the books on the shelves without an obligation to buy.'

He looked back at her, unblinking. Eve couldn't tell if he was interested in the history of the bookshop or if he thought she was showing off. Maybe he just wanted her to leave him in peace so that he could get on with checking out the books before closing time.

'Anyway,' she said. 'I should be going.'

The man didn't answer, so she shrugged, gave a slight dip of her head and didn't say, 'Bye. Nice to meet you,' as she ordinarily might have done, but instead pulled her stupid fake fur coat around her shoulders and walked away. The coat wasn't hers, in fact. It was Sascha's, and she wished she hadn't worn it.

'I hope you find him,' the man called after her gently, as she reached the steps to the upper level.

She turned and smiled, feeling self-conscious, then headed up the stairs.

3

Four months earlier

The nightmare began as it always did – with the noises: the scraping of a chair across the floor; the banging. The muffled shrieks: one, two, three. More banging, and then a loud crash. Bella woke with a start and lay still until almost all of the sounds had subsided – all but the gentle thud, thud, thud against the floor in the kitchen beneath her. Or was that her heart beating? She wasn't sure. At first she was too scared to get out of bed, but eventually she pushed back her duvet and swung her legs out, then made her way across the landing towards the stairs.

She was halfway down before she saw him.

'Shh!' he said, putting a finger to his lips. 'Your mother's sleeping. Go back to bed.'

And then she woke again, her heart pounding, her body stiff with fright.

She squeezed her eyes shut and breathed deeply, in and out, waiting for her heart rate to return to normal. When she was as sure as she could be that she was no longer asleep, she took a chance and peeked out. The curtains were open, the way she always left them, a slant of light from the street lamp sloping down her bedroom wall. She was pretty sure this was real, although in the nightmare she was usually here, in her own flat in Kentish Town, not in the bedroom she'd had at her mum's house in Streatham or the one at her dad's, where she had lived after that, so it could be difficult to tell.

The nightmares had followed her from house to house. Even now, they were as vivid as they had been the day they started, although she couldn't actually remember when that was. After her mother died, obviously. Sometimes, she would go into the kitchen and see everything she saw that day – and more. Sometimes she would see her mother's skull, the flesh partially rotted away, and she would wake up screaming. More often, and especially lately, she never got as far as the kitchen or even the living room. The man would appear at the foot of the stairs, shushing her and telling her to go back to bed.

She didn't have any stairs in her flat, nor was there a kitchen beneath her, and now that she was fully awake, she was able to recognise this with relief, but she never seemed able to hack the nightmare to point this out. She had read that it was possible to influence your dreams; in fact, she and her former therapist had worked on the assumption that her subconscious had added the man as some sort of barrier or saviour – someone who would stop her from ever reaching the kitchen and finding her mother the way she had.

But the man didn't feel like a saviour; he scared her. He had always scared her, and lately she had begun to wonder if this part of the nightmare could be real. Her dad had dismissed this out of hand when she'd suggested it – it didn't fit with the evidence, he said. She had gone to bed straight after Jamie Clarke arrived and had slept through the night, not waking again until seven the next morning; that's what she'd told the police at the time, and she couldn't go changing it now.

Her boyfriend, Justin, agreed. 'I'm not being funny, Bel, but if you came downstairs and saw him, surely he would have killed you too?'

This was a good question, of course. And Justin was right: it wasn't funny. It was a horrific thing to think about, and so she tried not to. And it wasn't as if she had the nightmares every night. Sometimes she would go months without having one, and sometimes she would go weeks without thinking about Jamie Clarke at all.

But recently she'd been thinking about him a lot, which was understandable, of course, because she had just heard that they were letting him out of prison.

And she was the person who had put him there.

4

Sarah Kellerman pulled her laptop towards her and clicked the link on the secure file she'd been sent by her contact at Truth for Justice. She could hear her boyfriend, Will, in the kitchen, rattling mugs and teaspoons. He wasn't in court today. They both had trial preparation or other paperwork to do, which often meant working from home together. Separately but together. She liked it when they did that.

It was almost exactly three years since she'd left the job she'd hated at the high-street law firm on Highbury Corner, and when she woke in the mornings, she still wanted to pinch herself. Going freelance had been scary financially at times, but it was the best move she'd ever made. She had parked her duty solicitor slots with a firm in Warren Street and acted as a consultant for them, covering her own slots on the rotas and doing whatever else she could to help out when they needed an extra pair of hands. But she was now in the enviable position of being able to take on the work that interested her most.

And, of course, the financial burden had eased considerably since Will had moved in with her. His work as a barrister was no more secure than hers, but between the two of them they were able to manage the mortgage of her house and the bills. They'd met when Sarah had instructed him on the Ellis Stevens case, and they had finally got together the same year she'd left her last firm. Will had residency at 5 Temple Square Chambers in the City and his own heavy caseload. But – their romantic relationship aside – he was the best barrister she knew, and she continued to instruct him on her cases whenever she could.

She looked up as Will entered the living room. He was wearing his 'suit', as he called it: grey joggers and a white T-shirt. His feet were bare and his chin was covered in a light stubble. He placed a mug of coffee on the table in front of her.

'What have you got?' he asked.

'A new case. It's from Sam at TFJ.'

'The appeal charity?'

Sarah nodded.

'Anything interesting?'

'You remember Christy Nicholls? The woman found by her seven-year-old daughter after she'd been raped and killed in her own home?'

Will looked at her, surprised. 'South London. Streatham, if I remember rightly?'

'You do.'

'That was a while back.'

'Twenty years ago – 2003.'

'They convicted the boyfriend, didn't they?'

'Yes. He's just been released on life licence. Stuck in more than one appeal in the last two decades. Wants another shot to clear his name.'

Will sat down on the sofa beside her and studied her expression more closely, watching her eyes as they moved across her laptop screen. 'You OK?'

'Yeah.' Sarah sighed. 'It's just . . . pretty horrible stuff. If he did it, he must have really hated her. Or hated women,' she corrected herself. 'He beat her up pretty badly – choked her and gave her a fractured cheekbone and three dislocated fingers. Pushed a rag into her mouth to gag her, then used duct tape for good measure. The primary cause of death was suffocation.'

'What was the evidence?'

'DNA found on her bra and in two other "crime-specific" locations. And he was positively identified by three witnesses who all said they saw him that night.'

'What did *he* say?'

'That he was her boyfriend. The prosecution case was that he wasn't but wanted to be, that he was stalking her. Either way, she knew him. There was no forced entry. He'd been inside her house more than once, he said, and they'd touched and kissed.'

'Explaining the DNA.'

'Yes.' Sarah paused, still reading from her laptop screen. 'Although the vaginal swabs were "inconclusive".'

Will considered this. 'That could mean a few things – that there was no profile found at all, due to poor quality of the test material, or that there was a mixed one . . .'

'The prosecution case was that he'd used a condom. He denied it. Said they hadn't had actual sex. Other than that, the case was reliant on ID evidence, most crucially from the daughter. She'd seen him at the house before and told the jury she was one hundred per cent certain it was him. The case pretty much turned on this.'

'She gave live evidence?'

Sarah looked down again, perusing the case summary. 'No. It looks as though her ABE video evidence was admitted under the hearsay provisions.'

Will shrugged. 'It happens. It would take a judge with cojones to kick it out.'

Sarah nodded, her eyes moving back to the page. 'His first appeal challenged the daughter's reliability and also that of the two key witnesses.'

'On what basis?'

'They all knew who he was. They'd seen him before, so were bound to pick him out during the ID procedure, which had a bolstering effect on an otherwise weak case. That's what his lawyers argued. The Court of Appeal threw it out. Said there was no reason to believe the witnesses were mistaken, that the police had followed Code D and that the forensic evidence against the boyfriend was strong.'

Will nodded thoughtfully.

'And then in 2012, he applied to the CCRC to have the case sent back again. He asked for the victim's clothing to be retested on the basis that the vaginal swab had been inconclusive at the time, but that advances had since been made in forensic science. His request was refused.'

'What reason did they give?'

'Same again. There was already sufficient forensic evidence that he'd had sexual contact with her before she died.'

'Hmm,' Will said. 'Might be worth looking at that again. Maybe get your own testing done.'

Sarah eyed him. 'It does raise some questions, doesn't it?'

He smiled. 'If you're asking me if I mind you taking on a pro bono case, the answer is that I think you should do what you feel is right.' He leaned over, kissed her and stood up, then picked up his laptop and walked over to the table beside the window where he usually worked.

Sarah looked across at him, feeling grateful, once again, that she had both the freedom and the support to follow her instincts. Gareth, her old boss, would have been dead against her pursuing a case like this, one where there was no money. But Will didn't need to ask if Sarah was going to get paid. He knew it would fall on him to support them all – himself, Sarah and Ben, her nine-year-old son – for the time it took while she wandered down this particular rabbit hole, and yet he hadn't batted an eyelid. Because *she* cared, *he* cared, which meant the world to her.

Gareth should care, too, Sarah mused as she scrolled through the crime scene photographs, feeling sick as she always did. The prosecution should care. The Criminal Cases Review Commission should care. The Court of Appeal should care. Because if there was even the slightest chance that the person who'd been convicted was *not* the person who had committed this terrible crime, then not only had a man's entire life been ruined, but the person who had killed Christy Nicholls could still be out there, preying on vulnerable women.

He could, at this very moment, have found his next victim.

5

Eve cycled along the Banbury Road and turned left into North Parade, where she stood her bike up against the wall in the alley next to the produce store. She glanced down briefly at the baskets of apples on the bench in front of the window before opening the shop door. Mackenzie was coming for dinner this evening on her own – without her boyfriend, Simon – which Eve was really looking forward to. Not that she had anything against Simon. He was a nice man – a really nice man, in fact. But it wasn't often that she got her daughter all to herself.

Of course this was a pity visit, Eve knew that. Julia, Rich's fiancée, had asked Mackenzie to be her maid of honour and the two of them had been in cahoots for months about everything, from dresses to venues to wedding cakes. In less than a month, Mackenzie would be walking down the aisle behind Julia, who had just had her twenty-week scan and had told Mackenzie she was having a little girl, which had made the baby, the wedding – all of it – seem far more real, somehow.

Eve was glad her daughter cared enough about her to

recognise that she might be finding it all a bit hard, but she wanted this to be the nicest of evenings and she was determined to keep her feelings to herself. Mackenzie was delighted at the thought of having a little sister, and Eve knew that in time she, too, would get used to the idea of Rich being a father again. In a year from now, she would probably be buying wool from the yarn shop next door to the produce store and knitting cute little cardigans for the baby (who was going to be called Daisy).

In the meantime, she would buy the best ingredients and cook spaghetti bolognese, Mackenzie's favourite meal, and she'd say, 'Be careful. The sauce is hot,' the way she always used to when Mackenzie was little, which was guaranteed to make her daughter smile. They'd drink a little too much wine together and she'd let Mackenzie get out her make-up box and do smoky eyes for her and put the photos on Facebook, even if Eve started laughing as she'd done the last time, when her make-up had streaked and she'd looked like a clown.

'Hello, Eve. How are you?' said Pete, the shop owner, from behind the counter as she entered. 'What are you after?'

'Some mince for a bolognese.'

'Sure. Help yourself.'

Eve opened the fridge and selected a pack of grass-fed beef, which she knew would have been locally sourced. She then selected three artisan cheeses, some spelt sourdough and a large bulb of chicory to make a salad, then tapped her bank card against the card machine as Pete held it out. She turned to leave, conscious that the shop doorbell had rung while she was being served and that another customer was waiting, but then she remembered she'd need herbs. She had some dried basil, but that was all. 'I don't suppose you sell oregano?' she asked, turning back towards the counter.

'Sorry.' Pete shook his head. 'You could try the nine-to-nine on the corner.'

'Thanks. I will.' Eve turned again, stepping aside for the man behind her. As she did so, he moved in the same direction.

'Sorry,' they both said together, and their eyes met for a second or two. He wasn't wearing glasses this time, but she could see it was him – the man from the bookshop. Blackwell's. The one she'd bumped into in the Norrington Room.

The man backed away, looking awkward, then shot her a faint smile of recognition. Eve responded with the briefest of smiles before pushing her purchases into her rucksack and opening the door to the street.

'Hello again,' she heard Pete say. 'What can I get you?'

So, he's local, Eve thought to herself as she shut the door behind her, and then it crossed her mind that if she really wanted to – which, of course, she didn't – she could go back to the shop tomorrow and ask Pete about him.

But she wouldn't. Why would she?

Maybe because . . . well, it seemed . . . serendipitous? Didn't it? To have never met someone before and then to bump into them twice in the same week. Both times, she'd been feeling a little low, a little overlooked, a little invisible. And then he'd appeared and he'd . . . *seen* her. They'd seen each other. And there was something there – something between them – wasn't there? Some kind of chemistry? A connection of sorts?

Eve, she reprimanded herself, tutting out loud as she collected her bicycle from the alley and wheeled it down the street to the shop on the corner. You're just making something out of nothing because you're lonely, and because Online Chris appears to have done a runner, and because this is the first half-decent-looking bloke you've met since you broke up with Rich.

She leaned her bike up against a wall opposite the entrance to the convenience store and went inside. When she came out, there he was again, walking down North Parade in her direction. Eve immediately felt flustered and began fiddling with the straps on her rucksack to avoid making eye contact, but as he got closer, he altered his path slightly and came towards her, then stopped.

'Did you manage to get any?' he asked, his eyes fixed on hers.

Eve stared at him. What was he talking about? She cast her mind back to the last thing he'd said to her in Blackwell's, about her date. *'I hope you find him.'* Was he talking about *sex*? Was he being *lewd*?

She glared at him. 'What?'

'Oregano,' he said. 'Did they have any?'

Eve instantly felt stupid. 'No. Just . . . spices. They have all the spices but no herbs. I got cinnamon and turmeric, but . . .' She sighed. Maybe she should just stop talking.

'There's some in my garden,' he said.

He had a London accent, Eve noticed. South London, in fact. She'd grown up there and, like his biker jacket, it felt familiar. She hesitated. 'Oregano?'

He nodded.

'At this time of year?' Eve didn't doubt him, but if he had some, then maybe she did too. She wasn't a very good gardener, but she was fairly certain she had planted either sage or oregano in the communal garden last summer, along with some chives and lemon balm.

'Yeah,' he said confidently. He pushed his hands into his jeans pockets, shrugging. 'It's early, I know, but there's a little there and I don't need it.'

Eve hesitated. 'Are you . . . near?' she found herself asking.

'Five minutes away,' he said. 'I'm going home now, if you want to come and grab some. Otherwise, the gate's usually open. It's twenty-one Norham Gardens. You could just go round the back and help yourself.'

'Norham Gardens?' Eve asked, surprised. 'You live in Norham Gardens?'

He looked slightly uncomfortable for a moment, then nodded.

'Wow. Those houses are—' Eve had been about to say 'worth millions', but stopped herself. Tens of millions, more like. 'Lovely,' she said.

He eyed her for a moment, then said, 'Yeah.' He hesitated for a second or two longer. 'It's in the border next to the lavender. There are secateurs in the bucket by the back door.'

He turned and began to walk away.

'Wait,' Eve called after him, pushing her rucksack over her shoulders and grabbing her bike. Norham Gardens was literally on her way home. 'If it's OK, I'll come now. I kind of need it for this evening. If that's OK?' she repeated.

'Sure.'

She fell into step beside him, pushing her bike as they walked the few yards to the Banbury Road. He stopped to cross, so she followed his lead, waiting for a break in the traffic and wheeling her bike along quickly. It was a blowy afternoon and she had to grip the handles hard. She followed him into the road opposite, where they walked side by side on the pavement in silence, him with his hands in his pockets, her with her bike alongside, trying not to run it into him or into the parked cars that lined the street.

A spattering of rain dotted her handlebars and she looked up at the trees swaying above them. 'It's getting a bit wild,' she observed.

'Yeah,' he agreed. 'It won't last.'

'You've seen the forecast?'

He nodded but didn't elaborate.

They turned right. Norham Gardens was the next road. When they had almost reached it and he still hadn't spoken, she filled the silence. 'I'm making a spaghetti bolognese for my daughter. She's coming over for dinner tonight.'

He didn't answer straight away and Eve felt even more awkward.

'How old is your daughter?' he asked, after a beat.

'Twenty-six,' Eve said. 'Twenty-seven next month. Do you have children?'

He shook his head. 'No.'

The conversation wasn't exactly rolling along, Eve thought. She wondered what he did for a living that allowed him to own a house in Norham Gardens, but it felt rude to ask. Maybe he was some kind of entrepreneur, or maybe it was inherited and he didn't need to work.

'I'm Eve, by the way,' she said as they neared the end of the street.

He hesitated, then said, 'I'm Joe.'

There was a big, noisy building development going on at the top of Norham Gardens and she followed Joe around the site hoarding, trying not to wheel her bike through the mud. They walked a little further down the street until Joe stopped outside a beautiful Victorian red-brick detached house, which had the traditional gothic turrets of the rest of the architecture in the road.

'This is me,' he said, walking onto the gravel driveway, where a light grey Volvo was parked in front of a garage. There was a black metal gate to the side of the house and he opened it. 'You can leave your bike there,' he said, pointing back towards the driveway. 'It will be fine.'

Eve smiled to herself, thinking that if a thief were lurking nearby, her old bicycle would probably be way down at the bottom of the list of items they'd choose. The Volvo wasn't exactly new, though, she noticed. In fact, it was a little beaten up. But she wasn't altogether surprised; in the past, she had known a couple of fairly well-off people who had owned old cars and worn scruffy clothes, and she had liked them for it. She had assumed they didn't want, or need, to flaunt their wealth.

She followed Joe into the garden, which wasn't big but was beautiful. Perfectly landscaped, it had a pretty antique gazebo in the middle and a spread of wild flowers that looked curated. The trees at the bottom bordered the Parks. She looked up at the back of the house, which was surrounded by scaffolding. There was clearly building work going on here, too.

'What are you doing?' she asked, still looking up.

Joe followed her gaze. 'A loft conversion. I've just put the windows in.'

'Wow. You'll have the best bedroom in Oxford,' she said, then felt herself flush. 'I meant . . . you know. You'll have the best view.'

He smiled. It was the first time he'd smiled since they'd bumped into each other in the shop. 'I know what you meant,' he said.

'You'll probably be able to see *my* bedroom.' Eve laughed, then cringed again and added, 'I just meant that . . . I live over there, on the other side of the park.' What the fuck was wrong with her? She was normally far more relaxed around men. At least, she had been when she was with Rich. It was weird, she reflected, how much more self-assured you were when you were in a relationship, when you had someone at home who loved you, and you weren't looking for anyone else. She now doubted everything: her looks, her intellect, her social ability. She remembered how critical Mackenzie had been of her during her teens, the way she'd walked ten paces behind her mother in the street or shrunk down in the car seat next to her, trying to disappear from view. 'You're so *weird*, Mum,' she'd said, so often. 'Why can't you be *normal*?'

Did Joe think she was weird? Did everyone?

But Joe didn't seem interested in her gaffes, she realised, as she watched him fetch the secateurs and walk over to a sprawling plant in a border next to the patio. He was entirely focused on the task in hand, and that was the problem, she supposed. She was trying to connect with him and wasn't getting anywhere.

'Here you go,' he said, using the secateurs to snip at a small branch of tiny leaves. He held it out. 'Do you need a bag?'

'No, don't worry. I'll just stick it in here.' She removed her rucksack from over her shoulder and opened it.

'Do you want some more?'

'Go on, then. A little.' She cast her eyes over the flower beds, which were already blooming with flowers she didn't know the names of. 'God,' she said, 'this is beautiful. Really. You're a far better gardener than I am. I think virtually everything I planted last year is either dead or dying.'

He shrugged. 'You may be surprised. It depends what you planted. It might just be too early.'

'Hmm,' she said. 'I don't know about that. I think the frost has taken the majority. I just don't have the time.'

'What do you do?' he asked, his back to her.

'I work at one of the colleges in Oxford,' she said. 'I'm a lecturer.'

'In law?'

'Yes. How did you—' she asked, before remembering which section of the Norrington Room he'd first seen her in. 'Oh, yeah.'

He handed her another branch and said, 'I can give you a cutting if you want.'

'Oh God,' she said. 'Now you're trusting me with your herbs.'

It sounded funny and this time they looked directly at each other and laughed.

'So, is it a special occasion?' he asked. 'This dinner for your daughter?'

Eve nodded. 'Yeah, I suppose it is. I mean . . .' She sighed heavily. 'I wish it *wasn't*. I wish I saw more of her, but . . .'

And then, to her horror, she started to cry.

Joe stood up straight, placing the secateurs on the edge of the wall.

'I'm sorry,' she said, wiping her eyes with the back of her hand. 'You must think I'm a complete idiot. Honestly. It's just that . . .'

Joe waited, blinking, saying nothing.

'I think I'm losing my family,' she said.

Joe nodded, and she could see that he was, indeed, making a judgement about her, but it wasn't a negative one.

'It's like that song,' she sniffed. 'That one by Keane. "Everybody's Changing". But . . .'

'But you're not. You can't.'

'No.' She shook her head. 'I'm not. I can't. And it's not that I don't want to. It's just that . . .' She wiped her eyes again, feeling a weight in her chest. She breathed deeply. 'It's just that I was with someone for over a quarter of a century and . . . and even though I have friends and a good job – a good career – it's not enough. I'm ashamed to admit that, and it's such an anti-feminist thing to say, but it still feels as though my whole identity was bound up in being a wife and a mother, and . . . and now that I'm not . . . I just don't know where to begin.'

She looked up at him, feeling the most raw and vulnerable she'd felt in years.

Joe looked back at her, his eyes soft, and said, 'Can I make you a cup of tea?'

6

Mackenzie arrived for dinner at six thirty that evening. Eve boiled the spaghetti, heated the pasta bowls and set out trays on the worktop.

'Red or white?' Mackenzie said, holding up a bottle of each.

'Red, I think. Thank you.'

Eve watched her daughter moving around her small, soulless kitchen, fetching glasses from the cupboard and pouring the wine, and she wondered what she thought of the way her mother now lived. Eve's home was not really a home; it was just the upstairs floor of a boxy 1970s semi-detached house in New Marston that had been divided into flats. It was a far cry from her old house in Headington, the house Mackenzie had grown up in, and it wasn't the kind of property in which Eve had ever imagined herself living, but first Rich had gone, then Mackenzie had moved in with Simon, and then Rich had offered to buy her out. At the same time, a work colleague had offered her this rental, and she had just wanted it over and done with. She had enough money from the sale to buy something nicer, but it had felt like such a huge and time-consuming decision, one that seemed easier to put off. And it was convenient here; in fact, the location was superb. She could cycle to work in fifteen minutes, and it was roughly the same distance into Oxford, through the Parks.

'Have you come straight from work?' she asked, eyeing her daughter's belted trench coat and smart black trousers.

Mackenzie nodded, taking a gulp of wine. 'I've been in town all day. I got a bus here from the station. I had a merchandising event at Harrods.'

'Ooooh. Harrods,' Eve said. 'How posh.'

Mackenzie shrugged dismissively. 'It's what buyers do, Mum. It's market research. I don't work for Harrods.' She took off her coat and draped it over a chair.

'I love your blouse,' Eve said.

Mackenzie glanced down at herself, as if she'd forgotten what she was wearing. 'Thanks. It's from Zara.'

Eve drained the spaghetti and tipped it into the bowls, then spooned the sauce on. 'Be careful,' she said. 'The sauce is—'

'Hot,' Mackenzie finished for her, smiling and picking up her tray, but her smile was tight, Eve noticed.

'So, what have you been up to?' Mackenzie asked, walking into the living room with her food and sitting down on the sofa.

Eve felt a stirring inside her. 'You mean . . . today?'

'Well, any day, really.' Mackenzie picked up her fork and folded the sauce into her spaghetti. 'I meant, generally.'

'Oh, you know. The usual,' Eve said, sitting down in the armchair and balancing her tray on her knees. 'Lectures. Tutorials. Lesson planning.'

'Aside from work.'

Eve hesitated. 'Well, I met someone,' she began.

'What? Online?' Mackenzie smiled and put down her fork.

'Well . . . no.'

'Where, then?'

Eve hesitated, taking a sip of wine. 'I bumped into him in Blackwell's, actually, and then bumped into him again and . . . and he invited me back to his house to . . .' She paused.

'Mum!' Mackenzie grinned. 'You didn't tell me about this!'

'Well, there wasn't really anything to tell until today, and actually, there still isn't. Not really. It was more of an opportunistic thing.'

'Opportunistic?' Mackenzie scoffed.

'Well, I needed some oregano and he overhead me asking for it in the shop and invited me back to his garden to pick some.'

Mackenzie burst out laughing. 'Oh yeah. That old chestnut.' She lowered her voice, imitating a male one. 'Wanna come back to my place and see my oregano?'

Eve smiled at her. 'It wasn't like that at all,' she said. 'It definitely wasn't a pick-up line – in fact, he was kind of cool with me to begin with, as if he wished he hadn't offered, and if I'm honest, I still don't really know if it's anything, but . . .' She trailed off.

'But?' Mackenzie persisted. 'Go on. What did you talk about?'

Eve hesitated, trying to sort out the conversation she'd had with Joe into the bits she could tell her daughter about and the bits she couldn't, but she already knew she wouldn't be left with much. The truth was that she'd mostly talked about Rich and Mackenzie and how she felt about the way that Mackenzie had bonded with Julia over the wedding preparations, and how she'd come to realise that Mackenzie and Julia were more alike, and had far more in common than she and Mackenzie had ever had, which hurt, but it had somehow made her feel better to say it out loud. And to give Joe some context for the way she felt about Rich's new baby, she'd told him that she hadn't been able to have children of her own, which had necessarily meant telling him they'd adopted Mackenzie when she was seven. And because Joe had been such a good listener, she'd told him quite a lot more than she'd originally intended to.

'Oh, nothing important,' she said now. 'He made me a cup of tea, that's all, and we just chatted about this and that.'

Mackenzie frowned and swallowed a mouthful of food. 'Well, you're still here, so it looks as though he didn't try to poison you.'

Eve thought about this for a moment. She supposed, with hindsight, that drinking a cup of tea that had been made for her by a complete stranger – someone she'd only just met – wasn't the wisest thing she'd ever done. But, on the other hand, she'd been upset and he had felt sorry for her. What was he supposed to do? Besides, he hadn't exactly lured her there secretly. It had been broad daylight. Anyone could have seen her with him, watched her walking down the street with him and going into his house.

'He lives in Norham Gardens,' she said, watching her daughter's face, knowing this would impress her.

'Norham Gardens? Are you serious? As in . . . the most expensive street in Oxford?'

'Well, I'm not sure if it's that, but . . .'

'What does he do?' Mackenzie blinked slowly at her.

'I'm not sure,' Eve admitted. 'I didn't like to ask.'

'Why not?'

'Because it might seem . . . I don't know. Vulgar?'

'Well, it should be easy enough to find out,' Mackenzie said eagerly, setting her tray down on the coffee table and picking up her phone. 'What's his surname?'

'I don't know,' Eve said. 'I didn't ask.'

'What number does he live at?'

'No,' Eve protested. 'Please don't google him. I don't want you to try and find out. I just . . . I just want to let things happen naturally.'

Mackenzie dropped her phone into her lap. 'So, do you think you will see him again?'

Eve considered the question. 'Honestly?' she said. 'I don't know.'

Mackenzie left an hour later, saying she and Simon were going to visit his parents in Dorset the next day and wanted to make an early start. Eve stacked the dishwasher, sliced and wrapped the sourdough before putting it in the freezer, and put the uneaten cheese and salad into the fridge. As she wiped the surfaces down, she found herself daydreaming about the possibility that this might not be her kitchen for much longer, that – instead of living like one of her students – she might, one day in the near future, find herself living in a nice house, with a nice man.

She was thinking about Joe – she knew that. What was it she liked about him? Mackenzie hadn't asked the question, and Eve had barely had time to think about it herself, but there was definitely something, something more than just the fact that there wasn't anyone else on the horizon. Was it because of where he lived? She didn't think she was that shallow.

Eve walked into the bedroom without turning the light on and went over to the window, ready to close the blinds. She hesitated, then flung the window open instead, breathing in a lungful of cool air as she peered out into the vastness of the night sky. A band of cloud bordered the horizon. Up above – stable, dependable, ever present – was the bright, silver orb of the moon along with a few lone stars. Directly ahead, she knew, was the park, and behind it, Norham Gardens.

She smiled. This was the very same stretch of sky that Joe could see from his bedroom window, if he were looking out. She thought of his intense blue eyes and the aura of sadness around him as they'd sat together at the table in his kitchen, as he'd listened to her talk. It was as if there was something missing for him, as there was for her; something they both craved. Something dark had happened in his past, she felt sure of it.

As she climbed into bed and closed her eyes, she could almost feel his pain, his hurt, his *need* radiating towards her as he lay in his own bed on the other side of the park.

7

Sarah stopped reading and looked up as she heard Will's footsteps on the path outside and his key in the front door, which then slammed shut.

'Hi!' he called out.

'In here,' Sarah called back.

Will opened the living-room door and peered round. 'Cup of tea?'

'Glass of wine, I think.'

'Hmm. That bad?'

Sarah sighed. 'No. Not really. It's just that it's like pulling teeth, trying to get anything from the court. Or the police.'

Will walked over and sat down on the sofa beside her, shrugging off his coat as he did so. 'What have you got so far?'

'The prosecution bundle. Well, some of it. The IDPC. Several witness statements. Jamie's pre-cons.'

'What has he got?'

'Not a lot. A couple of cautions as a teenager. A criminal

damage from 1999. He got a fine, so it can't have been anything much.'

'And?'

'That's it.'

'So, nothing for violence?'

'No.'

'Doesn't mean he didn't attack anyone, of course,' Will murmured. 'It just means he didn't get caught.'

Sarah smiled. 'Have you been prosecuting today, by any chance, Mr Gaskin?'

'I have, Ms Kellerman,' Will nodded. 'But this evening, I am definitely defending.'

'Who are you defending?'

'You.' Will pulled her into his arms and kissed her. 'First, I'm going to bring you that glass of wine, then I'm going to cook you a delicious frozen pizza, and make a salad to go with it. Then I'm going to go and collect Ben from Andy's while you put your feet up and binge a bit of *Boston Legal* or *The Good Wife*, or whatever it is you consider to be switching off but actually isn't. And then, after I've got Ben bathed and off to bed, I'll let you catch me up with whatever you're watching and I'll watch an episode with you. And massage your feet.'

Sarah smiled. 'What have I done to deserve all this? Or . . . wait. Am I yet to do it?'

Will eyed her, his own smile fading. 'I just think you need fortification.'

Sarah shifted in her seat, pulling away from him slightly. 'You think I'm wasting my time on this case?'

'I'm not saying that.' Will shook his head. 'But we both

know that when it comes to the defence getting access to what the police and the prosecution get access to, it's already far from a level playing field. And that's in an ordinary trial. When it comes to an appeal – and especially one that's twenty years old and has been refused twice before – well . . . you're still playing uphill, but this time you're two nil down.' Will scratched his chin. 'And you're well into injury time.'

Sarah smiled briefly at his sporting analogy, then sighed. He was right. 'There's no money for a start,' she agreed.

'Of course there isn't,' Will said wryly. 'The state is never going to pay to prove itself wrong.'

Sarah looked up at him. 'Are you OK with this, Will? With me working for nothing? I mean, we'll get some administrative support from the City law firms, and likely get some money for testing and stuff, but you can't Crowdfund something like this.'

Will gazed at her for a moment, then said, 'We'll make it work, Sarah. Don't worry about money. If Sam thinks there's a case, a route to appeal—'

'She thinks there might be. But we'll only know for sure if I can get hold of all of the defence papers, the police file, the analogue tapes from the original trial. And then I've got to get the tapes listened to and transcribed, and I'll have to get funding for that, and that's assuming they still have them and they haven't degraded to the point where that's impossible.'

'You'll find a way.'

Sarah looked at him plaintively. 'All of this . . . it might take a year. Longer, even. Maybe three to bring it to a conclusion.'

Will inhaled deeply. 'I know, and that's fine.'

'Are you sure?'

Will looked into her eyes. 'Would you do it if it was for me?'

Sarah nodded, feeling her throat tighten. 'I'd fight forever. I'd never give up.'

'Well then, you need to take the case,' Will said, squeezing her hand. 'He deserves a chance. And I'm here for you to bounce off, if he's OK with that?'

Sarah nodded. 'Thank you. I'd love that, and I'm sure he will too. I'm speaking to him tomorrow.'

'Good,' Will nodded. 'I'll help as much as I can.'

8

Bella lay rigid in bed after yet another nightmare. They were getting more frequent, more vivid, more terrifying. Sometimes Justin would be with her and he would wrap her in his arms and hold her until her limbs loosened and her heart stopped pounding, but there was nothing he could do to stop the bad dreams from coming. He knew, as well as she did, that they were happening because of Jamie Clarke.

It had been quite a shock, when she'd been told he was getting out of prison. She had thought it might never happen because he had refused to admit what he'd done to her mother. But first he'd been moved to an open prison, then he was up in front of the parole board, and then she had been contacted by her victim liaison officer, who had dropped the bombshell. Bella had written a victim impact statement and could have gone to the hearing to read it out, but the thought of coming face to face with Clarke had been too terrifying. In any case, she had been told it would be unlikely to make any difference to the decision, which would be based on his risk to the community, not on how she felt.

And then last week, Kathy, her VLO, had contacted her to give her the news that a bed had come up in a hostel and he had been released.

Kathy couldn't tell her where the hostel was, only that it was nowhere near where she lived, and that he would be given conditions, including an exclusion zone, to stop him from coming into contact with her. Even so, Bella had found herself obsessing about exactly where the hostel might be and where he might end up living after that.

She imagined it would be somewhere in South London, where he had lived before he went to prison, and when she had suggested this, Kathy hadn't corrected her. Bella now lived north of the river, but her dad and Jenny, her stepmother, still lived in the same house in Streatham. What if she bumped into him during a visit? she'd asked. Kathy hadn't ruled this out as a possibility. He had to spend at least eight weeks in the hostel, she said, and after that, he had to be allowed to choose where to live and go about his day-to-day life.

Bella knew she could avoid Streatham. The truth was that she didn't often visit her dad. After her mum died, she'd had no choice but to go and live with him and she had stayed for ten and a half years, but they had never really got on. In fact, they had clashed so badly during her teens that when she was finally old enough to leave home, her social worker had helped her get this flat, which she'd found through a housing association because she had been considered vulnerable, and it had been her home ever since.

She had done OK, though. She had even managed to leave school with three A levels and had done a foundation year in art at Middlesex University. But her heart hadn't been in it and she had left to work as a teaching assistant at a primary school in Tottenham. She liked the school and the staff and she loved the children, and then two years ago, she had met Justin, who taught Year Four.

Justin kept telling her that she should go back to uni and do her teacher training, but she didn't want the responsibility that came with being a fully qualified teacher. She couldn't commit to him either. Sometimes she'd feel scared and would need him, but other times she would feel trapped by him. There was a void inside her that she worried nothing would ever fill. Sometimes she dreamed of running away. She would exit the school gates at half past three and wander through the stifling streets of Tottenham to the tube station, where she would get on the Victoria line, but instead of changing at Euston, she would imagine staying on until Victoria, then crossing the road to the coach station. There were hundreds of destinations you could go to from there. She could get on a bus – any bus. She could go literally anywhere. She could go up north to Scotland, or south to Plymouth, or through the Channel Tunnel to Europe – to Paris or Brussels or Warsaw – or to the airport, where she could get on a plane to the other side of the world.

She had suggested this to Justin, more than once. 'We could just take off,' she said. 'Grab our passports, put our finger on a map and just go.'

But Justin had a five-year-old kid from a previous relationship and he would always say, 'When Robbie's older.'

Bella knew he didn't want to go away anywhere with her. He liked his life how it was and simply wanted her to get her shit together so that they could marry and she could be a stepmum to Robbie, but although she thought Robbie was cute, she didn't want to be a stepmum. She had one of those and knew what it could be like.

But she never did run away either. She never seemed to be able to make a decision about anything. It had been suggested to her that she was subconsciously too afraid – or too guilty, or both – to find happiness after her mother's life had been cut short, and Bella did find it hard to imagine being older than thirty-three, the age her mum was when she died. Justin kept saying what a great mum she would make and how, once she had her own children, everything would fall into place, but Bella wasn't sure this was the answer. She loved the children she worked with and she was happy to take Robbie out at weekends, but she didn't feel ready to be a mum herself. Something was holding her back.

What she really wanted was to know her own mother better – to find out more about her. But her dad wouldn't talk about her – he never had. He had simply clammed up whenever Bella raised the subject, and there was no one else who seemed to have known her well. Bella's maternal grandparents had never really recovered from what happened to their daughter and didn't want to talk about her either. They lived in Chester and Bella had spent time with them as a child, but their sadness had been all-consuming and she had felt smothered by it, and by them. Her mum had been an only child, like her, and although people pretended to have known her well – the

Blenheim Road neighbours, for instance – there was no one who could tell her who she really was. What she thought about, what she cared about.

Bella missed her mum every day, but she could barely remember anything about her either. It was the worst combination. There was a gaping void in her life that she couldn't fill with happy memories the way other people did. She couldn't summon up the kitchen at Blenheim Road without remembering what had happened in there, and so she had blocked out everything.

But the nightmares were here to remind her. Jamie Clarke was here to remind her.

9

Eve was sitting in her sister's kitchen. Sascha's was the same sort of kitchen she used to have. Sascha's house was the same sort of house she used to have, too: an Edwardian semi-detached with box bay windows, oak floors, marble worktops and a dark oak kitchen table covered with a tablecloth and cluttered with the kind of paraphernalia that belongs to a family – a fruit bowl, magazines and newspapers, a laptop, an iPad. In the corner, between the dining table and the hallway, there was a soft sofa with bright throws and cushions where Pooh, Sascha's old springer spaniel, was fast asleep. Sascha's kitchen felt warm and full of colour. It felt like a home.

Sascha poured filter coffee into a mug, fetched a milk carton from the fridge and placed both down on the island in front of her sister.

'So,' she asked, sitting down opposite. '*Are* you seeing him again? I mean . . . how did you leave it?'

Eve cast her mind back, remembering how it had felt to be in Joe's kitchen, to watch him make the tea while the winter sunlight glinted outside the windows. How he'd removed his jacket, and how she'd tried not to stare at the rise and fall of the muscles in his back and shoulders. How close he'd sat to her at the table – to her right, rather than opposite – so that she could very easily have reached out and touched his hands.

'Well, I'm not really sure, to be honest,' she said.

Sascha looked impatient. 'What do you mean? How can you not know? What was the last thing you said to each other?'

'I said I had to get home,' Eve told her. 'Because Mackenzie was coming at six thirty and I had to make dinner.'

'And before that?'

'Well, I was a bit emotional,' Eve confessed. 'So it's hard to remember everything that was said, and in what order. I was talking quite a lot about Kenz and Rich, and he was just . . . well, listening, really, at that point. And when I finally stopped talking, he said something about a song. We'd been talking about a song.'

'A song? Which song?'

'"Everybody's Changing". By Keane. You know . . .'

Sascha started singing the words.

'Yes,' Eve said. 'That one.'

'What about it?'

'Well, I told him that's how I felt. That everyone was moving on, and that my friends were all at a different stage in their lives, and that I was finding it hard to . . . I don't know. To know where I belong. And that's when he quoted some of the lyrics back at me. You know, the ones about finding it hard to stay awake and remember your name, which he said is about the existential struggle to make sense of your place in an indifferent world.'

'Oh, come on, Evie,' Sascha frowned. '*Indifferent*? You really think that?'

'Yes, Sascha,' Eve said insistently. 'That is how I feel sometimes. Not all of the time. But sometimes – yes. And he *got* that. He felt it too. He said, "Some days are better than others." And he also said, "You just have to take each day as it comes and never stop hoping that something good could suddenly happen to you when you're least expecting it."'

Sascha grinned. 'That's what he said?'

Eve nodded. 'Yes. I found it quite uplifting, actually.'

'You big berk!' Sascha laughed, then reached a hand out and gripped her sister's fingers. 'You're so naive! He was talking about you!'

'I don't think so.'

'Yes!' Sascha exclaimed. 'Go on, then. What happened next?'

'Well, we talked about that song and he said it meant something to him too. He said he remembered it being released for the first time in May 2003, but it didn't get much airplay, and then it was re-released a year later on a bigger label and suddenly it was massive. It was being played everywhere. He said that both times it was released, something monumental had just happened in his life and he knew nothing was ever going to be the same for him again. He said he froze in time and the world moved on without him.'

'What did he mean by that?'

Eve shrugged. 'He didn't say. But I suspect it was a

relationship that ended badly. Or maybe he lost someone he loved. I got the impression it was something pretty big.'

'You didn't ask him?'

'No.' Eve looked up at her sister. 'I could see by the look on his face that he didn't want to tell me. So I just said that I was sorry.'

Sascha sipped her coffee. 'Well, nobody comes without baggage at your age, Evie.'

'I know that. I didn't say I minded. It drew me to him, actually.'

'Good,' Sascha said, putting down her mug. 'You can have your midlife crises together. Keep each other company. So, when are you going round there?'

'I'm not. He didn't ask to see me again. That's what I mean. It was kind of left in the air.'

'Do you like him? Do you fancy him?'

'Yes,' Eve admitted.

'So, go round. Knock on his door.'

'Are you serious?'

'Why not? What have you got to lose?'

Eve pondered the question. 'The fantasy that he likes me back.'

'Are you stupid? Of course he bloody likes you!' Sascha sighed. 'If you don't go round there and knock on his door, I will.'

Eve waited until the following Sunday, an intoxicating blend of dread and excitement creeping up on her all week as she talked herself in and out of what she was about to do. She ate an early lunch, then washed and straightened her hair and put on a bit of mascara and eyeliner – not too much – and at two o'clock, she set off across the Parks, a handwritten note with her phone number folded up in the pocket of her bumbag in readiness for the possibility that Joe might not be home. She had decided to walk instead of cycle to give herself time to think about what she was going to say if he *was* home, and because she felt so nervous. She went along the path that led to the High Bridge, then over it and past the duck pond where she used to take Mackenzie when she was small, then stopped and sat on the bench by the water, remembering her date with Online Chris and how she'd been stood up. Was she really ready to deal with another rejection?

Her fingers found the note in her bumbag, the one it had taken her all morning to write. She pulled it out and read it:

Hi Joe. Eve Shotton here. We met a week ago on Friday. You gave me some oregano and a cup of tea! I wanted to thank you for the chat, which really helped, and I wondered if you'd like to get a coffee sometime? Or tea!

She'd added her phone number and signed off with a smiley face.

It was fine, she decided, tucking it away again; the tone was about right. And if Sascha was wrong and there was nothing between them, then at least she'd be able to move on. Get back online again. Chat to someone new.

She continued up the path towards the exit by Lady Margaret Hall, noticing how lovely the snowdrops now looked, interspersed as they were with crocuses – a huge carpet of purple and white lining the way.

The house was still and silent as she approached. The Volvo was outside, the back gate shut. Joe had said it was usually unlocked, but was it better to knock at the front or back door? She wasn't sure. She stood outside on the pavement for a moment or two, trying to decide what to do, when the gate opened and Joe stepped out onto the driveway carrying a ladder. He moved like a ghost towards the garage door, then saw her and stopped. For a brief second, she thought she saw an expression that could have been displeasure, or could have been fear, but then he smiled, faintly, and put the ladder down on the gravel, standing it upright.

'Hello,' he said.

'Hello,' she replied. 'I'm sorry to just turn up, but—'

'You want some more oregano.' Once again, she couldn't tell if he was joking.

She took a breath. She could say yes. It would make things less awkward. He could cut her some oregano, they could chat for a minute, then she could leave. No harm done.

'No,' she said with resolve, stepping forward. 'I came to see you.'

He looked taken aback for a moment, then their eyes met and it hit Eve once again how striking his were, the absorbing shade of blue, the heavy lids, the creases in the corners. It was his eyes. They had captivated her from the get-go.

He hesitated for a moment, blinking a little, then nodded towards the garage. 'OK. I'll just . . .'

'Of course.'

Unable to move, Eve watched as he pulled a fob from his pocket and pointed it at the garage door, which then clanked and clattered open. He picked up the ladder and took it inside, re-emerging a moment later and again pointing the fob at the door, which swung back down.

He turned to face her. 'Do you want to come in?'

'Sure.' She stepped onto the drive and followed him into the garden, closing the gate behind her and watching as he jumped up at a scaffolding board and grabbed some belongings – a small radio, a denim jacket – and then opened the back door.

'Don't let me stop you if you're working,' she said apologetically.

Joe shook his head. 'It's fine. I was just doing a bit of prep ready for tomorrow. It's getting cold out here. Let's go inside.'

He stood back to let her go first. Eve stepped into the kitchen and then moved aside for Joe to get past her. As he did so, she felt his arm brush against hers and a spark of nervous energy made her jump away.

'Sorry,' they said at the same time, and because they'd both danced this particular dance more than once before, they laughed.

'How did it go?' he asked. 'The dinner with your daughter?'

'It was fine.'

'Just fine?'

Eve inhaled. 'Just fine. She didn't stay long. She'd had a long day and they had an early start the following morning – she and her boyfriend. They were off to Dorset.'

Joe filled the kettle and flipped her a sorry smile, scrunching up his nose in recognition of the fact that her daughter's early departure couldn't have helped the way she'd been feeling that day.

'It's OK,' Eve said, then added, feeling brave, 'Talking to you helped. I was less . . . fragile about it than I might otherwise have been.' She smiled. 'But I'm sorry for getting upset.'

'Not at all.' He turned to face her, leaning back against the worktop. He was wearing a navy-blue cable-knit fisherman's jumper and jeans. His hair was tousled from being outside. He looked lovely, and Eve felt the strongest of urges to walk over, to put her head against his jumper, to feel his arms around her. Instead, she pulled out a chair and sat down.

Joe made the tea, then carried it over to the table. Eve liked that he'd remembered how she took it – a generous splash of milk, no sugar. He pulled out the same chair he'd sat on the last time, and as he slid it in next to her, Eve was, once again, conscious of how close he was to her, how intimate it felt, just the two of them sitting side by side in this big house.

'I see you like listening to the radio,' she observed, in case he wanted to switch it on.

'Yeah. I've usually got Radio Four on. Or Radio Two. A bit of background music.' He hesitated. 'Do you want it on?'

She shook her head. 'Only if you do.'

He scrunched up his nose again, that same gesture. 'It's fine. It's just company. But you're here now.'

A glow of optimism stirred inside her. Whatever this was, this thing between them, he liked her. He didn't mind that she'd turned up out of the blue.

'Have you lived here long?' she asked tentatively.

He gazed at her for a moment before answering. 'No,' he said. 'Not long. Just a few weeks.'

'Ah.' Eve nodded. 'You're still making it your own, then? Not that you have to do a thing to it. It's lovely as it is. It's . . . well. It's an amazing house, obviously.' She gave a small laugh. 'I just meant that . . . you know. You're doing the loft conversion. So you obviously know a thing or two about renovating houses.'

He took a sip of his tea and nodded. 'I do, actually.'

'Oh?' Eve raised an eyebrow.

'Well, I used to work on a lot of renovations,' he said. 'Back in the day.'

'Where?' Eve asked.

'In London. Where I grew up.'

'Which part?' Eve asked.

He eyed her. 'Clapham.'

'I knew it,' she said. 'I could tell by the accent. I'm from Dulwich. Although I've lived in Oxford since I was eighteen, so I'm not sure if I've got much London left. Or should I say, *Lan-den*,' she repeated, pronouncing it with a cockney accent.

'You have a little,' he said, smiling. 'So, are your parents still there?'

'No. They moved to France a few years ago. I have a sister and two nieces, though. And a brother-in-law. They live in Kew.'

'Kew. Nice,' he said.

'Well, yeah. It is. And her house is lovely.'

He nodded. 'And yours?'

Eve pulled a face. 'Unfortunately, mine isn't. It's only a

rental. I need to buy somewhere, really. Yet another thing I keep putting off.'

'You said you lived in Marston?'

'Yes. Just across the Parks from here.'

'So, where would you like to live?' he asked.

Eve thought about this. 'You know what? I really have no idea. I don't even know what I can afford. Maybe that's why I haven't got round to it.'

'Would you be looking for a project?'

'I wouldn't be frightened of a bit of work, if that's what you mean. This might sound weird,' Eve said, nodding towards the window behind the sink, 'but I've always felt a little excited by the sight of scaffolding.'

This made him smile.

'It's just the potential, you know,' she explained. 'For something amazing to happen, for a sad, jaded space to be transformed into something incredible. Something new.' As soon as she said it, she flushed, thinking this sounded like a metaphor, as if she were that sad, jaded space waiting to be improved.

Joe gazed at her for a moment, then he said, 'I can show you it, if you like.'

'The loft conversion?' Eve asked, surprised.

'Yes. Do you want to see it?'

'Yes please!' Eve couldn't think of anything she would like more.

Joe scraped his chair back, looking pleased. 'Come on, then.'

She followed him out of the kitchen and into the hallway,

which was light, bright and beautiful. Through an open doorway, she could see a room that looked like a study, with a desk and a piano and a wall-to-wall bookcase stuffed with hundreds upon hundreds of books. She followed him up the stairs to a huge landing, past a table with an antique clock and a chair with a tartan throw over the back, and then up to a further landing that had an open door to a bedroom with wooden floorboards, where she caught sight of an oriental rug and more books. There were pictures and paintings on every wall, not necessarily all to her taste, but they contributed to the overall atmosphere, which was unreservedly one of old money, of wealth, so much so that Eve was now doubting herself all over again. What on earth could she have that Joe wanted? She wasn't poor, but they clearly lived in very different worlds.

They went up yet another flight of stairs and when they got to the top, Joe opened a door that led to another, smaller staircase. They had to duck their heads a little as they went up. Joe climbed onto the chipboard floor and Eve took his place on the step above, her head peering over the edge, and there it was. For a moment, she was stunned into silence by the vastness of the space around her, by the light streaming in from the series of windows that stretched from one brick gable-end wall to the other. All she could see was sky. So much sky. Up above them, a row of silver insulation boards had been cut into the rafters and were catching the sunlight, glinting like mirrors.

Joe eyed her, grinning. 'Do you like it?'

Eve's mouth was open. She reached up a hand and flipped it at her chin, pushing her jaw shut.

Joe laughed and said, 'There aren't any walls up yet. It

won't always be this big.' He reached out a hand to help her up. 'The floor's fine to walk on,' he said. 'Just watch out for the odd nail.'

Eve took his hand. His touch felt warm, his grip strong. He tugged her up and together they walked across to the window. Eve felt a little giddy as she looked out. In the distance was a magnificent view of Oxford: the spires of the university colleges, St Mary's tower, Carfax. Immediately below her was the wide green stretch of the Parks, and to her left, the river.

'This view,' Eve said. 'It's to die for. Literally.'

'*Literally?*'

She shot him a smile. 'Yes. If this were my final view of the world, I'd be happy.'

Joe laughed. 'Well, then, wait until you see what it's like from the outside.'

'We're going outside?' Eve asked warily.

Joe's answer was to tug open a window. A gust of air made Eve catch her breath. 'This,' he said, pointing to a chair on the scaffold plank just below them, 'is my temporary balcony. Would you care to join me?'

'Oh my God,' Eve said as he climbed out of the window and onto the scaffold board, then turned and helped her do the same. 'Oh my God,' she said again as she walked tentatively towards the front edge of the platform. It reminded her of the times when, as a child, she'd stood on the top diving board at the local swimming pool, shaking as she looked down at the sheer drop beneath her, only this was a drop that could be deadly with one wrong move. All it would take was a brief loss of balance or one misjudged step.

Joe moved over and stood beside her.

'Oh my God,' she said for a third time, turning to her left as the wind caught her hair. 'You *can* actually see where I live.'

'Really?'

'Yes. Just there,' Eve said, laughing and pointing. 'You see the bridge? And then the path beyond it? And then the rooftops of the houses behind the trees?'

He nodded, following her gaze.

'Well, I'm just there. That's where I live.'

'Good,' he said. 'I can wave to you.' And then, still gazing outwards, he said, 'I'll come up here and say goodnight to you before I go to bed.'

Eve eyed him, feeling a small thrill at his words. She had never been very good at flirting, but . . . was that what this was? 'OK,' she grinned.

'Unless I'm with you, of course,' he added.

Eve felt his words in her stomach, and then in her chest. She felt the kind of butterflies she hadn't felt for two and half decades. Her sister had been right. Those words were unmistakable.

She turned to look at him and he smiled.

10

She left shortly afterwards.

It had been cold out on the scaffolding and they'd gone back inside and climbed down the stairs, then Eve had said she'd better be going, wanting to get home and hug this day to herself, to think about what Joe had said, to process it, savour it. It had been a lot for one day, but now everything made sense. He had wanted her to know he liked her too, she realised, but was waiting for her to make the next move, to set the pace. By the time they'd gone all the way back downstairs and into the kitchen, she no longer felt afraid to tell him she'd like to see him again. She gave him the note she had written with her phone number on it, and he said he'd find his phone and message her so that she had his too.

At the back gate, as they'd said goodbye, he was more like his former silent, diffident self, but he was smiling.

Eve found herself smiling, too, as she walked briskly back through the Parks and over the bridge, then along the dirt track and through the field that led to her street. The world was now brimming with possibility. The end to her loneliness had arrived at long last. The melody to the Paul McCartney song 'No More Lonely Nights' popped into her head and, glancing around to make sure no one was nearby, she began to sing the words, then laughed out loud at how ridiculous she was being. She thought about the video to the song, the one with Paul McCartney singing from the rooftop of his building, and she imagined Joe standing on his scaffold balcony in the moonlight, singing the same words, and she laughed out loud again. She felt glad she'd had a chance to burn off all this nervous energy with no one watching.

As she walked up the path to her front door, she heard a car door slam and the sound of footsteps behind her. She turned to see a man walking purposefully towards her. He was wearing a bomber jacket and jeans and had cropped grey hair and a humourless expression.

'Eve Shotton?' he asked.

Eve stopped. 'Yes,' she said. 'Who are you?'

The man unzipped his jacket and pulled out a warrant card holder, opening it up to show her. 'I'm Detective Inspector Jon Carver,' he told her. 'From Thames Valley Police.'

'What's happened?' Eve gasped. 'Is it Sascha? The girls? Oh my God, is it one of my parents?'

'This isn't about your family, Eve.'

'Then . . .?'

He stepped forward. 'Can I come inside?'

'Why? What's happened?' Eve asked again, her heartbeat quickening.

The detective pursed his lips. 'We need to talk about Jamie.'

The Stranger on the Stairs

'Jamie who?'

'Jamie Clarke.'

Eve frowned.

'OK. So, what name has he given you?'

'Who?' But as soon as Eve asked the question, she knew.

OFFICIAL – (when complete)

MG5

POLICE REPORT

5 May 2003   URN: 40BP/28769/03

Defendant(s) name:	Anticipated Plea	Adult/Youth
James Clarke	N/G	ADULT

Child Abuse   Domestic Abuse   Drugs Test   POCA   Hate Crime

1. **Summary of the Key Evidence:** 'Key evidence' establishes every element of the offence and that the defendant committed the offence with the necessary criminal intent.

- Set out the facts in chronological order, telling the story and covering the 'points to prove'
- The summary must be balanced and fair
- Record address and contact details of all civilian witnesses along with all dates to avoid on MG9

Summary of the Key Evidence:

VICTIM:- Christy Jane Nicholls – DOB 2/2/1970 (Age 33)

DEFENDANT:- James Joseph Clarke – DOB 21/6/1974 (Age 29)

On Friday, 2nd May 2003 at 08.05 following a 999 call, police were called to 17 Blenheim Road, Streatham Hill, South London, and directed through the open front door to the rear of the property where the body of a woman was reported to have been found. They located the victim on the kitchen floor, where she was only partially dressed and was curled up in a foetal position. Officers could immediately see that she had been bound and gagged with silver duct tape. Her eyes were unresponsive. Life was pronounced extinct at the scene by medical staff from London Ambulance Service.

The victim was identified as Christy Nicholls, who had lived at 17 Blenheim Road with her seven-year-old-daughter, Bella Duncan. Bella told officers that she had woken that morning at approximately 07.30 and had come downstairs. She had discovered her mother lying motionless on the kitchen floor and had gone out through the front door to alert the next-door neighbour, Brenda Barlow.

Mrs Barlow informed police that Bella had arrived on her doorstep crying at 07.45 that same morning to tell her that, 'Mummy has been hurt. A man tied her up. She can't move.' Mrs Barlow followed Bella back into the property and through the lounge to the kitchen where she could immediately see that the victim was no longer alive. She made the 999 call.

Officers at the scene established that there had been no forced entry into the property. Specially trained officers questioned Bella, who revealed that 'the same man came again and kissed Mummy and I had to go to bed.' When asked how the man got into the house, Bella said 'through the back door. He just came in.' Officers found the back door to be unlocked with the key missing.

Area intelligence revealed that a burglary had taken place in the same street six weeks previously and that officers who had conducted house-to-house inquiries had taken statements from witnesses who had seen a man entering 17 Blenheim Road on more than one occasion during this time. They described the man as being of medium build, approximately 6 feet tall, in his late 20s to early 30s with mousy brown hair and piercing blue eyes.

The description matched that of the defendant, who arrived in Blenheim Road while police were present and was pointed out by local residents. Two of these witnesses told police they had seen this same man emerge from the back of 17 Blenheim Road the previous evening at around 21.45 p.m. The defendant was arrested for the offences of rape and murder and taken to Farringdon Police Station, where he agreed to give DNA samples and to take part in identification procedures.

Identification procedures took place the following day and Bella Duncan and the two Blenheim Road resident witnesses, Carly Benfield and Anthony Norris, attended. All three witnesses made a positive identification of the defendant.

On Monday, 5th May, Dr Crighton performed a forensic autopsy and the provisional cause of death was ascertained as suffocation. There was also evidence of airway interruption in the form of strangulation along with significant injuries to the cheek, left breast and middle three fingers of the right hand. The victim was right-handed and these were consistent with defensive wounds. Toxicology analysis was negative for pathology and there was no evidence of anatomical natural disease. The time of death was placed at sometime between 9 p.m. and midnight on the evening of Thursday, 1st May.

Items of the victim's clothing were sent away for forensic analysis and swabs were taken which provided a positive match with the defendant. The vaginal swab results were inconclusive.

In interview the defendant denied the allegations or that he had attended the address on the evening of Thursday, 1st May, stating that he had instead visited the victim at home earlier that same day when he had been intimate with her, and that this could account for the presence of his DNA. He stated that this was a case of mistaken identity, and that he was at home at the relevant time.

The defendant was remanded to Central London Magistrates Court.

Key witnesses and their role:-

BELLA DUNCAN – daughter of victim, age 7, witnessed a male arrive at 17 Blenheim Road on the evening of Thursday, 1st May, heard the back door being locked and saw the early stage of the attack on her mother, before being sent to bed. Identified the defendant as the attacker.

BRENDA BARLOW – next-door neighbour of victim. Made the 999 call the following morning after being alerted by Bella Duncan. Heard Bella say, 'Mummy has been hurt. A man tied her up. She can't move.'

CARLY BENFIELD – resident of Blenheim Road and neighbour of the victim. Saw the defendant emerging from the rear of 17 Blenheim Road at the relevant time.

ANTHONY NORRIS – resident of Blenheim Road and neighbour of the victim. Saw the defendant emerging from the rear of 17 Blenheim Road at the relevant time.

11

Eve followed the detective into the living room, where he sat down on the sofa and placed his jacket by his side. He looked up, grim-faced, as she sat in the armchair next to him. He was in his fifties, perhaps, not quite old enough to act paternally towards her, but she could see that he pitied her, that whatever he was about to tell her was going to make her feel like a fool.

'I'm here about the man you've been visiting at twenty-one Norham Gardens.'

Eve's heart fluttered. 'What about him?'

'So, he hasn't told you?'

'Told me what?'

'That he's been in prison?'

Her stomach sank. 'No.'

He nodded. 'Well, I'm sorry, Eve, but I'm here for your own protection. You may have heard of Clare's Law. It enables the police to disclose information about a convicted criminal to potential partners, if they feel a woman may be at risk of violence from him.' There was a pause, and then he said, 'I'm here to tell you that the man you are seeing is a convicted murderer and rapist.'

Eve's breath stopped in her chest, her mind unable to process this. 'Are we talking about *Joe*?'

The detective looked hard at her. 'His name's not Joe. It's Jamie. Jamie Clarke. He's not long come out of prison. He was convicted in 2004 of the rape and murder of a thirty-three-year-old woman. He bound her up, gagged her, raped her, then strangled her in her own kitchen while her little girl was asleep upstairs.'

Eve's tongue felt thick in her mouth. 'Are you sure we're talking about the same person?'

He looked sorry for her. 'He's a sex offender, Eve. He's on the register. He shouldn't even be talking to you without telling his probation officer, let alone inviting you into his house – which is not his house, obviously.'

'But . . .' Eve hesitated, confused. 'It *is*. I mean . . . he lives there. I've been there. We went upstairs.'

He looked interested. 'You've had sex with him?'

'No!' she protested. She lowered her eyes, overcome with shame at the way this had sounded, at her naivety. 'He took me up to show me the loft conversion he's building, and . . . and he definitely lives there.' She hesitated, now doubtful. 'Doesn't he?'

'Did he tell you it was his house?'

Eve cast her mind back. Had Joe ever actually come out and said that it was his? 'I can't remember,' she admitted. 'Maybe I just assumed he owned it. I mean, he had access to it. He had a key to the back door. I saw him open it. And I didn't see anyone else.'

'The owner's away. He's also been in prison. I suspect that's how they met.'

'And they live together?' Eve felt her throat tighten. 'How could that even be allowed to happen?'

'Well, that's a good question, but the probation service seem to have approved it.'

Eve shut her eyes, blinking back tears. When she opened them again, the detective's face had visibly softened.

'Are you OK?' he asked her.

'Isn't he on licence?' Eve asked. 'Isn't he supposed to be supervised? I've been to that house twice. Why am I only being told this now?'

'Unfortunately, that's the way it works. Convicted criminals get to live in the community and go about their business and it's left to us to keep an eye on them, but, as I'm sure you understand, we can't do that twenty-four seven. And they have rights. But I also have a duty to protect you, which is why I'm talking to you now.'

'I could have been hurt,' Eve whispered. 'I could have been killed.'

'Yes. You could.'

'And yet I've been there twice and he has only ever been nice to me.'

'But you haven't rejected him yet, have you?'

'I don't . . .?'

'That's his MO, Eve,' the detective said. 'He sees you. He likes you. He lures you in. And he seems like a nice guy at first.'

Eve swallowed hard, listening.

'But before long, his true colours begin to show. He starts to say things – and do things – that creep you out a bit, and then you get frightened and realise that this isn't someone normal, so you change your mind and tell him you don't want to see him any more, which you are perfectly entitled to do, Eve. But he doesn't like it. It makes him angry. He doesn't like being told to go away. It makes him mad. And so he rapes you, to teach you a lesson. And then he kills you, because if he doesn't, you'll tell the police and he'll go to jail. And then, because you're no longer there to tell the truth, he says he was your boyfriend and that there was consensual sexual activity between the two of you that very same day – but a bit earlier, of course. And *that* . . .' He paused and Eve felt the weight of his gaze. '*That* will explain away any DNA that might be found on your body. Right? Because he's your boyfriend and he's already been intimate with you.'

Eve thought about Joe making her a cup of tea, about him reaching out a hand to pull her up into the loft, how he'd helped her out onto the scaffold board. How much longer would it have been before he'd touched her in the kinds of places that would need to be explained away by a rapist? By a murderer? She felt a shiver of ice run down her spine. 'Are you telling me he's done this more than once?'

The detective gave her a sardonic smile. 'They've always done it more than once – and they'll always do it again. Until somebody stops them, that is.'

He paused and Eve met his gaze. He wanted something from her, she could tell.

'So, you've met him twice?' he asked. 'Just twice?'

Eve thought about this. Did the first time count, that time in Blackwell's? She supposed that would depend on whether their meeting had been by chance or not. She shivered again as she realised how foolish she'd been. Where was her due diligence? She hadn't even asked Joe's surname. She'd stopped her daughter from trying to find him online.

'Think carefully, Eve,' he said. 'Because he's got conditions on his licence and if he's breached them, he's going back to jail.'

'We met three times,' Eve said. 'But the first time was in a public place. We were only alone together at his house twice.'

'It doesn't matter.' The detective looked pleased. 'He's in breach. I'll let the probation team know. He also gave you a false name, which he's not allowed to do. They'll almost certainly recall him. And then he'll be off the streets and you'll be safe – you and all the other women in Oxford.' The detective looked at her. 'OK?'

Was this OK? Eve thought of Joe being handcuffed and escorted out of the house in Norham Gardens, then taken to a police station and held in a cell until he could be put into a van and carted off back to prison. There wouldn't even be a trial. There would be no need for him to be proved guilty; it was in the hands of his probation officer, who only needed to press a button and he'd be back inside. And all because of her, because of what she'd told this detective, who was now getting up from the sofa and putting on his jacket, ready to leave.

'OK?' he asked again.

Eve nodded, slowly. She'd done the right thing; she knew she'd done the right thing. So why did she feel so terrible?

12

There was someone in the house. Bella lay in the darkness for a few moments, then pushed back her duvet and made her way across the landing. She reached out for the light switch, but when she pressed it, nothing happened, and that was when she realised: this was real. The man had come for her, and this time he was on the stairs. She could see his outline in the darkness.

'Who are you?' she said loudly, trying to appear confident, although her whole body was trembling.

'Shh!' he said, putting a finger to his lips. 'Your mother's sleeping. Go back to bed.'

And then a hand touched the base of her neck and a scream ripped from her throat.

'Shh,' said Justin, drawing her into his arms. 'Bel. Shh. It's OK. It's just a dream.'

Bella opened her eyes. The room was dark, the air close and musty. Justin was here with her. She was in her own bedroom, in her own flat. Slowly, her heartbeat returned to normal.

'You closed the curtains,' she complained.

'Sorry. I didn't—'

'I need them open.'

She heard a sigh, felt the bed move. A moment later, she could see the familiar orange glow from the street light outside.

'You need to sort this out, Bel,' Justin said, getting back into bed. 'You need to go back to therapy.'

'It's too expensive.'

'Well, we need to do something. You can't live your life like this.'

'You mean, *you* can't.'

She knew she was being unfair. Justin was only trying to help, and he had been infinitely patient with her throughout the two years they had been together. But she sometimes resented the dynamic this created between them.

'Look, I know what this is about,' Justin said. 'I know you're worried about you-know-who. But you have to remember what Kathy said. He's going to have a ton of conditions. He'll have to go to meetings. They'll be monitoring him.'

'I know that,' Bella said. 'It's just that it's dragged things up.'

He put his arm around her again, kissed the top of her head.

'But it's made me realise . . .' She paused.

He hesitated, too, and that moment's hesitation spoke volumes. 'Realise what?'

'That it could really have happened. That I could have come downstairs in the night and seen a man on the stairs.'

Justin fell silent. 'But we've been over this,' he said finally. 'We know why you created this character.'

'I'm not sure that I *did* "create" him.'

'Bel, the neighbours saw Jamie Clarke. They saw him leaving the house.'

'I know.'

'So who else could it be?'

'Well, that's what I'm wondering, but I can never see his face in the dream.'

He stroked her arm. 'You've got to stop feeling guilty.'

Bella felt annoyed. 'You think I made him up because I feel guilty?'

'You've told me you feel guilty,' Justin said, sighing. 'I'm not saying you should.'

Bella fell silent. Of course she felt guilty. How could she not? She had gone to bed and slept while her mother lay dying beneath her. She had explored this with her former therapist, who had come to the conclusion that this was why Bella wanted to believe she had come downstairs in the night. Bella was supposed to keep an elastic band on her wrist and snap it every time she began to think about this.

'You were seven, Bel,' Justin was saying. 'Kids sleep deeply. You know what Robbie's like. Once he's out for the count, it would take a hurricane to wake him.'

'But what if I *didn't* sleep through it?' Bella turned onto her side to face him. 'What if I'm not imagining it? What if I really *did* hear noises? Maybe I came downstairs and blocked it out?'

'I don't know what to say,' Justin said, sighing.

'I think he might have removed the light bulb,' she persisted. 'So that I couldn't see his face.'

'Look,' he said. 'It's nearly three o'clock and I have to pick Robbie up at eight. Shall we try and get some sleep?'

'Of course,' Bella agreed, but she suddenly didn't feel like taking Robbie out with Justin today. She would make an excuse.

13

As soon as the detective had gone, Eve opened her laptop. James Clarke might be a common enough name, but when linked in the search engine with the word 'murder', she found him easily, and it made her wonder how she could have been so oblivious. How did she not remember this happening? How did she not know about him? The horrific details were set out in black and white on page after page: the national newspapers, the BBC website, the locals. He even had his own Wikipedia page. *James Joseph Clarke*, it said, *is an English murderer, sex offender and rapist.* This identity – this horrible, vile identity – was ascribed to him in various forms all over the internet.

And then there was his photo, the pictures of him in handcuffs. He was younger back then, of course, but the man in the mugshot was unmistakably the same man she'd drunk tea with that very same afternoon in that sunny whitewashed kitchen. She winced, the acrid taste of bile rising in her throat and making her want to retch as she remembered thinking how nice he'd looked in his blue cable-knit jumper, how she'd wanted to feel his arms around her. And then she looked again at his photo, at his prison-issue grey sweat top and the expression in his eyes – those eyes that she'd been so incredibly drawn to – as they gazed out at her from the screen of her laptop. *Hello, Eve*, they seemed to say. *So, now you know.*

According to Wiki, he'd been born in Clapham in 1974, one of three children, to Dorothy and Gerald Clarke. Gerald worked in construction and Jamie, the oldest, had followed in his father's footsteps, securing work on building sites in and around South London as a teenager. In May 2003, he'd been working on the renovation of a house in Streatham Hill, just a short walk away from Blenheim Road. His victim, Christy Nicholls, had mentioned to a neighbour that she'd met Jamie in a nearby shop and he'd offered to come round to fix a faulty door. Three days later, there had been a burglary at a house four doors away from Christy's, and just six weeks after that, Christy had been found dead by her traumatised daughter. The neighbourhood around Blenheim Road was considered to be a safe one and the burglary had been the first to be reported in several years. First a burglary, and then a woman was raped and murdered. Coincidence? The residents thought not.

And besides, he'd been identified by the daughter, who had seen him in the house at the time of the murder. The poor, poor girl, Eve thought. It was hard to think about what she must have gone through, what it must have been like for a seven-year-old to come downstairs for breakfast one morning to find her mother motionless and semi-naked on the floor. She imagined Mackenzie – who had a key to her mother's apartment – letting herself in and finding *her* like that, and she began to sob gently, not for herself but for Mackenzie and because she'd been so, so careless. What happened to Christy Nicholls could so easily have happened to her, and it would have had a traumatic and devastating impact on her daughter, and her sister, and her nieces, and on her poor parents, and even on Rich, who she knew still cared about her. Her stomach lurched as she thought about the parallels. She, too, had met Joe in a shop. Was DI Carver right? Was this his MO?

But at the same time, it was so hard to believe that the gentle, diffident man she had drunk tea with could have so much hatred inside him. He'd listened to her so sympathetically, been so understanding. His face had fallen when she'd cried and he'd comforted her with words that had actually helped, that had shown he understood what she was going through. *God.* She closed her eyes. So *that* was the monumental thing he'd alluded to: getting arrested for Christy's murder and then being convicted the following year and going to prison. *'I froze in time and the world moved on without me.'*

He'd seemed so . . . so thoughtful. He hadn't seemed like someone who could hurt a woman in that way. But she didn't know him. That was the thing. She didn't know if he had any genuine feelings for her. She didn't know if anything about him was genuine. She didn't know him at all.

Eve buried her face in her palms. She stayed like that for several moments, the plummeting sensation in her stomach finally subsiding to the point where she could at last think and breathe, but then a sudden sound jolted her upright, making her heart skip a beat. It was her phone, moving and vibrating on the coffee table. She reached over and picked it up. She could see straight away that it was Joe.

She opened the message with trembling fingers. *Eve, I'm sorry*, it read. *I know that the police have been round to see you. I'm so, so sorry that I didn't tell you, but I was going to. I really was. Please, please hear me out, Eve. I'm not a rapist and I'm not a murderer. I can explain everything. Please don't give up on me.*

Eve stared at the message for several long moments.

Please don't give up on me.

He said this as if she meant something to him, as if they meant something to each other, and it was hard not to be moved, harder still to comprehend that it had only been a matter of hours since she'd skipped across the park, imagining her future, only to find a police detective on her doorstep waiting to drop a bomb into her life.

But the detective was right. She knew nothing about this man she'd been seeing, or at least nothing that was good. He didn't own the house in Norham Gardens. He possibly didn't even live there. He might just have had a key because he was working there; she couldn't remember what he'd told her. But he must live somewhere nearby, and he couldn't have been arrested yet, not if he was still able to use his phone.

Whose house is it? she typed. *The one in Norham Gardens?*

She waited, watching the ellipsis as he entered his reply.

His name's Chas Cauldwell. He's a music producer.

Do you live there?

Yes. For now.

The police say he's been in prison.

He was wrongly accused, came the reply. *He was exonerated.*

Eve paused, wondering what Chas Cauldwell had been accused of, although, if a court *had* overturned his conviction, that shouldn't matter, she knew. But it would be easy enough to find out. *So how do you know him?* she typed.

I've taken my case to an appeal charity in London. One of their lawyers acted for Chas. The woman who runs the charity told him about me and he felt sorry for me because he'd been through the same thing. He offered me a place to stay and then he told me he wanted a loft conversion and I said I'd do it.

So, where is he now?

Abroad. He'll be back next month.

Eve considered this for a moment. *Your name isn't Joe*, she typed.

It's my middle name. It's the name I use now.

Does your probation officer know that?

Yes. She approved it. Eve, my name's all over the internet. I wanted a new start. But I was going to tell you. I promise, I was going to tell you everything.

There was a long pause, then the ellipsis began to move again.

Eve, please. I need your help.

Eve closed her eyes and took a long breath. Was she the most gullible person on the planet? Was she all that was on offer for someone who had hit rock bottom?

The ellipsis was moving again, then stopped.

They said you've breached your probation, she typed.

I haven't, came the reply. *Not unless you say I have! Please, Eve. Will you speak to my probation officer?*

Eve felt her breath catch. Did he want her to lie for him?

Why? she typed. *Why would I do that? I don't even know you.*

You do, Eve. You do know me, he typed back. *We know each other. I haven't lied to you, not once. Please trust me. My probation officer's name is Debbie Stroud. I just need you to talk to her. I'm not going to coach you. I'm not going to do anything except give you her phone number. Please?*

14

Charles Phillip Cauldwell was a fifty-five-year-old British music producer from West London who was known for the success of a couple of bands Eve had heard of and several she hadn't. He'd been accused of drug trafficking four years ago after a large stash of heroin was found in the boot of a Mercedes he'd hired and left at the airport before a trip abroad. He was suspected of having been involved with an international organised crime group. He'd denied this from the outset, had appealed immediately post-conviction and had been successful. It transpired that the police had withheld phone data from the defence that would have cleared his name had it been available at his original trial. He'd spent a total of eighteen months in prison, but didn't appear to be at all bitter; in fact, he considered himself fortunate to have had good lawyers and had gone on to become a trustee for a London charity, Truth for Justice, which helped convicted prisoners who maintained their innocence but didn't have any money to fund an appeal. Meanwhile, he had continued his work as a music producer and had bought the house in Norham Gardens not long after his release from prison.

Eve tapped in the phone number Joe had given her.

'Debbie Stroud,' said a tired-sounding female voice at the other end of the line.

'It's Eve,' she said. 'Eve Shotton. I've been asked to call you.'

'Oh, yes. Just a second.' Eve could hear the sound of a yapping dog and a television in the background, both of which faded to silence as a door was closed. The voice came back. 'Is this about Jamie?'

Eve hesitated. 'I know him as Joe. He said you had approved that.'

A pause. 'We know he's using his middle name, yes.'

Eve breathed deeply. 'So, what is it that I need to confirm?'

'Are you fully aware of his situation?'

'Well . . . no,' Eve said. 'I can't say that I am.'

'But you know why he was in prison?'

'Yes. The police told me.'

'And you know he was released last October?'

'I didn't know it was October,' Eve said. 'But yes, I know he was inside for murder and rape and that he came out quite recently.'

'OK,' Debbie Stroud said. 'Well, as you'd expect, he's on a life licence and has a number of conditions attached. One of them concerns the disclosure of new relationships. He is required to notify us of any developing relationship with a woman.'

'That sounds a bit vague.'

'It's because he is an ongoing risk to females.'

'Yes. I get that,' Eve said. 'But we haven't . . .' She let out a breath. 'You know.'

'The relationship needs to be disclosed, whether intimate or not.'

'When?' Eve asked. 'At what point?'

'By the second meeting. That was made clear to him. And this is for your own protection, Eve. He knows this. He is required by his licence conditions to explain his circumstances to you as soon as possible. It's something we would have assisted with if he'd told us sooner. I would have sat down with the two of you together and helped him to explain the situation.'

'But the police got to me first.'

'So it seems. But there's nothing to stop them from doing so. And there's a delicate balance to be struck. I'm sure if it was your daughter, you'd want her to know.'

'So, what did they tell you?' Eve asked.

'Who?'

'The police.'

'Well, nothing yet. It was Jamie—'

'Joe,' Eve interrupted. 'His name's Joe. You said you'd approved this. So can we please call him Joe?'

A pause. 'Yes. Joe.'

Eve realised what Debbie had been about to say. 'Hang on. So Joe *did* tell you about me?'

'Not until this afternoon,' Debbie said. 'Not until *late* this afternoon.'

'It sounds like he must have called you straight after I left his house?' Eve said, surprised. This wasn't quite the picture the detective had painted.

'Yes, but my concern is that he left it longer than he should have done.'

'Well, I'm not sure that's correct,' Eve said. 'I've only known him for a couple of weeks.'

'So how many times have you met him?'

Eve cast her mind back, thinking it through carefully. 'OK. Technically, I've met him three times,' she said, truthfully. 'But the first time we were strangers who bumped into each other in a bookshop and had a brief conversation.' She paused. 'In fact, it was mostly me who did the talking. He barely said a word. Then we bumped into each other again in a shop in North Parade a few days later. We recognised each other and he offered me some herbs from his garden because I hadn't managed to buy the ones I wanted, and I walked back to his house with him. I was upset about something – something to do with my family – and he took pity on me and made me a cup of tea.' She paused again. 'And then today, the third time, he didn't know I was coming. I turned up at his house and surprised him. Honestly, he looked taken aback to see me. He definitely wasn't expecting me. He offered me a cup of tea again and we chatted for an hour or so, and then I left . . . and then he phoned you.' Eve concluded: 'Look, I'm not trying to protect him, but to be honest with you, I can't see how he could have done things any differently. Can you?'

There was silence on the other end of the phone as Debbie considered her response. 'I'm just making some notes,' she said.

Eve waited.

'OK,' she said, finally. 'That's been very helpful.'

'Are you going to recall him back to prison?' Eve asked.

'Possibly not, based on what you've told me. But you need to know that we consider him high risk.'

Eve felt a small jolt to her stomach. 'What makes him high risk?'

'He hasn't admitted the offence. He hasn't done any of the reoffender programmes. He hasn't accepted responsibility or shown remorse.'

'Could that be because he didn't do it?'

A pause. 'They all say they didn't do it, Eve. I'm getting the sense that this might be wishful thinking on your part.'

'He's still fighting his conviction,' Eve pointed out. 'He's been released, but he's still fighting it.'

'Eve, he's on life licence. He is on the sex offenders register. He has multiple conditions that are going to continue to restrict his freedom for many years to come, and some of them will do so for the rest of his life. They'll dictate where he can go, where he can't go, what kind of work he can do. Whether anyone will want to be in a relationship with him.' She paused for the message to land. 'Look, if you want my honest opinion, you need to be careful. You may not like what I'm telling you, but I have a duty to tell you nonetheless, and I'm going to be making a note of this conversation so that it's on record that I've warned you: the man you're seeing is dangerous.'

15

Eve woke early the next morning with a headache. She showered and dressed for work, then drank a cup of coffee and ate a banana seated by the kitchen window before going downstairs and out into the garden to unlock her bike.

Joe took up residence in her mind for the rest of the week, but he didn't contact her. Eve wondered if Debbie Stroud had had second thoughts and if he'd been recalled back to prison after all, and she badly wanted to know if this was the case. But the thought of ringing Debbie made her feel weak and desperate; nor did she want to contact Joe in case this gave him false hope that she believed in his innocence, because she honestly didn't know what to believe. She also worried that if he *had* been recalled and was on his way back to prison, then the police might have his phone.

Not that there was any rule to stop her being in touch with him, she didn't think, not now that Debbie had been made aware of her existence. In fact, she suspected her name was already in circulation between the police and the probation service and who knew how many other government officials? How could she contemplate any kind of relationship with Joe now, even one of friendship? How *could* she?

And what about her colleagues? The head of her department at college – what would he say? Could her link to Joe threaten her job? It would hardly reflect well on the college to have one of their senior law lecturers hobnobbing with a convicted rapist and murderer. And what about her family? Her daughter? Her sister? Her nieces? How would they feel about her ongoing contact with a man who was considered a high risk to women? And could they, too, be in danger?

Debbie Stroud's remarks crawled around her mind on a loop: *'If you want my honest opinion, you need to be careful . . . the man you're seeing is dangerous.'* Despite the stance Eve had taken on the phone, she now felt foolish and naive. While she regretted the part she had played if Joe was sent back to prison, she couldn't help but suspect that Debbie was right and he was just one more in a long line of guilty offenders who claimed to be innocent, and that to believe otherwise would be wishful thinking on her part.

Monday was a struggle. Exhausted and preoccupied, she dragged herself through the day, finding the gaps between lessons hardest of all. Tuesday and Wednesday were better. She had a full timetable of lectures on both days and was able to throw herself into her work and gain a little reprieve from her thoughts. She continued in the same vein for the rest of the week, distracted by classes and lesson planning for stretches at a time, but during the moments in between, as she walked between the lecture halls or to the café, Joe would lurch back into her mind and her heart would skip a beat.

On Friday morning, she congratulated herself on having almost got through the week, but at the same time she dreaded the weekend. The weather was going to be unseasonably warm and Oxford would be busy. There would be clear blue skies and picnics, and punts setting off along the river from Magdalen Bridge through the Parks, which would be full of students playing volleyball or strolling along the pathways holding hands. Everyone would be living their lovely lives and she would be on her own with nothing to do except ruminate over her foolishness.

It was also Rich and Julia's wedding in just over a week's time and Rich was bound to call to ask her if she was still coming. She had said she would go, but her ex-husband's happiness was now even harder to think about, and she felt herself descending deeper into despondency. She knew the reason: she had been harbouring a hope that her relationship with Joe might have developed to the point where she could ask him if he'd like to come along as her 'plus one'. The idea was, of course, now as mortifying as it was disappointing.

At lunchtime, she decided not to bother going across to the café. She wasn't particularly hungry. The milder weather was already here and the blossom was out on the campus, which was buzzing with students and staff enjoying the sunshine. As she exited the law faculty, she found herself walking up the lane, away from the college grounds and in the opposite direction of the student village, so that no one she knew would see her and try to strike up a conversation.

She took a side street and ended up at a small park in the middle of a housing estate, sitting on a bench and gazing into the distance. She watched a magpie as it swooped down from a nearby fence, startling a baby squirrel, which darted away into a bush, and she wondered what was wrong with her. There were other men out there to date. Who on earth would choose a convicted rapist and murderer? Why take that risk, especially as she'd only known Joe such a short time? Most women would tell themselves that they'd been lucky, that they'd found out just in time, and would then move on with their lives. So why was she still thinking about him?

She took out her phone and opened his messages. *You do know me*, the last one said. *We know each other.* A familiar tightening gripped her abdomen. It wasn't just her; he'd felt it, too, this invisible cord between the two of them that was still tugging at her, squeezing her heart and her lungs and her head so that at times she couldn't think or breathe.

But maybe he was a natural predator, just like the magpie she'd been watching, who had now given up on the squirrel and was casting his eye around for his next prey. And sure, Joe hadn't lied to her outright, but he'd lied by omission. She would never have gone up into the loft with him had he been truthful with her about his past.

She cringed for the hundredth time as she remembered how eager she'd been to go upstairs with him, how naive she'd been to follow him into the remotest part of the house. And then it hit her right in the gut: she could have spent her final hours there. She could have been raped on that chipboard floor under those silver insulation boards while the sunlight danced above her, and then she could have been killed. *'There aren't any walls up yet,'* she remembered Joe telling her, and a chill ran through her as she imagined him hammering away, a nail in his mouth, the radio playing as he built the frame for the wall inside which he would bury her. *'I'll come up here and say goodnight to you before I go to bed.'* Eve closed her eyes as the words took on a new meaning. By the time her family missed her, he could have put her inside the wall cavity and boarded her over. No one would ever know she'd been there.

But he *hadn't* done that. He hadn't hurt her.

Eve forced herself to think about all the reasons why Joe might be telling the truth, the first of which was that she'd *been there*. She'd been there in the loft with him and she knew how it had felt to be with him, to talk to him. He'd been a little reserved and she'd sensed he was holding something back, but there was nothing about him that had set off alarm bells. Nothing at all. She needed to have faith in her own instincts, the instincts that had told her he was a safe person to be alone with. And the parole board must have considered him safe to release, mustn't they? Most importantly, he'd found an appeal charity that was willing to take on his case. One of the trustees had given him a place to stay after being told about him by the woman who ran the charity. That had to mean something, didn't it? Chas Cauldwell believed in him. The charity believed in him. They must do.

She held on to this thought for the rest of the afternoon, waiting until she got home and could use her own laptop before looking him up again. This time, she moved on past the headlines of the first few pages, digging deeper into the history of his case. He'd lodged two unsuccessful appeals based on inconclusive forensics and weaknesses in the ID evidence, and had served twenty years of a life sentence, although his minimum term had been fifteen. He could have been out five years sooner had he admitted his crimes.

Eve looked through her search history and found Chas Cauldwell's name, which in turn led her to the name of the charity Joe had mentioned: Truth for Justice. She wrote down the phone number. It was the weekend now, but she'd call them first thing on Monday and see what else she could find out.

16

The weekend passed slowly. On Sunday morning, Eve woke feeling listless and deflated. At half past nine, the local church bells started up their usual ringing and it reminded her of how upbeat she had felt this time last week. She remembered the intoxicating blend of dread and excitement that had coursed through her as she washed and straightened her hair, gearing herself up to go to Norham Gardens and surprise Joe. She'd been nervous, but in a good way. She'd had everything to look forward to.

And then she realised she couldn't stand not knowing – not knowing if Joe had been recalled to prison; not knowing if he was guilty or innocent. By lunchtime, she realised she couldn't go back to work the next day feeling like this. She needed answers. The same blend of dread and excitement began to creep through her as she made her decision, as once again she washed and straightened her hair, put on a bit of mascara and eyeliner and set off across the Parks. Joe might not be at home, she told herself. He might be in prison. But she wasn't going to find out by doing nothing.

When she arrived at Norham Gardens, the Volvo was outside, but she realised she didn't even know if it belonged to Joe or Chas. Chas, most likely, she decided. How could Joe own a car?

She walked onto the driveway and peered through the metal bars of the gate into the back garden. She couldn't see anyone, but the garden hose was out on the path, snaking its way from the tap on the wall onto the grass by the planters, which looked wet. She could also see Joe's radio and jacket on the bottom scaffolding plank. The radio was playing softly. She couldn't hear the song, just the sound of the notes pulsing through the still air.

She hesitated, her heart beating faster as she pushed open the gate, stepped over the hose and walked towards the back door. She paused, ready to knock, and then she saw him at the window and her heart skipped a beat. He disappeared out of view for a second and then appeared again right in front of her, unlocking the back door and opening it. His eyes were wide and fearful, but he said nothing. They stood staring at each other and then he stepped back a little so that she could come in. He closed the door and stood beside the sink, still looking at her.

He was wearing a white T-shirt and jeans, a simple combination that Eve found attractive. His expression, his hair, his face, his posture all felt so familiar to her. He looked as though he wanted to cry, and Eve felt a strong urge to comfort him.

She stepped forwards, uncertain, and reached up to stroke a strand of hair away from his forehead, then moved closer until he was right there in front of her. He leaned in, his breath stirring her hair as he murmured, 'Eve.'

And then his hands were either side of her head and he was looking into her eyes, and he was kissing her, his mouth soft and warm on hers. He leaned against her and she had to step backwards, then at the same time he stepped forwards, so that she was pressed against the wall next to the door. Eve felt a thrill rip through her as his chest pushed up against hers and squeezed the breath from her. He lifted her into his arms. Eve felt dizzy with longing. She knew that she was going to allow herself to fall off the cliff edge and into the abyss.

17

They were in a bedroom on the first floor – wide, white-walled, high-ceilinged. Opposite was a box bay window with four vertical glass panes, each with its own rucked linen blind. A pair of heavy curtains hung each side of the bay, almost ceiling to floor, and a chest of drawers stood in front. At the foot of the bed was a chaise longue with a series of cushions, and on either side of the room, a clutter of furniture: wingback chairs, a heavy oak wardrobe. A writing desk.

Eve couldn't believe what they had just done. She'd thought about it, but that had just been a fantasy, one which had come to an abrupt end when DI Carver had turned up on her doorstep. What had just happened, on the other hand, had been startlingly real.

But nice. So very nice.

Yet wild. Reckless. No condom. Not that *that* side of it mattered any more, but . . .

She felt herself flush as she thought about the frantic way they'd begun to take off each other's clothes right there in the kitchen, in full view of the back-door window – in full view of all the windows. She thought about the way Joe had kissed her, his tongue finding hers, and how he'd then leaned down and kissed her breasts. Her stomach lilted as she remembered him finding his way into her knickers and putting his fingers inside her, then taking her hand and pulling her towards the door to the hallway and up the stairs.

She glanced across at Joe. 'Is this your bedroom?' she asked, realising that it might not be.

'No,' he admitted. 'But it's not where Chas sleeps either.'

'Would he mind us being in here?'

'Honestly, I don't think so. It's just a spare room.'

Eve smiled. '"Spare Oom",' she said.

Joe gave her a quizzical frown.

'Sorry,' she laughed. 'It's just that's what Mr Tumnus says in *The Lion, the Witch and the Wardrobe*, and it reminded me. In fact, this whole house reminds me of the one in the story. From the outside, as well – it's just how I imagined it.' She grinned and eye-pointed to the wardrobe across the room to her right. 'Is there a magical world in there, by any chance?'

'Maybe.' Joe shot her a smile. 'You'll have to step inside and find out.' His smile faded. 'I . . . I didn't mean that,' he said. 'That sounded creepy.'

'No. It was funny,' Eve reassured him, then continued swiftly: 'It was my favourite book as a child, probably because everyone in Narnia kept calling the two girls "Daughters of Eve". It reminded me that I had the same name as the very first woman on earth. It made me feel kind of important.'

'You're Eve, Daughter of Eve,' Joe mused.

'"*From the far land of Spare Oom*",' Eve quoted, '"*where eternal summer reigns around the bright city of War Drobe*".'

Joe eyed her. 'That's the faun, right? The one who asks her to come to his house for a cup of tea?'

'Yes!' Eve glanced at him, pleased he knew the story, but also now thinking about the parallels between Joe and the troubled Mr Tumnus, who had, of course, lured a female to his home for tea before turning her over to the forces of evil.

'Well, I suppose I've already done that,' Joe said, reading her mind. 'And quite a bit more besides,' he added, and they looked at each other at the same time and smiled.

'Are you glad?' she asked, after a beat.

He nodded. Pink patches appeared on his cheeks as he asked, 'Are you?'

'Yes,' she said. 'Maybe a little surprised at myself – at us – if I'm honest. It was a bit unexpected . . . well, *very* unexpected, and I wouldn't normally have . . .' She trailed off a little. 'But . . . yes, I—Ouch!'

She was cut off abruptly as Joe shifted onto one elbow to face her. As he did so, the hard plastic of his electronic tag collided with the bony part of her own ankle, making her gasp out in pain.

'Oh my God,' he said, looking distraught, his blue-grey eyes seeking out hers. 'I'm so, so sorry! Are you OK?'

'It's fine,' she reassured him, taking a deep breath. Then, seeing the extent of his discomfort, she added, 'Really, Joe. It's fine. This . . .' she flipped her gaze between the two of them, side by side in bed together, '. . . it's all fine.'

Joe nodded, his Adam's apple bobbing in his throat, then he sank back down onto his side of the bed.

Eve reached out and took his hand. He gripped hers tightly, then brought it to his lips and kissed her fingers. He closed his eyes, still clutching her fist and holding it against his shoulder. She could feel him trembling and gazed at him, realising that whatever this was – whatever this might be, or could be – it was going to be way more complicated than she could ever have imagined. She rolled towards him and put her spare hand on his cheek. He opened his eyes and looked into hers.

'I was worried you'd been recalled to prison,' she said. 'I'm so glad you weren't.'

'Thanks to you.'

'Well, it wasn't really thanks to me, was it? I was the one who got you into trouble in the first place, turning up like that last Sunday.'

'No. It was my fault. I should have told you.'

'I get why you didn't.'

He let out a shaky breath. 'Thank you.'

'For what?'

'For . . . this.'

They fell silent. Joe squeezed the hand he was still holding, then placed it on the bedcovers, letting go. 'Most women would have run a mile by now,' he said, shooting her a look that she couldn't decipher. 'But you're not most women, are you?'

'I don't know what I am,' Eve confessed. 'I don't know what I'm doing here, if I'm honest. I just knew I had to see you.'

'I'm glad.' Joe swallowed. 'And grateful. And if you're

here for answers, you can ask me,' he said. 'I'll tell you. I'll tell you anything you want to know.'

Eve turned her head to meet his eyes. She had so many questions. 'The song,' she began, tentatively. '"Everybody's Changing". You said that both times it was released, something monumental had just happened in your life. You said you froze in time and the world moved on without you. Was that what you were talking about – getting arrested? Then going to prison?'

'Yes.'

She waited.

'The first time it was released was the twelfth of May 2003. I'd just been remanded to Pentonville.' He looked up at the ceiling. 'The second time was the day I was convicted,' he continued. 'The third of May 2004. They took me back to prison and it was playing in the canteen, in the common room. Everywhere.'

'It was re-released the same day they found you guilty?'

He nodded. 'Do you remember the first couple of lines – about wanting to wander your own land and not being able to?'

She nodded.

'Well, that was the day I knew for sure that I wasn't coming out of prison again for a very long time. Three weeks later, I was sentenced. The judge gave me life with a minimum of fifteen years.'

'But you did twenty,' Eve pointed out.

He shrugged. 'I had to admit I'd done it and I couldn't do that, because I hadn't.'

'So, what happened?'

'At the trial?'

'Yes, but . . . not just that.' She paused, hating herself for asking. 'I meant, what happened to Christy, the night she died?' She looked into his eyes and could see the hurt there.

'I don't know,' he said. 'I wasn't there.'

'I know,' Eve said, although she didn't, and they both knew that. 'I just meant, why did they think it was you?'

'I was seeing her.'

'As in . . . dating?'

'Kind of. It was early days. It was a bit like . . .'

'Us?'

'Yes.' He nodded. 'Except that we hadn't . . . I didn't have sex with her,' he said. 'I'd only known her for around six weeks.'

There was a pause as they both realised he'd known Eve half that time.

'So, how did you meet?' she asked.

'I was working in Streatham Hill, a few streets away from where she lived,' he said. 'There was a 7-Eleven, or whatever those corner shops used to be called, and I was there buying a cold drink and a newspaper. She was doing a bit of shopping and . . . well, I fancied her straight away.' He paused again and glanced at Eve, as if to check whether she minded him talking about another woman like this at the same time he was naked in bed with her. 'I mean, she was just . . . beautiful,' he explained. 'She had long dark hair and big brown eyes, and . . .' He paused. 'Sorry.'

'Don't be silly,' Eve said.

'She was funny. Like you,' Joe added, glancing at Eve. 'I told her I was a carpenter and she said . . .' He paused and smiled, and his eyes glinted. 'She said, "So was Jesus, and they say *he* was a good 'un."'

Eve smiled too.

'And then we got chatting and she told me her back door needed fixing and I said I'd come round after work and take a look if she liked, so she told me where she lived.'

Eve remembered reading about this. It was the prosecution's case that this was how he had gained access to Christy's house on the night she died.

'And then what happened?'

'I fixed the door – it was just sticking. I planed a bit off, and then she made me a cup of tea and we chatted for a bit, but then she said her daughter was going to be home from her dad's soon and that she needed to get the tea, so I went home. I couldn't stop thinking about her, though.'

'And so you went back?'

He nodded. 'A few times, after I finished work. We didn't swap numbers or anything – that's one of the things the police zoomed in on. I didn't have her phone number. But she always seemed pleased to see me. She always invited me in, and we got into a bit of a routine. I'd pop round after work a couple of times a week – one night during the week, usually, when her daughter was at her dad's house, and sometimes on a Saturday, when it was his weekend.'

'So you didn't meet her daughter?' Eve asked, surprised.

'No. I did.' Joe nodded. 'Once or twice. But Christy was a good mum. She wouldn't have wanted the girl . . .' He paused.

'Bella.'

'Yes. Bella. She wouldn't have wanted her to know she had a boyfriend, not until she was sure that's what I was.'

'But she identified you,' Eve said. 'Bella. She said you were there the night Christy died?'

'She got that wrong.' He shook his head vehemently. 'I wasn't there. Not *then*. Not that night. I'd been there earlier that afternoon, but . . .'

'So she got the time wrong?'

'I don't know, but she was mistaken. She didn't see me that evening. She couldn't have done.'

Eve braced herself as she asked the next question. 'So, who do you think did it?'

Joe frowned. 'If I knew the answer to that question, then I wouldn't have spent the last twenty years in prison.'

'I'm sorry,' Eve said. 'I just meant, was there anyone else on the scene? Another man who liked her, perhaps?'

He shrugged. 'I don't know. But three days after I met her there was a burglary in the street, and they never caught the person that did it. Everyone thought it was me. I saw the way people were looking at me. At first, I thought it was because I was a builder. It was a nice street and I thought they were just looking down their noses at me because of the way I was dressed. But then, after what happened . . .' He hesitated, his eyes misting. 'As soon as I got there, as soon as I got to the street, I knew. Not that it was Christy,' he corrected himself. 'But I knew it was something very, *very* bad. I walked up the road towards her house and there were people standing around outside, and then I saw the police cars, and then I got closer and saw the cordon across the front of her house, but before it even had time to register, I noticed the way everyone was looking at me, and I knew straight away that they were going to have me for it. I knew that what had happened to Christy was the very worst thing that could happen to a woman, and I knew they were going to blame me.'

He looked up at the ceiling again and Eve felt the mattress move underneath her as a shudder went through him. 'They just took me,' he said, looking bewildered. 'They just grabbed me and that was my life gone. My life and Christy's. Two lives destroyed.'

Eve reached out a hand and closed her fingers around his. 'Joe,' she said. 'Do you want to stop?'

He glanced at her gratefully, his chest rising and falling. 'Maybe we should get dressed?'

Eve nodded, realising how inappropriate it suddenly felt to be lying in bed naked, talking about what had happened to Christy. But then, as Joe got out of bed and went off to use the bathroom, she realised he had probably told her more here, like this, than he might otherwise have done. And the evidence was there in his body, she realised; she had felt it. He had been devastated by the terrible thing that had happened to Christy, and by the monumental thing that had then happened to him. 'Fragile' was not a strong enough word to describe him.

She glanced across at the empty space in the bed beside her and then at the bedroom door through which Joe had just left. Nobody could be that hurt – that *harmed* – surely, she thought to herself, not if they'd really done something so vile and hateful to another human being? They'd have to be the best actor in the world, or have spent a long time studying human behaviour and learning how *not* to be a psychopath.

18

It was 3 a.m. the following day and Eve was awake. *My God*, she thought. *I had sex with Joe. I went round to his house. We kissed and we touched each other in intimate places, and then we fucked each other in the spare bedroom in that great big house.* She screwed up her eyes in an attempt to shut out the image, but her thoughts continued. *And we didn't use a condom. I shared bodily fluids with a convicted murderer and rapist, a man who has spent the past twenty years locked up in an institution with God only knows what kind of people. I had sex for the first time in years – and that's who I chose.*

She was now back at home in her own bed, but the truth was inescapable: she'd got naked with a man she barely knew, a man who had been convicted of the most heinous and violent act a man could commit. When she had left his house earlier that evening, she had been convinced he hadn't done it and had gone to bed believing this, but now, with the darkness, came the doubt.

She kept her eyes squeezed shut, though she knew it was

futile; there was no way she was going to be able to go back to sleep, not after the shot of cortisol she had given herself. She breathed deeply and evenly from her diaphragm, telling herself that what she was feeling was an old, evolutionary response, a relic from the past; this was the time of the night when humans were biologically programmed to be alert and ready to fight or to flee from a nocturnal predator – a lion or tiger, perhaps.

She got out of bed and went into the kitchen, where she switched on the fairy lights that she used to decorate a vase on the windowsill, then filled the kettle. As it boiled, she walked herself through everything that had happened that afternoon. While Joe was in the bathroom, she had got dressed and gone downstairs into the kitchen, where he had found her a few minutes later. He had made tea – more tea – and then he had sat down at the table next to her and told her that he thought they should keep what had happened between them. He didn't touch her, or even look at her, as he spoke, and Eve had thought to herself, *So that's it, then. I'm being dumped.* But she had seen the conflict in his eyes. He would have to tell his probation officer, he'd said, if their relationship was to continue to be a physical one, and that wasn't what he wanted for her.

Eve had nodded, imagining the conversation he would have with Debbie Stroud, who was no doubt unused to many women sticking around after being told that the new man in their life had been to prison and was 'high risk' and dangerous. She would think Eve stupid, or reckless, or desperate, or mad, or all four things. Eve couldn't help but wonder, too, what her colleagues and family would think of her, especially

Mackenzie, who already managed to find a million ways to be critical of her mother.

Joe had detected her disappointment. 'You make me feel things I didn't think I'd feel again,' he had said. 'But there are too many problems, too many obstacles.'

He didn't want Eve's personal life to be aired in public, or for her to be tainted by the stigma attached to him, or restricted by his licence conditions. He had a night-time curfew, for one; he couldn't even take her out for dinner. Over time, with good behaviour, he might be a little freer, but he didn't feel free and he didn't think he ever would, not unless and until he was able to successfully overturn his conviction. Until then, he had nothing to offer a woman.

Eve had opened her mouth to protest but stopped herself. This was the truth – *his* truth – and anything she said to the contrary would seem false and trite. And besides, he was right: there *would* be shame for her in going out into the world as a couple. How could there not be? She would be sustained for a while by the memory of what had happened between them – she might even enjoy hugging their secret to herself – but was she ready to face the world if someone found out?

'Do your lawyers think you have a case?' she asked.

'I don't know yet,' he said. 'I'm seeing someone on Friday. She's been waiting for the papers. It takes time,' he said. 'All of it. It takes so much time.'

Eve nodded. 'But they must think there's something there, to even be considering it?'

'I hope so. But my lawyer said she won't know until she gets disclosure of everything she's asked for from the police.'

Eve had wanted to ask about his previous appeal, but could tell that Joe was emotionally spent, so she'd got up to leave, saying she had lesson planning to do before tomorrow, and he had looked sorry that she was going and at the same time relieved. Then, as if reading her mind, he'd told her that the appointment with his solicitor on Friday would be here, at his home, and had asked Eve if she wanted to be there.

'In your capacity as a lawyer, in case anyone asks,' he said.

Eve had been pleased. Friday was her quiet day at college and she would be able to move things around and get away for a couple of hours.

'You can be my innocence project,' she'd told him. 'Some academics have them.'

As she left, they'd kissed awkwardly in the doorway – a chastened kiss on the cheek, nothing more. She had walked back home across the Parks. As she entered her street, she'd wondered if anyone had seen her leaving Joe's house and had almost expected the detective to appear on her doorstep again. She had got a little paranoid about it and spent a few minutes walking up and down the road, peering inside the parked cars.

Now, she made herself a cup of chamomile tea and took it into the living room, where she settled down on the sofa, pulling a throw over her and a cushion beneath her head. It was still dark outside, but the moonlight was streaming in through the window, bringing with it an aura of comfort and a reminder that Joe was asleep – or awake, perhaps? – on the other side of the park. She closed her eyes, remembering how hurt he had looked as they lay, side by side, in bed together, how he'd clung to her hand and the way he had trembled, and it occurred to her that if he *was* a fake and a fraud – and a murderer and rapist – then what would be the point in trying to convince her of his innocence? Yes, she knew the law, but he already had a lawyer, so why would he need her?

And that was a very good question, wasn't it, because if he were the kind of man who could do what he was accused of – tie up a woman, gag her, violently rape her and kill her – how could he be capable of genuinely caring for a woman as an individual?

19

Bella drove south to King's Cross, through Clerkenwell and across Waterloo Bridge towards Streatham. She needed to talk to her dad about her nightmares, and about Jamie Clarke. It was a warm day, the sun already high in the sky, softened by a gentle breeze that lifted the sparkle from the Thames into her eyeline. She wound down the car windows – all four of them. It felt encouraging, as if the wind and the spray from the water were carrying her forward, but still she felt uneasy at the thought of the impending conversation. For all her fights with her dad over clothes and make-up and friends and curfew times, she had never tugged too hard at the loose threads of the narrative of her life before she came to live with him. He had made it clear that she couldn't possibly remember things differently, and it was true that the trauma of the final few hours had pushed everything that came before it into the shadows.

Her father's neighbourhood was empty and quiet, his house still. Her stepmum, Jenny, let her in, her surprised look suffused with an undercurrent of dismay that told Bella she expected trouble. Her dad was in his favourite armchair in the living room, sleeping off his lunch with one eye on the football. He pulled himself into an upright position when he saw her, his expression wary.

'We weren't expecting you,' he said, looking confused, as if he had perhaps forgotten she was coming. His thin grey hair was matted to his head, and his glasses had slipped down his nose. He looked older and more tired than the last time Bella had seen him, and she was momentarily moved by this, but then he pulled his usual mocking face. 'To what do we owe this pleasure?'

'Do I need a reason to visit you?'

He shrugged. 'No Justin today?'

'He's got Robbie. They're going to the zoo.'

'You should have gone with them.'

'Instead of visiting you?'

'He's a good bloke, that Justin. He's good for you.'

'Like a vitamin pill?' Bella asked him.

Her dad huffed and absorbed himself in his newspaper.

'Or maybe a Valium. Or a zopiclone?'

There was no answer.

She sighed. 'I spoke to Kathy earlier.'

'Kathy?' he said, still reading, or pretending to.

'My VLO.'

'Oh yeah? What about?'

'About Jamie Clarke.'

Her dad looked up. 'What about him?'

'He's been released from the hostel. He's now free to live where he wants. Within reason.'

Her dad looked back down at his newspaper.

'*How do you feel about that, Bella?*' she mimicked. '*Would you like to talk about it?*'

'There's no need for sarcasm,' he muttered.

'Well, then . . . chuck the ball back, Dad,' she said, frustrated.

'What do you want me to say?'

'That I don't need to worry. That he's not going to hurt me.'

'Of course he's not going to hurt you.'

'How do you know that?' Bella argued. 'I was the star witness. I got him banged up for twenty years. He's not exactly going to be happy with me, is he?'

'You didn't do much. You didn't even go to court.'

'Yeah. And why *was* that?' Bella asked. She had often wondered exactly how it had come about that she had never been cross-examined by Jamie Clarke's defence team.

'Because you were too young to go on the stand.'

She hesitated. 'Maybe I was too young to know what I saw?'

'For God's sake, Bella,' her dad said irritably. 'Why have you brought this up again? You told the police you were a hundred per cent certain that it was Clarke.'

'I've seen the transcript of my interview with the police, Dad. I don't think that's what I meant.'

Her dad looked uncomfortable.

'I think what I meant,' she continued, 'was that I was a hundred per cent certain that I'd seen him before, which I would have done if he came to the house. If he was her boyfriend.'

'He wasn't her boyfriend.'

'You don't know that.'

Her dad straightened up in his chair. 'Seriously? You're sticking up for that piece of shit?'

'No, Dad. I'm sticking up for the truth.'

'The truth is that Jamie Clarke is a rapist and a murdering scumbag and your mum was too—' He broke off.

'Go on, say it!'

Her dad looked down at his paper again. Bella could see Jenny hovering in the doorway, unsure whether to intervene.

'She should never have let him in,' her dad said finally. 'She was too much of a . . .'

'What?' Bella insisted. 'Go on. What was she?'

'She was just a bit too trusting,' Jenny said, from the doorway. 'That's all he means.'

Bella felt a burst of rage. 'You don't know what really happened, Dad,' she said. 'You weren't there.'

The room fell silent.

'*Were* you?' Bella asked, the question suddenly entering her mind.

'Of course I bloody wasn't.'

'Well, then, you don't know. No one knows for sure – except me. And I don't remember who I saw that night. I only remember what I saw the next morning.'

'You told the police it was Jamie Clarke,' her dad said stubbornly.

'But I'm not sure any more. I've been having dreams, and there's someone there in the house. For years, he's been in the hallway, at the foot of the stairs, but now he's started to come up. It's like he's coming for me, and . . . and it doesn't feel like it's Jamie Clarke.'

Bella paused as this realisation hit her. She hadn't been able to put this thought into words until now, but as soon as she'd said it, she knew it was true.

'For Christ's sake, Bella, of course it was Clarke – and he's done his time and he's got conditions and he's—'

'I never see his face, Dad. The man on the stairs. I never see his face. And that's what's frightening me the most. I need to know who he is.'

Her dad flung down his paper. 'It's just a bad dream, Bella. For God's sake, grow up!'

Bella felt stung by this, but she persevered. 'I just need you to tell me,' she said, keeping her voice steady, 'if you can think of anyone else who could have been inside the house that night. Could one of the neighbours have come in, perhaps?'

Jenny stepped into the room. 'If one of the neighbours had come in, they would have found your mother. They would have seen her immediately and called the police.'

'Unless it was one of them who killed her,' Bella suggested.

'Don't be ridiculous,' her dad said.

'That *is* ridiculous, Bella,' Jenny agreed. 'I met every single one of those neighbours. They really cared about your mum. They did everything they could to help put that man away.'

Bella thought about the neighbours. There was that woman, Carly Benfield, from up the road, and Mr Norris from across the way, and Mrs Barlow, who had held her hand until her dad had arrived. A voice came to her. It was one of those neighbours. Which one? She didn't know, but she could picture her, sitting here on the sofa where Bella was now. *'You remembered right, love,'* she had said. *'It was his eyes, wasn't it? You couldn't forget those eyes.'*

Bella had seen Jamie Clarke's eyes. She had seen the scores of online articles describing them as 'chilling' or 'evil'. 'THE EYES OF A MONSTER!' the headlines had screamed out.

But twenty years on, these images were now all mixed up in her mind, and she could no longer say for sure which ones were memories and which were photographs.

R. v. *James Joseph Clarke*

DEFENCE SUMMARY OF EVIDENCE

(May–June 2003)

Civilian Witnesses – Blenheim Road:

15 Kerry Munt	17 **Christy** **Nicholls** **(victim)**	19 Brenda Barlow	21	23 Carly Benfield	25 Louise Coulter (Burglary victim)
		14 Tony Norris			20 Stacey Gillis

Kerry Munt: Lived next door to CN for 2.5 years. Would often chat to her over the fence. On Saturday, 15th March at around 5 p.m. saw a man go into CN's house with a tool bag, now knows him to be JC. Describes him as medium build, approx. 6ft tall, late 20s/early 30s with piercing blue eyes and looking a bit scruffy in jeans and 'work boots'. Heard a loud noise coming from CN's back garden and looked out of her kitchen window. Saw the same man using some kind of electric tool on her back door. Got chatting to CN in the garden the following day and asked about her door. CN told her it had been sticking and that she had met the man in the Spar on Stamford Road and he had offered to come and fix it for her. Three days later met LC in the street and found out that she had been burgled. Everyone in street worried. Says police did house-to-house and came to her house to take a statement. At approx. 11 a.m. the previous day (2nd May), heard police cars and ambulance outside and found out CN raped and murdered. Shocked, etc. Did not hear anything the previous night, but noticed that JC was 'hanging round' CN's house a lot before it happened. Never spoke to him but 'he made her feel uncomfortable'. Doesn't believe CN was interested in him romantically – he was 'punching above his weight'. CN was wonderful, warm-hearted, the kind of person who wouldn't want to hurt someone's feelings by telling them to leave her alone. STATEMENT MADE 3rd MAY 2003.

Carly Benfield: Eyewitness. Lives 3 doors down from CN. On evening of 1st May at around 9.45 p.m. was outside her house, putting out the bin for collection the following day, when she saw a man leaving CN's house. Describes him as medium build, approx. 6ft, late 20s/early 30s with 'piercing' blue eyes. He was wearing a blue jumper and jeans. She immediately recognised him as a man she had seen going in and out of CN's house on at least 3 or 4 occasions since the burglary that happened at no. 25 in March. Was paying particular attention to him because the police had told 'everyone' to be vigilant and because he didn't live in the street. Never spoke to him, but could tell he was an oddball, 'a bit weird'. He turned right out of CN's front garden, but even though it was dark, 100% sure it was him. STATEMENT MADE 2nd MAY 2003.

Stacey Gillis: Friends with CN. Lives 4 doors down from her on the other side of the road. At some point in mid-March police made her aware of a burglary at the house opposite in which several items were stolen. They did house-to-house inquiries and 'asked us all' to be vigilant. Saw a man hanging round CN's house a lot, who she hadn't seen before. Describes him as medium build, 6ft, late 20s/ early 30s with 'creepy' blue eyes. Now knows him to be JC. He said hello to her once when she was out with her 3-yr-old daughter. Didn't like the way he looked at her. Got a bad feeling about him. When she heard about CN being attacked immediately thought of him. Did not witness either crime but describes Blenheim Road as a lovely road to live on, affluent, friendly, community-minded, etc. Nothing like this has happened before. Describes CN as having been kind, caring, bubbly, full of life. Once asked her if JC was bothering her and CN said no, but she looked uncomfortable when she said it. Thinks he was harassing her. STATEMENT MADE 3rd MAY 2003.

Tony Norris: Eyewitness. Lives diagonally opposite CN (opposite her next-door neighbour Brenda Barlow). On evening of 1st May at around 9.45 p.m. was outside his house, putting out the bin for collection the following day, when he saw a man leaving CN's house. Describes him as medium build, approx. 6ft, late 20s/early 30s with 'piercing' blue eyes. He was wearing a blue jumper and jeans and TN immediately recognised him as a man he had seen going in and out of CN's house on at least 3 or 4 occasions since the burglary that happened at no. 25 in March. Was paying particular attention to him because the police had told 'everyone' to be vigilant and he didn't live in the street. Never spoke to him, but could tell he was 'a loner' and 'a bit weird'. He turned right out of CN's front garden, but even though it was dark, TN 100% sure it was him. STATEMENT MADE 3rd MAY 2003.

Louise Coulter: (Burglary victim.) Lives 4 doors down from CN. Knew her for 2.5 years – good friends. Extremely upset about her rape and murder, which immediately brought to mind what happened 6 weeks earlier, when she was the victim of a burglary. Burglar gained entry through her back door, which was damaged. Items taken included a pair of knickers from FatFace (pale blue with pink and white daisies and a lace trim). Was made aware by KM and other neighbours in the street that a man she now knows to be JC kept turning up uninvited at CN's house after coming to fix her back door. Believes he was becoming a pest or stalker. Told police about him as suspected he might be responsible for the burglary. Very traumatised by the thought that what happened to CN could have happened to her if she had been home at the time of the burglary. STATEMENT MADE 20th JUNE 2003.

Brenda Barlow: CN's next-door neighbour, other side from KM, opposite eyewitness Tony Norris. Hears banging at the front door at 7.50 a.m. on Friday, 2nd May, finds CN's 7-year-old daughter, BD, crying on the doorstep. BD tells her 'Mummy has been hurt. A man tied her up. She can't move.' Follows BD into CN's house through the open front door and through the lounge into the kitchen, where she sees CN on the floor, naked from the waist down, gagged and tied up. Can immediately see that she is no longer alive and calls 999. STATEMENT MADE 2nd MAY 2003.

20

Sarah stopped typing and gazed at the summary she'd prepared of the statements she had received so far. What stood out for her was that they were, for the most part, overwhelmingly prejudicial. The statements of Coulter, Munt and Gillis contained no direct evidence against Jamie relating to either the burglary or the charges on the indictment in his original trial, and yet the prosecution had used the burglary and the judgements the residents had made about him to portray him as a predator who had committed both offences. She noticed that Louise Coulter hadn't given her statement until 20th June, several weeks after Jamie had been charged, and as for Benfield and Norris, their statements were almost identical. She could see why his previous lawyers had raised this as an appeal point. There was a lot to object to here.

But she also knew how hard it could be to get an appeal case across the line into the 'for sure' territory that was needed for a conviction to be found unsafe.

She looked up as Will came into the living room with a

bottle of wine and two glasses, which he set down on the coffee table beside her. He unscrewed the cap, then poured them each a generous serving. 'How's it looking?' he asked.

She tilted her head to one side. 'Well, there are definitely things that concern me.'

'Like . . .?'

'Like the way they've used the burglary against him. He was never charged with it, and yet they've made it part of their case.'

'Have you spoken to him yet?' he asked, handing her a wine glass.

'Only briefly, on the phone,' she said, taking a sip. 'I'm seeing him tomorrow. And by the way, he calls himself Joe these days.'

'He's changed his name?'

'He's using his middle name. All approved by probation.'

Will nodded. 'So do you know what he's saying?'

'Not yet, but I know what he said in his police interview back in 2003. He gave a full account, denied it, cooperated fully with the investigation. Volunteered his DNA and semen and agreed to go on an ID parade.'

'Hmm.' Will wrinkled his nose. 'Sometimes that happens, even when they're guilty. Some murderers get overconfident and convince themselves they won't be caught. It's also common for them to return to the crime scene and insinuate themselves into the investigation. Remember Ian Huntley, speaking to the press?'

'Yes. I do,' Sarah agreed. 'Not that Joe had a chance for any of that. He was pointed out to the police and identified straight away.'

'Ah, yes. The two eyewitnesses.' Will paused. 'So, remind me, who were they?'

'Carly Benfield and Anthony Norris.'

'Were they a couple?'

'Not that I'm aware of. Tony Norris lived at number fourteen, which was across the road from Christy's next-door neighbour, Brenda. Carly Benfield was a few doors down on the same side as Christy, at number twenty-three. But they both saw Joe leaving Christy's house at around nine forty-five.'

'So, what were they doing out in the street at that time of night?'

'Putting out the bins.'

'Both of them?'

'The next day was bin collection day.'

'And how dark would it have been?'

'Completely. It begins to get dark at eight thirty in early May.'

Will considered this. 'Was a Turnbull direction given?'

Sarah nodded. 'The judge ran through the guidelines in his summing-up. Distance. Visibility. Obstruction. How long they had him in sight. Whether they'd seen him before and how often, and all the other stuff – "*An honest witness may be wrong, even if they are convinced they are right; a convincing witness may still be wrong . . .*" blah blah blah. He covered it all. But their evidence was accepted.'

'Juries like eyewitnesses,' Will murmured. 'They like nothing more than a human being standing in front of them, pointing a finger.'

They fell silent, both thinking.

'We need to eat,' Will said at last, rubbing his temples. 'What do you fancy?'

Sarah turned her gaze towards him, but Will could see her mind was elsewhere.

'Go on,' he said. 'What is it?'

'Remember when I went to put our bins out on Sunday evening and neither of us could remember whether it was the week for rubbish or recycling?'

Will nodded.

'Well, it was too dark for me to be able to see what colour bins everyone had put out, not even Jill's next door. I had to go back inside to get my phone and put on the torch.'

'I suspect it would be easier to identify a person. And the street lighting may have been better.'

'But it would still have to have been pretty dark. They both said he turned right out of Christy's front garden and went east towards Telford Avenue, in the opposite direction from where they were standing. So how could they have seen the colour of his eyes?'

Will frowned. 'Read the description for me again.'

Sarah tapped the trackpad on her laptop and brought her summary of the evidence back up. 'Medium build, approximately six feet tall, in his late twenties to early thirties with mousy brown hair and piercing blue eyes. Blue jeans, blue jumper. A few other things, but basically they were describing Joe. If you look at the online photos of him, his eyes are unmistakably blue and piercing, but I don't think they would have stood out in the dark.'

'Any inconsistencies in their statements?'

'No. They both said the exact same thing. That was part of the grounds for his first appeal, in fact. His lawyers said their statements were *too* similar, the suggestion being that they had talked before giving their statements, or that someone had coached them. But there was no foundation for that suggestion and the Court of Appeal threw it out.'

'What reason might they have had to lie, or to convince themselves it was Joe?'

'Well, the burglary. They believed he'd done it,' Sarah reminded him. 'They were all het up that the police still hadn't caught anyone for it. Joe was the newcomer to the street. Seems a lot of people thought it was him.'

'Was there any evidence to support that?'

'I don't know,' Sarah said. 'But I've drafted a disclosure application and I've asked for the police file.'

'On the burglary?'

'Yes. It wasn't made available to his lawyers during the original trial.'

'You think they'll give it to you?'

'I don't know.' Sarah put down her papers. 'But I think they ought to. The prosecution have painted a pretty good picture of a man on the prowl.'

21

Bella sat in her car outside her dad's house and had the sudden, uncomfortable sensation that she was being watched. She brushed it off as paranoia, brought on by the argument she'd just had with her dad and all the stuff about Jamie Clarke being released, and being here, all alone, in Streatham – which might well not even be where Clarke was now living. But she no longer wanted to feel spooked by any of this, that was the thing.

She started the engine and drove to her old home in Blenheim Road, where she parked opposite number seventeen and looked across at the front-room window. She hadn't dared to come back at first, partly because of the trauma of her final day there, and also because she hadn't wanted to run into any of the neighbours. But after she'd learned to drive, she would come back from time to time. She would just park up and sit there, gazing at the house, feeling nostalgic as she tried to remember her life with her mother. She sometimes had a flash of herself in the living room as a child, the sun casting a globe of light over the carpet as she lounged on her tummy and elbows, drawing. But usually it wasn't long before all the other thoughts would crash in.

She remembered the police arriving. The sirens and flashing blue lights outside the living-room window. The tight knot of fear in her chest as strangers in uniforms flooded the hallway, the living room, the kitchen. The deep, all-consuming ache in her gut as she was led up the stairs to her bedroom and told to pack up her belongings. How badly and suddenly she had needed the toilet; how mortified she had been at having to ask permission from the policewoman, who had watched her from her bedroom doorway.

But she couldn't remember what she'd packed, or what she'd owned, or even what her bedroom had looked like. She could only remember the atmosphere of fear and shame – the same atmosphere that still lingered in her nightmares – and so, in the days and weeks that followed, she had been left with little choice but to accept what people were telling her, to go along with their version of what had happened to her. She had done so without question because she was a child in a world full of adults who claimed to know more, and to know better. Even Jenny seemed to know more, though she hadn't met Bella's dad until the following year.

She looked over to the house next door, which was where she had run to that morning. She remembered the lady who had lived there, Mrs Barlow. She had been kind, Bella remembered. Warm. Gentle. Different from the other neighbours, who had all seemed a little too interested in the drama that had unfolded in their street. They kept turning up at her dad's house, pretending to have been good friends with her mother, which Bella knew wasn't true.

On a sudden whim, she got out of her car and walked over to the house. She paused, briefly, then opened the front gate and began to walk up the path. She knocked on the door, feeling weak with fright as the panic she had felt that day began to resurface. This was where she had stood. This was where she had rung the doorbell and knocked on the door repeatedly until Mrs Barlow's shocked face appeared.

A young woman with a pixie haircut came to the door, holding a baby.

'I'm sorry to bother you,' Bella said, holding back tears. 'I was looking for Mrs Barlow.'

The woman shifted the baby across to her opposite hip. 'I'm afraid she doesn't live here any more. We've been here five years now.'

Bella nodded and swallowed hard.

'Are you OK?' the woman asked.

Bella nodded again, not trusting herself to speak.

'I used to live next door,' she said, after a moment. 'Years ago. Twenty years ago, actually.'

'Oh. I see,' the woman said, recognition clouding her features. 'I'm sorry. I mean, if it was your mother who . . .'

'Yes. It was.'

The baby leaned forward and reached out a hand towards Bella, who smiled and held out her car keys, which the baby grabbed at, looking delighted. And then she and the woman both laughed as the baby snatched them.

'No, Livvy,' the woman said. 'Give them back.'

'My fault,' Bella said. 'I shouldn't have put temptation in her way.'

'She just loves people.' The woman managed to extract the car keys from her baby's chubby fist and handed them back to Bella.

'I love *her*. She's so cute.'

'Thank you.'

'Anyway, I'm sorry to have bothered you.' Bella turned to leave.

'Wait,' the woman said, her face softening in pity. 'You look like you need a hug.'

And then she stepped out of her house and put one arm around Bella, and Bella clutched the woman and the baby, who tugged at her hair, and she cried. And then a memory surfaced, as clear as day. Mrs Barlow holding her in her arms on that same doorstep, telling her she was brave.

'Do you know where she went?' Bella asked. 'The lady who lived here?'

'I'm not sure,' the woman said. 'But I might have a phone number somewhere, from around the time the sale went through. If you'd like to leave me yours, I could have a hunt for it?'

'Thank you. If you don't mind.'

As Bella walked back into the street, she saw a black saloon car driving slowly past. She felt sure she had seen the same car an hour earlier as she had driven to Blenheim Road from her dad's. She felt a rush of adrenaline as she tried to catch a glimpse of the driver, but the windows were too dark.

22

Friday arrived and with it another cloudless sky. Eve spent the morning on campus and then cycled to Norham Gardens. She met Joe in the back garden, where he was tending to the flower beds, a mug of tea next to him on the low wall. He offered her one and she said she would wait for Sarah. She realised how much she was looking forward to having an independent perspective on all the thoughts about Joe that were still crashing around in her head.

They heard the noise of a car engine outside and the sound of a vehicle pulling up onto the gravel behind the Volvo. Joe stood up and crossed the path to the gate, and Eve stood up, too. She waited as he walked out onto the driveway, returning a few moments later with a woman in her late thirties or early forties who had wavy fair hair pulled back into a loose knot. She was wearing a yellow crocheted vest-style top, three-quarter-length jeans and trainers. Her casual appearance immediately put Eve at ease.

'Hello.' Sarah smiled warmly and held out her hand. Eve took it.

'Eve is also a lawyer,' Joe added.

'Well, I'm an academic,' Eve said, a little dismissively. 'I haven't practised in decades.' She smiled. 'You know what they say. Those who can, do; those who can't, teach.'

Sarah frowned. 'You're training the next generation of lawyers,' she said earnestly. 'I wouldn't be here today without my law professor. She was brilliant.'

The introductions over, they went into the house through the back door. Joe offered Sarah use of the study next to the kitchen, but Sarah said, 'This is perfect, right here, if that works for you?'

Joe agreed that it did and turned to put the kettle on again while Sarah took a laptop out of her rucksack and Eve slid into her usual seat.

'I've made Joe aware,' Sarah said, setting herself up at the table to Eve's left and sitting down, 'that anything he tells me is confidential, but this doesn't apply to you. Obviously you are legally trained,' she said, fixing her eyes on Eve's, 'but you're not retained as his lawyer, which means that you could – in theory – talk to anyone you like about his case.'

'Oh, no,' Eve said, 'I wouldn't—'

'But you could,' Sarah argued. 'And that's what I need Joe to understand. It might help if you were able to reinforce this.'

'Sarah's right,' Eve said, turning to Joe. 'I could, in theory, go to a newspaper or to my family or to the police and tell them everything you've said here today. But I'm not going to,' she added. 'Of course I'm not going to.'

Sarah raised an eyebrow at Joe.

'I get it,' he said. 'But I trust Eve, and I want her here. I want *her* to trust *me*.'

'OK, then,' Sarah said decisively and turned her eyes towards the screen in front of her.

They both watched as Sarah moved a finger across the trackpad on her laptop and clicked open a document.

'The first thing I want you to know,' she said, looking up, 'is that we're going to be meeting a lot. As Joe no doubt realises by now, criminal appeals are notoriously difficult to bring, especially at this stage, post-conviction. You first have to apply to the CCRC – the Criminal Cases Review Commission – and it's not their job to decide if you are innocent or guilty. They have a different test. They have to decide – based on the evidence we present to them – whether the Court of Appeal is likely to come to a different conclusion from the one it came to previously.'

'They have to predict what another person might do,' Eve observed.

'What *three* other people might do, but yes,' Sarah agreed. 'Many lawyers consider it to be an irrational test, but until someone manages to change it, that's the law, and so it doesn't matter how weak, or suspicious, or worrying the evidence is that convicted you, if the Court of Appeal have already heard that evidence and the CCRC thinks it's unlikely to change its mind, they will refuse to refer it back.' She paused, looking at Joe. 'And that's the other part of the problem. The Court of Appeal often *won't* reverse a decision it has already made. It's very conservative and there is genuinely very little belief that the system gets it wrong. Also, the available grounds for appeal are very restrictive. There are only a handful of gateways. The upshot is that in Joe's case, it is going to boil down to whether we can find any significant new evidence that points to his innocence, something that hasn't been presented before and is hugely compelling. And then, as I said, you've first got to get past the CCRC – and to put this into perspective, out of every fifteen or sixteen hundred cases they look at each year, only thirty are referred back.'

'Only thirty out of every fifteen hundred appeal cases make it into a courtroom?' Joe said, looking shocked.

'Beyond the first right to appeal, yes. That's been the average for many years, and definitely since you last tried in 2012.'

'So why are they even there?'

'Well, in theory—'

'To sort through the slush pile?' Eve suggested.

'But in a very restrictive way,' Sarah said.

'So they're really there to block you,' Joe said.

Sarah exhaled. 'There were good intentions initially. The CCRC was set up after a series of wrongful convictions in the seventies and early eighties, their mission being to investigate potential miscarriages of justice and refer them back to the Court of Appeal. It started out well with a full complement of full-time staff before suffering the most horrific cuts, and now there's a skeleton crew of commissioners working only one day a week, so of course there's a huge backlog. Over the years, it has become clear that its mission is to act as a gatekeeper for the Court of Appeal, not to support those who potentially have a good case for wrongful conviction – so, yes, Joe, it *is* more likely to look for reasons *not* to refer.'

Joe took this in. Eve wanted to reach out and take his hand, but she knew any physical contact might alert Sarah to there being something between them that went further than friendship. She wasn't a good actor. She hoped Joe wasn't either – in fact, she was banking on this.

'Don't get me wrong,' Sarah said. 'I'm not here to tell you that it's going to be impossible. We just need to be realistic. Joe has already tried to get the CCRC to refer his case back once before and they refused. So this time we need to be in that "for sure" territory before we even try, which means that I am going to be reliant on every small nugget of information I can glean from you. I'm going to need you to tell me anything and everything, whether you think it's relevant or not, so that I can see if there is anything I can use – something that didn't come up at the original trial, perhaps, something that your previous legal team didn't know about, or didn't spot, or didn't consider important. I'm going to need you to tell me the whole story of what happened all over again, starting right at the very beginning, and I'm going to need as much detail as you can give me.'

'OK.' Joe nodded.

'Good.' She sat back and looked at him. 'So, we'll start in a moment. But first of all – putting aside everything I've just said – how are you bearing up, Joe? Are you doing OK?'

Eve glanced at Joe, giving him a half smile of encouragement.

'I'm OK,' he said, taking a shaky breath. 'I know how lucky I am to be living in a house like this, to have this support. I know most ex-prisoners aren't so lucky.'

'No,' Sarah agreed. 'They're not. And you're doing some work for Chas, too, is that right?'

Joe nodded. 'A loft conversion. It's the sort of thing I used to do before I went to prison, and when I told him, he saw an opportunity for both of us. He also liked the idea of having someone to look after this place while he was away, and so . . . well, like I said, I've been lucky.'

'But is there anyone else? What about family?'

Joe shook his head. 'Just my mum. My dad died in 2008 and my brothers both disowned me pretty much straight away after I got arrested. I haven't spoken to them in years.'

'I'm sorry to hear that.' Sarah typed this up. 'But your mum is supportive?'

'Yes. But she's in Woking now. My parents moved there after I went to prison. She's seventy-five and she doesn't own a car and she still works part-time, so she can't visit me easily, and I won't go to her house. I wouldn't do that to her. She spent a lot of years being spat at in the street.'

'Anyone else. Friends? Aunts? Uncles? Cousins?'

Joe shook his head. 'We weren't a close family. I got into trouble a bit as a kid. You probably know that. It took me a while to find my place in the world.' He glanced sideways at Eve. 'And you probably know that I got a conviction for criminal damage in my mid-twenties.'

'I saw that,' Sarah said. 'I was surprised it was adduced at your trial, though. What happened?'

Joe coloured. 'I broke my neighbour's wing mirror. I was angry. He kept parking in my space and I lost it. It was stupid. I was working long hours on building sites, so I was tired by the time I got home, and I had all this equipment to carry, and we got into a row.'

'And they used that against you in a murder case?' Sarah frowned.

'They said it showed a . . .'

'A propensity?' Sarah suggested.

'Yes. That's it,' Joe said. 'A propensity for violence. It was stupid and I regretted it straight away. I apologised to my neighbour and he didn't even want it to go to court, but he had already made a statement and I had already admitted it, so they had the evidence they needed. But I turned my life around after that and I was doing OK,' he said. 'I was saving up. I was going to buy a house and start working on my own renovations.'

'OK. We'll come back to that,' Sarah said. 'But first of all, is there anything else you want to tell me? Anything that might be unhelpful, I mean? We may as well get it out into the open.'

'Not that I can think of.' Joe coloured a little again and exchanged glances with Eve, who shook her head.

Sarah peered back down at her laptop. 'OK, so let's go over the information I already have. Do you remember what you said to the police when you were first interviewed?'

'I said the same thing I said at the trial – that I didn't do it.'

'You said you were dating Christy, or in the early stages of a relationship, one that became physical on the day she died.'

'Yes.'

'And that's why your DNA was on her T-shirt and bra.'

'Yes.'

'You said that on the day she died, you went round at four thirty, after you'd finished work?'

'Yes.'

'And this was a Thursday. Where was Bella?'

'Asleep on the sofa. She'd been off school with a stomach bug.'

'And did she see you come in?'

'No. She was asleep when I got there. Christy saw me from the front-room window. She waved to me, signalling that I should come round the back way, so as not to wake Bella. She opened the back door for me and I came into the kitchen. She made me a cup of tea and we sat at the table and chatted quietly. We were almost whispering.'

'But you didn't actually see Bella?'

'No. The door to the living room was shut the whole time.'

'And then at around half past six or so, you stood up to leave. Christy got up too, you said, and she put her arms around you, and so you kissed her and then you got a bit carried away.'

'Yes.' Joe flushed. 'I touched her . . .'

'Underneath her clothing?' Sarah asked.

'Yes. I put my hand under her T-shirt and I touched her bra and I . . .'

'Kissed her there?'

'Yes.'

'On her clothes? Under her clothes?'

'Both.' Joe's cheeks were pink and Eve tried not to think about him having done this to her only a few days ago. 'But it was me who stopped it from going any further. Bella was asleep in the next room, and we had only met a handful of times before and I didn't want to rush things.'

'And so you went home.'

'Yes.'

'And Bella didn't see you leave?'

'Not that I was aware of.'

'So, this was at around seven o'clock, you said. You had a job you had to price up for the following morning, and then you ate dinner and went to bed.'

'The job was a loft conversion, believe it or not,' Joe said, sighing. 'I was almost certainly going to get it.'

'And can anyone corroborate this?'

'That I was going to get the job?'

'That you were at home, pricing it up.'

Joe shook his head. 'My housemates were out. They always went to the pub after work on a Thursday. Most of us worked a week in hand and Thursday was usually pay day. I told the police that. They asked me why I didn't go to the pub, and I said I had this job to price up and I wanted to get an early night. They asked me what I watched on television that evening and I told them I didn't, that I went to bed and read a book. They didn't believe me. They thought it was weird that everyone else except me went down the pub after work on pay day, and my solicitor said they didn't find a book by my bed when they searched my room, and because I was so flustered and upset, I couldn't remember the name of the book when they asked me.'

'Can you remember it now?' Sarah asked.

'I've remembered it every day for the past twenty years,' Joe told her ruefully. 'And I've kicked myself every day, too. It was Alain de Botton's *The Consolations of Philosophy*, which is ironic because the title is a reference to the book of the same name by Boethius, a Roman senator who ended up in prison, on death row, for treason in AD 523. Little did I know at the time that was where I was going to be heading. Luckily, there were no plans to execute me.' He paused, then gave an awkward smile and asked, 'Is that too much information?'

'Nowhere near.' Sarah smiled back. 'So what happened to it? The book? Do you know?'

'No idea,' Joe said. 'But I lived in a shared house at the time, which was a bit like living in Piccadilly Circus. By the time the police came round to search my room, anyone could have gone in and taken it. There were no locks on any of the doors and it's the sort of thing my housemates would have found funny when they were drunk.'

'Who were your housemates?'

'Three other lads, I think. Or was it four? They were doing similar kind of work to me. I didn't know any of them before I moved in. I just rented a room. It was that kind of place.'

'Full of transients?'

'Exactly. Builders, mostly. There was a fair bit of work around there at the time. I remember one was an Irish lad and the others were Eastern Europeans – one Pole, I think, and two Latvians.'

'What were they like?'

'Big. Burly. Noisy. They drank a lot of beer and ate a lot of meat, I remember that. There were lots of barbecues.'

'And were they often drunk?'

Joe gave a half smile. 'More often than not, I'd say.'

'Were you close to any of them?'

Joe looked thoughtful. 'You mean, like . . .'

'Did you tell any of them about Christy?'

Joe looked at her steadily. 'I can see where you're going

with this, and I didn't know them well, but they weren't the kind of men to rape and kill a woman.'

'Were they the kind of men to commit a burglary?'

Joe paused. 'No.' He shook his head. 'They earned good money. They would have no need.'

'Which pub did they go to?'

Joe hesitated, then said, 'The one on Chadwick Road. On the corner. I can't remember the name of it. Oh. Yes, I can. It was The Chadwick.'

'And where was your house?'

'Harberton Street. Towards Balham.'

'And where was the building site they were working on?'

'Cavendish Road. Next door to The Chadwick. That's why they went there.'

Sarah typed quickly and Joe waited for her to catch up.

'Blenheim Road would have been on their way home from The Chadwick,' Joe said. 'If that's what you're looking up. And yes, I did tell one of them about Christy. They all started teasing me, making jokes about her wanting a bit of rough, and I refused to tell them any more after that, so I suppose, if they were drunk, it's possible that they could have decided to go round there, got the wrong house, done something stupid.'

'And did you tell your solicitor all this?' Sarah asked.

'Which one?'

'The one you had at the police station.'

'Not that I remember. I don't think they asked.'

'Did the police ask? Only, it's not in the transcript of your police interview.'

'It wasn't my housemates,' Joe said, shaking his head. 'They were just out for a laugh.'

'All the same,' Sarah said, 'I'm wondering why no one asked you these questions.'

Joe shrugged. 'I guess they didn't think it was important. They weren't investigating the burglary.'

'No. But maybe they should have been.'

'They thought I'd done it,' Joe said. 'The burglary. That's why they wanted me for Christy's murder.'

'I know.'

'But it wasn't me.'

Sarah held his gaze for a moment. 'And I think that's where I'm going to begin.'

'What do you mean?'

'The victim of the burglary was one of the witnesses against you,' Sarah said. 'She didn't come out and say you'd done it, but she might as well have done, and it helped to convict you. I shouldn't have to prove you didn't commit the burglary – I shouldn't have to prove anything, I should only need to cast doubt on the evidence and show that the conviction was unsafe. But if I can show you didn't commit the burglary, I think it's our best chance.'

Joe looked thoughtful for a moment. 'There was a psychologist, too, who gave evidence about rapists starting out as burglars. That didn't help me either.'

Sarah's eyes held Joe's for a moment, and then the room fell silent while she typed this up. When she'd finished, she looked up again, breathing in deeply.

'OK, so most people would think from what they see on TV

that it's like America, where someone appeals their conviction and the lawyer asks for the original file and gets it – trial transcript, statements, exhibits, the lot. But in this country, there's no transcript of the trial unless you ask for the recording and get it transcribed – which costs thousands of pounds – and everything else is scattered between former solicitors or family members, or the court or the police or CPS, who often don't want to hand it over, or it hasn't been kept, so after twenty years, it becomes almost impossible for me to get everything I need, or even to know if I've got everything. The judge's summing-up is designed to present the case fairly to the jury, but not to pick out any unfairness. I know it was a long time ago, but I'm heavily reliant on you being able to remember what happened, and this is exactly the kind of thing I need you to tell me.'

Joe nodded.

'So, everything's important, Joe,' Sarah said. 'Have we established that now?'

23

Eve tried to get an early night. Tomorrow was Saturday, the day of Rich and Julia's wedding, and although her head was still buzzing from the meeting with Joe and Sarah, she needed to switch off and get some sleep. All of her friends – all of Rich's friends and all of his family – would be there, and she had contemplated backing out, but Mackenzie – as chief bridesmaid and choreographer – had been behind much of the planning and Eve wanted to show her daughter how proud she was. Also, Rich had been a good husband to her and was still a good friend, and he had told her it would mean a lot to him for her to be there.

'Aww. He wants your blessing,' Sascha had told Eve on WhatsApp earlier that evening. 'I think it's sweet.'

'He doesn't need my blessing,' Eve had replied, feeling cross, although she knew she was mostly just cross about having to go to the wedding.

'He still feels guilty about leaving you.'

'Well, he doesn't need to,' Eve said. 'I have my own life now.'

'Oooh, yes, and I want to hear all about *that*.'

Eve had closed down her messages then and gone to bed, but this last comment loomed large in her mind. Sascha had asked about Joe numerous times in the past three weeks since she had persuaded Eve to knock on his door. Each time, Eve had fobbed her off with 'It's complicated' or 'I'll tell you when I see you,' but she knew she was going to have to come up with something to tell her sister, who was also coming to the wedding and would be picking her up at half past eleven the following morning.

Eve set the alarm and lay in the dark, turning everything over. She couldn't tell anyone the truth about Joe. There was no one she trusted. Sascha would adopt the conventional 'no smoke without fire' approach, as, indeed, would Mackenzie, and the wedding wasn't going to be the time or the place for her to set about convincing them otherwise. She could already see the fear and alarm on their faces; she could already hear the questions: *He's just come out of prison? Twenty years? He's on the sex offenders register? He did that to a woman? And you believe him? Are you crazy?* Eve was at risk, they would say, as were they through her connection with him, and Eve could understand why they might think that, but if they had been at the meeting that afternoon, they would feel the same way she did, she was sure of it.

Sarah had stayed for three hours. While the trees swayed in the breeze outside the window, the atmosphere in the kitchen at Norham Gardens had been still and calm. Sarah had finished going through the transcript of Joe's police interview and had then read out loud from a number of the witness statements she had managed to get, the details of which had been eye-opening for Eve, but no doubt traumatic and triggering for Joe, who had last heard it all twenty years ago from behind a glass cage in a courtroom (and by the way, where was the presumption of innocence in that?). Nevertheless, he had patiently repeated the account he had given to the police and to the court, which was that there had been consensual sexual activity between him and Christy that same afternoon, hence the forensic link between them. The eyewitnesses were either mistaken or lying; he didn't know which.

Sarah said she would apply for funding for some further forensic testing of Christy's clothes and would also make a disclosure application to the police for the burglary file. The eyewitness statements raised red flags for her, she said. There was no evidence that they had colluded, but the accounts of the two neighbours were strikingly similar, and she had doubts as to their claim that they were able to see the colour of Joe's eyes in the dark.

But the Court of Appeal had already heard and rejected this argument, which meant that Sarah couldn't use it again without significant new evidence. *Something hugely compelling. Something Jamie's previous legal team didn't know about, or spot, or consider important.* What might this be? Eve turned it over and over in her mind.

At two o'clock, she swallowed a sleeping pill. When she woke, she realised with a jolt that she had slept through the alarm and had only left herself an hour to get ready for the wedding. She edged out of bed and got into the shower, then opened the bedroom blinds. The weather was still mild and she dressed in a pale blue top and a flowery Marks & Spencer's midi-length skirt which Mackenzie had picked out for her. She dried and straightened her hair, then glanced at the kitchen clock, deciding she just about had time to paint her nails, although she'd need to flap her hands around outside the window or get the hairdryer out.

She rested her fingers on the kitchen counter and began painting, while thinking again about what to tell Sascha about Joe.

We're playing it cool.

We're in a relationship and it's going well, but he couldn't come.

It didn't work out.

Eve didn't fancy that last option. She might not officially be part of a couple, but she didn't want to be completely single again, not even for her sister's benefit, and it would be so much nicer to tell all her old friends that she was seeing someone. Joe didn't need to be the *real* Joe, did he? Why couldn't he just be a faceless man that she couldn't bring to the wedding for whatever reason? He was away on business, or he had a child from a previous relationship and it was their birthday. She didn't see the harm. It *was* her life, after all, and no one else's business, and Joe wasn't actually a danger or a threat to anyone.

She was sure of it.

24

Eve's nails were still wet when Sascha and Graham arrived, and she asked Sascha to lock up her flat and carry her handbag and wedding gift to the car so that she didn't have to touch anything. She sat in the back seat as they drove to the venue, letting her nails dry out of the window, in the breeze, which Sascha said was 'typical Eve' and which Graham found amusing. Mackenzie would have been mortified, Eve knew.

They arrived at the venue on time, and as she got out of the car, Eve breathed in hard. It was going to be a civil ceremony and two hundred guests had been invited. She didn't feel quite ready to start milling around, making conversation with people she hadn't seen in years. But everyone was already seated inside and so they walked straight in, taking seats near the back, next to Mackenzie's Simon, and Lorna and Pete, two of Eve's oldest friends, whom Eve was pleased to see.

In the moments before the ceremony started, she was able to relax a little and take in the room. Mackenzie had done an amazing job. The seating was white with lilac bows and there were lilac flowers everywhere. The music began and Eve was surprised to find herself feeling emotional as Julia came down the aisle looking radiant in white, notwithstanding her very obvious baby bump. The music was lovely, Rich looked happy and Mackenzie was stunning in lilac as she took charge of a slightly unruly entourage of much smaller lilac bridesmaids whose antics made Eve and Lorna laugh.

Afterwards, they were led to a huge glass dining area at the back of the building, which held forty or so round tables with white cloths and chairs. Eve had a glass of champagne thrust into her hand and was soon saying hello to everyone she knew. As she circulated, a few people asked if she was seeing anyone, and Eve said she was, but he couldn't come today. Although one or two friends had wanted to know more, Eve was somehow spared as more people arrived and the conversation opened up to include their children, old times, the fantastic job Mackenzie had done of organising the wedding, what an eye she had for colour and design, and how Eve must be so proud of her. Eve *did* feel incredibly proud of her daughter.

The light faded outside as afternoon turned into evening. The waiters distributed candles, more food was served, the champagne flowed freely and Eve realised that, very soon, she would have got through this difficult day and could probably even persuade Sascha to let her take a cab home without anyone minding. It wasn't that she had anything against any of her old friends; it was just that she was no longer the right fit for them. Julia had taken her place in the old gang, and Eve didn't mind that. She really didn't. It was fine, because everything was changing for her. *She* was changing. She was on the precipice of a new and different phase in her life, she could feel it.

A lot of people were now on the dance floor, and she had lost Sascha and Graham, so she found an empty table at the far side of the marquee where she could sit quietly for a while and listen to the band. She spotted Simon and Mackenzie with the gaggle of bridesmaids, who were all jumping around excitedly and begging to dance on Simon's feet as Mackenzie organised them into an orderly line. Eve thought about what great parents Simon and Mackenzie were going to make, if and when they got around to having children of their own, and it was a nice thought, but she also felt a small twinge of horror at the idea of being a grandma. The truth was that she no longer needed the role she had cherished for the past twenty-five years, the one where she took care of other people.

The music mellowed and the band began to play love songs. More couples stepped out onto the dance floor and began to slow dance, and as Eve watched them through the flickering candlelight, she allowed her thoughts to wander back to Joe. Not his legal case. Joe. Her and Joe, to be specific. The two of them by the back door in the kitchen, his mouth on hers and his arms lifting her up against the wall. Eve's heart skipped a beat as she remembered the pressure of his body against hers, and although she knew it couldn't – or shouldn't – happen again, she very much wanted it to.

'There you are!' Sascha's voice cried out triumphantly from behind her as she sank down into the seat next to Eve. 'So.

Come on, then,' she said, grabbing two glasses of champagne from a passing waiter and pressing one into Eve's hand. 'Spill!'

Eve frowned, glancing down at her glass. 'What are you talking about?'

'I'm talking about the beans. Spill them. What's going on with this new man of yours?'

'Oooh. You didn't say, Eve. Anyone we know?' asked Lorna, who had suddenly appeared and was sitting down opposite, looking interested.

'Oh, no,' Sascha said, drawing out the *oh* and shortening the *no*. 'Evie's gone and got herself a millionaire.'

Lorna was wide-eyed. 'Really?'

Pete and Graham were pulling out the two seats between Lorna and Sascha. Then, as the band took a break, Mackenzie arrived too, swishing up the big lilac skirt of her bridesmaid's dress and flopping onto the seat on the other side of Eve. 'Who are we talking about?' she asked dreamily.

'Your mum's boyfriend.' Sascha smiled. 'Her secret billionaire.'

'Bloody hell,' Lorna said.

'How did he go from being a millionaire to a billionaire in two seconds?' Eve asked, laughing.

'Well, which is it, then?' Sascha asked. 'Come on. You've been completely mysterious about him.'

'Yeah. You have, Mum,' Mackenzie agreed, pulling her long brown hair out of the tightly coiled French knot she had been wearing all afternoon. 'You've been doing that thing politicians do. Answering a question with another question.'

'Well,' Eve said, enjoying herself a little. 'It's all brand new.

You don't always know how things are going to go in the early stages, do you? I didn't want to jinx it.'

'But?' Mackenzie prodded Eve in the waist, making Eve recoil, laughing.

'You're sleeping with him!' Sascha announced loudly, her voice still pitched to compete with the music, which had stopped five minutes ago. 'Whoops,' she slurred, looking round at the faces at the neighbouring tables. 'But you are. I can tell.'

'Mum?' Mackenzie prodded, her eyes widening, and even Pete and Graham looked interested.

Eve felt herself flushing. 'I am not,' she said in a *don't be ridiculous* tone of voice that told them she was.

'He owns a huge, fuck-off house in Norham Gardens,' Sascha told Lorna, leaning forwards.

'Norham Gardens?' Lorna asked. 'Is that the one in North Oxford, by the University Parks?'

Eve felt an alarm bell ring inside her. Norham Gardens was a well-known street and Oxford was a small city. She realised that she was going to have to be a little more careful about what she said.

'Good God. What does he do?' Lorna was asking.

Everyone turned to look at Eve.

'Is he like ... a musician or something?' Mackenzie suggested.

'What's his name?' Lorna asked.

'Joe,' Sascha said.

'Joe what? What's his surname?'

They all turned to look at Eve again. Even Graham and Pete were listening.

'Cole,' Eve said. It was the first name that popped into her head.

'Joe Cole. Oh my God. Not the actor?' Sascha gasped. 'The one from *Peaky Blinders*?'

'Or the footballer?' Graham suggested.

Pete turned and grinned at him. They didn't believe this; they were clearly just enjoying the joke.

'*Is* he a footballer?' Lorna asked.

'Who?' asked Simon, sitting down next to Mackenzie.

'Joe Cole,' said Pete and Graham together.

'What about him?'

'Eve's dating him,' Graham said, laughing.

'Oh, fuck off!' Eve smiled, balling up a paper napkin in her fist and throwing it at him. Graham ducked.

'Mum! The candles! Be careful!' Mackenzie cried out.

Simon looked from Eve to Graham and back again. 'You're dating Joe *Cole*?'

'Who's Joe Cole?' Lorna asked Pete.

'Only one of the best footballers the country's ever had.'

Eve stood up abruptly. 'Look, I'm not dating a footballer, or an actor, or a musician,' she said, exasperated. 'And I'm not talking about this any more, so can you please all shut up.'

They left just after nine. Graham drove Eve home and waited in the car while Sascha, under the guise of wanting to make sure that Eve was safe, walked her sister upstairs to her front door. 'Is he married?' she asked, wide-eyed and tipsy, picking up the conversation again the minute they were alone together. 'Is that why you can't talk about him?'

Eve hesitated, but she didn't like the idea. 'No,' she said. 'He's not married. And his surname's not Cole. I just said that to get you all off my back.'

'Why? Why are you being so secretive?'

'Well, it's just that . . .' Eve sighed. 'He *is* quite well known and he doesn't want people to know about us, not just yet.' This part, at least, was true. 'Or where he lives,' she added.

Sascha's eyes widened. 'So he *is* famous?'

'Not famous exactly, but . . .'

'OK, but you will be able to tell me?'

'Soon,' Eve promised.

'And can you just tell me the terrible secret from his past?'

Eve froze. 'What?'

'The big thing. Remember? You told me you thought he'd had a bad break-up or lost a child or something.'

'Oh, yes. No. I can't tell you that. Not yet.'

'But you'll tell me soon, right? When you've been together a bit longer?'

'Yes. I promise.'

'OK. Love you.' Sascha left, seeming satisfied with this.

When Eve got inside, she shut the door behind her and breathed a sigh of relief. The early stages of a champagne headache were already threatening, and having nothing to be up early for the next day but not wanting a hangover, she decided that it would be best to drink a couple of pints of water and give it an hour before she went to bed. She filled two glasses and put them both on the coffee table, then sat on the sofa with the lights off and the curtains open. She placed her phone on the sofa next to her and thought about Joe, about how much she would like to call him and hear his voice, about how much she would like to be with him right now. Would he be missing her, too? she wondered.

She needed to be more grown-up about him, she decided, reminding herself that Joe was vulnerable and in the wrong place for a relationship. She needed to focus on doing whatever she could to help with his case. She was about to close down the app, drink her water and go to bed when the word 'typing' appeared on the screen in front of her. Her heart lifted. She waited, her fingers poised, for his message to appear.

How did it go today? Are you home yet?

Yes, she typed. *Just got back.*

How was it?

It was fine, she wrote. *I got through it!*

Well done! All over. Now you can relax.

Yes. Going to bed soon.

Me too. Shall I wave to you from the balcony?

Eve hesitated, smiling to herself. *I'd like that*, she typed, then paused and added two kisses.

Waving now xx, came the reply.

A familiar tightening gripped her abdomen and her heart filled with hope. He was innocent, she was sure he was. And that was why she was going to help him.

25

To Do:

1. Chase burglary file
2. Forensic testing of Christy's clothes – where are they? With police or lab?
3. Court – request/find tapes of hearing and get costing for transcript
4. Missing statement: Dr Christian (psychologist). Who has this?
5. Body map – Jamie. Custody suite: Farringdon PS. What injuries did he have on arrest?
6. Find Jamie's landlord in Harberton Street. Name?
7. Call schedules – finish going through
8. Crime scene/forensic attendance – any more statements?
9. Police station papers from rep
10. Attendance on Jamie's mother – does she have any of the above?

As Sarah looked at the list she'd created on the screen in front of her, a blast of music sounded from the living room, making her jump. She saved the document and got to her feet. Her nine-year-old son, Ben, was home today. There had been a power outage at his school, which had unexpectedly closed. Sarah exhaled deeply as she went along the hallway to investigate, but, as she did most days, she felt grateful that the particular brand of stress that had come with being the employed single mum of a severely autistic and learning-disabled child was now broadly a thing of the past, although there had been a lot she wanted to get through today and watching Ben hadn't been on the agenda.

'No, Ben, too loud,' she told him, entering the living room to see that he had paired his iPad to the TV and turned up the volume. She bent down to pick up his glasses, which he had thrown on the floor. She turned the TV off and led him away to his computer, where she sat him down and flicked on the monitor, pushing the mouse towards him. Within seconds, he'd opened five different tabs and was simultaneously playing *Peppa Pig* clips on YouTube in five different languages. Sarah watched as, with an earnest expression, he clicked on each tab in turn and rewound each of the videos so that they were all playing at the same time. She wondered, as she often did, how it was that Ben could bear to listen to five different sets of sounds simultaneously, yet found the background buzz of voices inside a restaurant or shop so overwhelming that he would bolt and run or, more often, refuse to enter in the first place. But that was Ben – her beautiful, wonderfully unique and endlessly intriguing boy.

Back in the kitchen, she scrolled through her emails, looking for one from the data control department at Farringdon Police Station, which looked after the records for all their cases, but still there was nothing. She picked up her phone, called the number and was passed around the department for a minute or two before eventually being put through to an officer.

'I'm phoning about my disclosure request in the case of James Clarke. You said I'd hear from you by today, but I still haven't had a reply.'

'We've read your request,' the officer said. 'We can't disclose the records you're asking for unless you can be more specific about your reasons for wanting them.'

'I've given you my reasons,' Sarah said. 'The burglary was used to convict my client in his murder trial and I need to know if there was any evidence that he was responsible.'

'That's not specific enough, I'm afraid. Our rules require you to demonstrate why you want each statement and what you expect it to show.'

'I won't know the answer to that until I've seen the witness list.'

'Well, we can't disclose that without good reason. We have to protect the data of the witnesses.'

'This isn't a data protection issue,' Sarah said, taking a long breath. 'I'm asking you to disclose information about a criminal investigation in which the witnesses gave statements, fully expecting them to be disclosed to third parties, and especially to lawyers. If the prosecution of the murder case was predicated on the two cases being linked, this should be reason enough for you to at least disclose the list.'

'Our rules are that we can't disclose it unless you can tell us what you expect the statements to show.'

'How can I possibly know what they'll show until I've seen them?' Sarah said, through gritted teeth.

'Well, then, I'm afraid I can't help you.'

'The Supreme Court case of Nunn says that you should cooperate with me, not block me,' Sarah said, her voice rising.

'I'll cooperate when you are able to be more specific about your reasons for wanting the records.'

'I've already told you I can't be!'

'Well, it sounds as though you're on a fishing expedition. We can't disclose what you've asked for. You'll get our email later today.'

Sarah hung up and called Will. 'You're not going to believe this,' she began crossly. 'Sorry.' She paused. 'Are you busy?'

'Judge has stood the case down for ten minutes,' he said. 'What's up?'

Sarah recounted the conversation she'd just had.

'Ah, yes,' Will said. 'The catch-22. It's a good catch, that one.'

'No, it's bloody not,' Sarah muttered.

Will laughed. 'There's an article about it online. It's by Dennis Eady in *The Justice Gap*. Check it out.'

'I'm too angry.'

'Ah, but you do your best work when you're angry.'

'It's so unfair.'

'So, take the police to court.'

Sarah sighed. 'Looks as though I'm going to have to. But that will take time and money and I don't have any. I'll have to get costs protection via legal aid, and to get legal aid I'll need counsel's advice. I know you'll try and help, Will, but it's going to be the same old story – we'll have to prove they've got something we're entitled to.' A notification vibrated on her phone. 'Hang on,' she said. 'Don't go away. The police email has arrived.'

'OK.'

She leaned over her laptop. 'They're telling me that I can apply to the CCRC and they can request the statements if they consider them to be important enough. Aargh.' She let out a frustrated scream. 'But they won't. They never do. I'm going to need some evidence from the police to have a chance with the CCRC, but if I had that evidence, I wouldn't need to ask the CCRC in the first place.'

'You couldn't make it up, could you?' said Will.

Sarah sank down into her chair and put her face in her palm.

'Has Joe got any money?' Will said.

'None whatsoever. He's surviving, but only just.'

'Family?'

'No. His mum lives in social housing. Dad's dead.'

'Hmm. I'm being called into court, love. Sorry. Find me some more reasons why we need these burglary statements and I'll do the advice.'

Sarah ended the call and sank back into her seat at the kitchen table. The volume in the living room had risen again but was just about bearable. She reread the email from the data controller and dug her nails into her palms. She was so fed up with having these circular arguments about disclosure.

Her phone vibrated on the table next to her and a notification told her that she had missed a call and there was a message. She dialled her voicemail and listened.

'Hi, Sarah,' the voice said. 'It's Eve Shotton here, Joe's friend. You said that it was going to take time to get the funding for the court transcript and the forensic tests and – probably – to get the disclosure you need from the police, too, and I want to help with this. I want to help Joe.' Sarah heard her take a shaky breath. 'I have some money put aside to buy a house, and I want to use it to pay for anything you need. I don't want this appeal to take months or years if it doesn't have to. I know what you're going to say – that it's going to cost thousands, not hundreds, but I have the money sitting there in the bank and I can't think of a better way to use it. If you are happy with this and it will work for you, please can you let me know and then I'll talk it over with Joe.'

Sarah hung up, feeling heartened but wary of the expectation behind the offer, and concerned for both Eve and Joe. She wondered how long Eve had known him. Were they already in a relationship? This was going to be a big step, and there was no guarantee either Joe or Eve would get the results they wanted. Eve would have to pay the police legal costs if the challenge failed and those could amount to tens of thousands of pounds. It was one thing for Sarah to work on Joe's case pro bono, but something else entirely for Eve to use her life savings to bankroll it.

And to succeed in court, Sarah would still have to convince the judge that her request was proportionate. If she had all the statements from the murder trial – all the evidence she should have and was already entitled to – she would have a much better picture of the weaknesses the statements exposed, but even her requests for the original file were being frustrated.

She opened the police email again and typed a reply, asking for the original statement of Louise Coulter, the burglary victim:

> Her statement in my client's case was made over seven weeks after he was charged with the offences of rape and murder. He would already have entered a not guilty plea and been indicted in the crown court, and it therefore appears that this statement has been taken to bolster the case against him. It is highly prejudicial and contains no direct evidence against my client. I wish to know – for context – what other items were stolen in the burglary. I expect Louise Coulter's statement made in the burglary investigation to show that it was not considered to be a sexually motivated crime at that time, and that it should not have been introduced in evidence in this case.

The reply came straight back:

> As already mentioned, you can apply to the CCRC and they can request the statement if they consider it to be important enough.

Sarah threw her head back in frustration. If she was sitting here with the court transcript or even half the paperwork she was already entitled to, she might stand a chance, but the police data controller's response was that it had been given to his solicitor twenty years ago and they were under no obligation to supply a second copy. The original solicitor didn't have it. She was getting nowhere fast.

She took a deep breath and typed back:

Has the victim's clothing been located yet? As mentioned, we wish to undertake our own testing.

Then she picked up her phone again and called the number Eve had left.

26

Bella's new therapist was called Adele. She lived in Belsize Park, in a lovely flat in a Victorian building that was much nicer than Bella's. The hallway in Bella's building was grubby and smelled of cabbage and occasionally of cannabis, and the paintwork on all the front doors was chipped and peeling. Adele's block, on the other hand, was pristine, the staircase carpeted and clean, her front room bright and welcoming. Everything looked expensive: the soft cream carpet, the cream sofa and chairs, the solid oak furniture, the blue and white abstract seascape paintings.

Over the years, Bella had had a few courses of therapy from various different providers (with a child psychologist at the hospital soon after her mother died, once through college as a teenager, a couple of times through the NHS), however there had only ever been a finite number of sessions on offer and she hadn't been able to afford to pay privately. But recently the school she worked at had introduced an 'employee assistance scheme', one that included free counselling to help with 'any problems, big or small', as the head had cheerfully phrased his announcement at the weekly staff meeting. Bella had wondered what constituted a 'big' problem and whether having come down for breakfast one morning to find her mother lifeless and semi-naked on the kitchen floor might be 'too big'.

She had often worried about this and had got used to pre-empting any awkwardness about the shadow in her past, which Bella had sensed was 'too big' for most people she met. The conversation would go something like this:

'What about you, Bella? Where do your parents live?'
'Dad's in Streatham. Mum died a while back.'
'I'm sorry. How old were you?'
'Seven.'
'God, I'm sorry. How did she die?'
'Oh. Um, actually she was murdered.'
'God. What happened?'
'Erm, actually, she was raped and killed in our kitchen at home.'
'Oh my God, I'm so sorry. Did they catch him?'
'Yes. He's in prison.'
'So, who found her?'
'Oh. Erm. Me, actually.'
'Oh my God. How terrible.'
The End.

She would immediately be classified as 'damaged' – how could she not be? – and nobody wanted a damaged friend, except other people who were damaged or people like Justin who wanted to help people who were damaged. So she would reassure them. 'Oh, it's OK,' she would say dismissively when the inevitable discomfort registered on their faces, and then she would make a joke to demonstrate how OK she actually was.

But with Justin's encouragement, she had finally put herself forward for the programme at work and had been referred to Adele, who she liked way better than all of her previous therapists, and now here she was, in her fifth session. Bella had emerged from the previous four feeling churned up inside, but in a good way, a way that made her feel in touch with herself, and in touch with her mother. Each time, she had needed to lie down and cry afterwards and had then felt drained and sleepy for the rest of the day, but she liked the feeling better than the feeling of being empty, which wasn't complete emptiness anyway – it was emptiness tinged with guilt.

'Guilt is a useless emotion,' her previous counsellor – the one she'd had in college – always used to say. Or, 'You were seven. You couldn't have done things any differently.' Or, 'You can't change the past.' But no matter how many times Bella had repeated these affirmations to herself, it hadn't changed the way she felt. She had concluded that her problem was 'too big', and this had been confirmed to her when her ten sessions were up: she could see the relief on the counsellor's face.

Adele, on the other hand, didn't seem fazed by anything Bella said. 'That's interesting,' she would say, resting her chin on her fingers. 'Tell me more about that.'

So Bella had. She had told Adele pretty much everything, including the worst and most awful parts about finding her mother, and Adele hadn't once looked shocked or tried to steer her away.

And so, now, Bella was able to talk about Jamie Clarke.

'What would happen if you saw him?' Adele asked her.

'I don't know,' Bella admitted.

'What would you like to say to him?'

'Apart from, "Did you kill my mother?"'

This was said with Bella's usual pre-emptive smile, but Adele's face remained solemn.

'I wouldn't know where to begin, actually,' Bella said. 'There's so much I'd like to say to him.'

'Like . . . ?'

'Like, do you hate me?'

Bella blurted this out and Adele allowed a short pause for it to register with them both.

'You think he hates you?'

'He might do,' Bella said, in a small voice.

'Why would he hate you?'

'Because . . . it was my evidence that sent him to jail. And I'm now beginning to wonder, what if it wasn't him? What if I got it wrong?'

Adele nodded slowly. 'I wonder . . .' she began, fingertips to chin, head to one side in the way she did whenever she was about to ask anything challenging. 'I wonder how it would feel if you *had* got it wrong?'

'You think I might have?' Bella froze. This was a first. Everyone else she knew was quick to dismiss the idea out of hand. Nobody had ever acknowledged that it might be a possibility.

'Maybe. Maybe not. I have no idea. But how would it feel if you had?'

Bella shook her head, her stomach sinking. 'It would be unbearable. To know that a man had spent twenty years in prison because of me.'

A raising of the eyebrows. 'Just you?'

'No. There were other people who said it was him.'

'So, what is it that's causing you to question it?'

'Him, I suppose,' Bella said. 'The fact that he has never admitted it. The fact that he could have been out a lot sooner if he had.'

'Is that the only thing?'

Bella thought hard about this. 'No. I mean, lots of rapists and murderers say they didn't do it.'

'Almost all of them, I should think.'

Bella nodded. 'I suppose it's because of what he said at the trial. I wasn't allowed to go, and for years, my dad wouldn't let me have a phone or a laptop because he didn't want me to read about it, so I didn't find out until much later that he hadn't just put his hands up to it. Everyone talked as though it was a foregone conclusion that it was him, and they kept telling me how brave I'd been and how I'd done the right thing – the police, the victim support people, everyone. And our neighbours. They acted like I was some kind of hero.'

'That would have been very powerful.'

'It was. They lined the streets. I've never forgotten it. I had to leave the house for good that same day, while the police were still there. It was before they had even taken my mother away, I remember, because I didn't want to leave her. As I came down the path with my teddy and my little suitcase and got into my dad's car, they were all standing outside their houses. When we drove away, it was like a military parade. And for weeks after that, they would turn up at my dad's and congratulate me on being the one who caught him.'

Adele frowned. 'That's a huge responsibility to place on a seven-year-old.'

'I think they thought it was a good thing, but it wasn't.'

Adele frowned and shook her head in agreement.

'But I was part of it,' Bella said. 'I played my part, and I can't help but wonder, did I pick him out because he was the person I saw – the man in the kitchen kissing my mother – or did I pick him out because, when I saw the line-up, his was the only face I knew? That's what he said when he appealed to the court, and I've been wondering ever since I found that out. I don't think I've ever been sure about it. I said I was at the time because that seemed to be the right thing to say. They asked me, "One hundred per cent?" and I said yes, and my statement was read out to the jury with those words – "one hundred per cent" – but lately I've been thinking that I don't remember being one hundred per cent sure about anything. It was all so confusing. And yet, I definitely saw the man who killed my mother. I saw him come in, and I saw him grab her and start to kiss her, and if it wasn't Jamie Clarke, then who else could it have been?'

Adele waited.

'What I can't understand,' Bella continued, picking at a scab on her finger and turning to look out of Adele's big bay window, 'is why I went to bed. I saw the man throw Mum's phone across the room, so I must have known something bad was about to happen.'

'What do you think you should have done?'

'I should have run next door to Mrs Barlow. If I'd done that, then she'd have called the police straight away.'

'And why didn't you?'

Bella froze for a second time. She had never been asked this question before either. This was the part where she normally snapped an elastic band against her wrist or told herself that she had just been a kid and hadn't known any better or that she couldn't change the past. She felt the usual stress symptoms rising inside her: the sweaty palms, the knot in her stomach, the dry mouth, the racing heart.

But Adele wasn't judging her, she knew.

'Because of my mum's eyes,' Bella said, remembering. 'She lifted her eyes towards the ceiling.'

'Her eyes,' Adele said, nodding. 'She spoke with her eyes.'

'I know it sounds weird, but I was a good kid,' Bella said. 'She only had to look at me. I mean, I don't remember now how she looked at me, but that's what I said in my statement to the police. I would have done what I was told. But maybe I misread her expression. Maybe I got it wrong?'

'Let's just assume for a moment that you got it right. OK?'

Bella nodded, her stomach unknotting, her heart rate slowing. She wiped her palms on her jeans.

'So, why might she have sent you to bed instead of next door to the neighbour?'

'Because . . .' Bella paused. 'Because she wanted to protect me and pretend that everything was fine.'

'That sounds about right. I might do the same thing in her position. I might want to shield my daughter from what was happening, pretend to her that it was consensual and report him later.'

'But then he tied her up and killed her,' Bella said, her eyes glistening.

'And she wasn't expecting that.'

'She can't have been,' Bella said. 'Otherwise she wouldn't have sent me upstairs. And I wouldn't have gone.'

'So there's your answer,' Adele said, gently. 'That's why she sent you to bed.'

'With her eyes,' Bella said, suggesting again that she'd misread her mother's expression.

'With her eyes,' Adele said firmly. 'Like this, perhaps.' She turned her expression into a hard one and glared at Bella, raising her eyes to the ceiling and frowning.

Bella burst into tears, feeling the weight of the stare. 'Oh my God. Yes. That was it exactly.'

'But then you came down again,' Adele offered. 'Because you heard the noises and knew your mum was in trouble.'

'Do you think so?' Bella asked, wiping her cheeks.

'I do think so,' Adele said. 'And I think you've been trying to tell yourself the truth about this for a very long time.'

'But everyone says I couldn't have done. They said it doesn't fit with what I told the police, but maybe I just didn't remember it until later? Maybe I just thought it was a bad dream.'

'Maybe the thought that you came face to face with your mother's killer was too horrific for you to acknowledge until now,' Adele suggested.

Bella felt a wrenching in her gut that threatened to knock her over. 'But why didn't he kill me too?'

'Perhaps because he knew he could convince you that everything was fine and that your mother was asleep. Maybe because he knew you were a good little girl who would do as she was told and go back to bed. Maybe because he was someone who hated grown women, but didn't have anything against little girls.'

Bella nodded. 'You know, I never see his face in the dreams, but when I see him in my head, I see him as someone frightening but at the same time someone you would trust, someone in authority. Someone you would believe.'

The minute the words left her mouth, Bella was smacked with the most intense, gut-wrenching confusion, but also the certainty that this felt right.

She swallowed. 'I think I came downstairs in the night because I heard noises and the police were already there, and they told me to go back to bed because they had already found my mother and didn't want me to see her like that . . . but . . .' She hesitated. 'But how could that be right? I was the one who found her in the morning and nobody argued with that. How could the police have come in the night and found my mum, then gone away again?'

27

It was the Monday after the wedding and Eve had just finished work. Joe looked apprehensive as he let her in and closed the door behind her. He was wearing a plain white T-shirt and jeans again, and his face and arms were brown from the sun. Eve felt an intense desire to kiss him, but something told her not to. She placed one hand on his arm instead, feeling the muscles tense up.

'Are you OK?' she asked him.

'I'm being spied on,' he said.

'By the police?'

He nodded. 'I think so. I don't know. I'm just getting a bad feeling. I'm doing everything probation have asked. I'm sticking to all my licence conditions and I'm trying to contribute to the probation meetings, but they're still trying to get me to talk about something I didn't do. I'm never going to say I did it, and I'm pretty sure that's being fed back to the police.'

'I'm sorry,' Eve said. 'I'm sorry this is so hard, Joe.'

'It feels like they're not going to leave me alone until they've got me again.'

'I'm sorry,' Eve said again. 'Have you spoken to Sarah about it?'

'No,' he said, leaning back against the worktop next to the sink. 'She's doing enough already and she's doing it for free. I don't want to give her extra work.'

Eve nodded slowly. 'So, when did you last speak to her?'

'Not since our meeting on Friday. Why?'

'Look, Joe. I want to give Sarah some money,' she said, raising her eyes to meet his. 'For the forensic tests and for . . . well, whatever else she needs. I've offered to pay for it all and she's accepted – if you agree, that is.'

Joe shook his head. 'No,' he said. 'I can't let you do that.'

'But I want to,' Eve insisted. 'I have the money in the bank, and—'

'That's for your house!'

'The house can wait,' Eve said, gently.

'No.' Joe shook his head again. 'I can't ask that of you.'

'You're not asking anything. I'm offering, and Sarah agreed it would help. She wants to take the police to court to get disclosure of everything she's asked for, and then there are the forensic tests, which she might get legal aid for, but there are still hoops to jump through with that, and then there's the court transcript, which she needs if she's going to find out exactly what the witnesses said at your trial, and she'd have to submit applications and fundraise and it could all take ages, Joe. This will speed everything up.'

'It will cost thousands of pounds,' Joe protested, concern

clouding his features. 'And even if they exonerate me, I might not be able to repay you. I might not get compensation. Not everybody does. In fact, hardly anyone does. To get compensation, Sarah would have to prove I didn't kill Christy, not just that my conviction was unsafe. She told me that right at the beginning. It was the first conversation we had.'

'I know that. I don't care about getting it back. I care about you.' Eve felt herself flush. 'I've thought about nothing else for days, Joe, and it's what I want. I don't want you to feel indebted to me or pressured in any way, and if things don't work out between us and you find you don't want to be with me, then that's absolutely fine too, but I think there *is* something between us, and I am pretty sure you feel it too, and I think it could be something really good and I'd like the chance to find out – and I'd like that to happen sooner rather than later.' She stopped, running out of breath, out of words, and held his gaze.

He stiffened. 'Eve, you must know how I feel about you. But I just can't think about anything happening between us. Not right now. It's all too much. I'm sorry. I'm so sorry if I've led you on, but I just can't think straight at the moment. I just . . . can't.' He put his head in his hands.

Eve took a deep breath. This was all wrong. Joe had already made it clear that he was in no fit state mentally for a relationship and all she'd done was pile pressure on him.

'No, it's my fault,' she said. 'I shouldn't have said all that. Of course you can't think about us being together. It's the wrong time. I get it.'

Joe looked up slowly, his eyes tired. 'It's not that I don't want things to be different,' he said. 'What we did last Sunday was ... well, it was lovely. Of course it was. But after you left, I started having flashbacks to the day I was arrested. I got worried. What if you'd gone to the police and accused me of raping you too?'

'Joe, I would never—'

'I know, Eve,' he said. 'I know you wouldn't. But the last time I was with a woman in that way, I was accused of doing something terrible to her. I was pulled off the street and thrown into prison, and it haunts me. It's still haunting me.'

'I'm sorry,' Eve said, tears springing to her eyes.

Joe reached out a hand and held hers. 'Eve, don't cry. Please.'

'It's just that this is all so unfair.'

He nodded, his cheeks hollow. 'I know. But it doesn't change the fact that I'm not a good prospect.'

'I understand, Joe. I really do. But please let me help.'

Joe hesitated. 'How can I? How can I, when I can't give you anything in return?'

'I told you,' Eve said. 'It's unconditional. No strings. It's just money, Joe. It's sitting in the bank doing nothing.'

'But it's for your house.'

'The house can wait. I'm in no hurry. And anyway, it's the wrong time to buy. I'll probably get a better deal later in the year, and when I find something, you can give me a quote for an extension or a loft conversion. What do you say?'

A glimmer of hope shone in his eyes, but his voice cracked as he said, 'I knew there was something special about you, the first time I saw you.'

The Stranger on the Stairs

Eve smiled. 'Is that a yes?'
'If you'll let me work for free.'
'Mates' rates,' she said.
He smiled back. 'Mates it is.'

28

Happy would be the wrong word to use, but Bella definitely felt heartened as she left Adele's house later that afternoon. She now knew what she had to do: she had to find Jamie Clarke. Bella knew this wasn't quite what Adele had meant when she'd said that it was 'within her power to find out the truth', but she couldn't get the idea out of her mind, and what other choice did she have?

She couldn't involve her VLO or the police or anyone else from MAPPA, the multidisciplinary team who would be monitoring Jamie, and there was no public access to the sex offenders register. Nobody would tell her where he was, and Kathy, her VLO, had already been clear that a prearranged meeting was out of the question. Restorative justice was only available to those who admitted their crimes, and he never had.

Finding him was going to be tricky, though. Her internet searches had revealed nothing useful, and even if there was a way to find out which hostel he had been released to, he would in all likelihood have moved on by now.

The logical step was to search for his parents. She knew Jamie had grown up in Clapham. His mother was called Dorothy and his father Gerald, so she typed these combinations into Google, but up came all the same old entries she'd found already, with only one or two additional reports. Gerald had died in 2008, and from the few photos she could find of Dorothy – at Gerald's funeral, looking browbeaten and downcast, her chin tipped away from the camera – she didn't have the appearance of someone who was likely to want to hang out on Facebook or Instagram. Bella did a brief search anyway, but Dorothy must be in her seventies now, and none of the profiles Bella opened were of a woman that age.

But then she struck lucky: Gerald's building firm, although dissolved many years ago, was still registered on the Companies House website with Gerald as its director and his address as 8 Morely Crescent, Woking. A Street View search on Google Maps revealed this to be a 1980s mid-terraced red-brick property on a housing estate. What else could this be but his home? There was no guarantee that Dorothy still lived there, and his brothers – who had disowned Jamie after he went to prison – were bound to have moved on a long time ago, but it was her first real clue.

She made an excuse to Justin about a friend from her first year at uni who was unexpectedly in town the following Saturday and wanted to meet up. When Saturday arrived, she drove her Fiat Panda out of London. On the motorway, she rehearsed the conversation she might have with the neighbours. Bella knew from her own experience of being a minor celebrity for all the wrong reasons that people felt strongly about Jamie

Clarke, and that even in a new neighbourhood, twenty years on, there was a good chance someone would remember his arrest and conviction, or would know about it second hand, and might have some information about the family and where they were now.

It was late March and the weather was warm. Woking town centre was busy with shoppers strolling around the streets. Bella followed Google Maps along the dual carriageway to an estate bordered by grassy knolls on the outskirts of the town. She drove past a builders' merchant, a row of shops and a pub, through a number of identical-looking streets with identical-looking 1980s red-brick houses, then turned into a side street, and there it was: Morely Crescent. She parked in a lay-by and got out. Number eight was near the end of the row. She stood outside for a moment before pushing her bag onto her shoulder and walking up the front path.

She could feel her heart beginning to race as she stepped up to the front door and pressed the bell. She waited, but there was no answer. It didn't look as though anyone was home. She stood there for a moment longer, trying to decide her next move, when the next-door neighbour's front door opened and a woman stepped out holding a trike in one hand and a toddler's chubby fist in the other.

Bella seized the opportunity. 'Hello,' she said. 'I'm looking for someone who I think used to live here. Her name's Dorothy Clarke. She would be in her seventies.'

The woman nodded. 'She'll be at work. She always works Saturday mornings.'

'She still lives here?' Bella stepped back, speechless for a moment, and her heart raced harder.

The woman let go of the toddler's hand and set the trike down on the path. 'Are you from the press?' she asked, narrowing her eyes.

Bella shook her head. 'I'm Dorothy's niece,' she lied. 'Great-niece, in fact. I haven't seen her since I was a child, what with . . . you know. Everything that happened.'

'Oh. Yes. Well—' The woman stopped to call after the toddler, who was climbing onto the trike and taking off down the path, then turned back to Bella. 'We've only been here a couple of years, so I don't know too much about it all, but I think she lost a lot of family when it happened. Friends, too. So now she keeps herself to herself.'

'Understandable,' Bella said.

The woman's eyes widened and Bella saw another question forming, so she cut in quickly with, 'It's fine. I can see you're busy. I'll just wait for her. Thank you.'

She walked quickly back over to the lay-by and sat in her car with her head down, making herself as inconspicuous as possible and only glancing up from time to time at the sound of a front door opening and closing, or a car stopping or starting. Every time she heard footsteps on the path beside her, her heart rate would go up. If anyone saw her here and worked out who she really was, she could be in trouble.

Half an hour went by, and then an hour. Eventually, Bella caught sight in her rear-view mirror of a woman who walked past her car and turned onto the path to number eight. Her heart racing, Bella got out of the car. She shut the door gently, but with the instincts of someone who had no doubt spent twenty years being alert to trouble, the woman turned round. For a moment, they looked directly into each other's faces. In the few online photos Bella had seen, Dorothy Clarke had been wearing glasses with light-blocking lenses or had been looking away from the camera, but Bella was now staring directly into her surprised, sad, sea-blue eyes.

'I'm Bella,' she said, under her breath, 'I'm Christy Nicholls' daughter. I've come to talk to you about Jamie. It's important.'

Dorothy Clarke nodded, her eyes flitting towards the windows of the neighbouring houses. 'You'd better come in, then,' she said.

Bella followed her down the hall to the small kitchen.

'I'm sorry for turning up unannounced,' she said, standing in the doorway. 'I didn't know if you lived here.'

Dorothy looked worried. 'Have they published my address?'

'No,' Bella said quickly. 'I had to look hard to find it. And I know I shouldn't be here. Your next-door neighbour's the only person I've spoken to and I told her I was a relative.'

'Which one?' Dorothy asked, lifting her shopping bags onto the countertop.

Bella swallowed. 'Erm. Your great-niece.'

Dorothy nodded, seemingly OK with the lie. She turned round to face Bella square on, inspecting her face, eyeing her clothes. 'Please. Sit down.'

Bella pulled out a chair at the table, which had a PVC

tablecloth with roses around the edge. She waited while Dorothy put the kettle on, then took out a tin of biscuits, placing them down in front of her. Bella felt movement beneath the table as a cat began to wind its way back and forth between her legs. She reached down and stroked it.

'I'm very sorry about your mother,' Dorothy said, placing two mugs and a pot of tea on the table. She leaned against the counter and her shoulders dropped a little. 'But it wasn't my son that did that to her. He loved her.'

Bella felt her gut tighten. 'Did he tell you that? That he loved her?'

'Yes. He'd not known her long. But he'd known her long enough to know that she was special. I didn't have a chance to meet your mum, but I know I would have done. They would have been together, he was sure of it.'

Bella felt a rush of pain rise to her chest. 'But how do you know?' she asked, swallowing back tears. 'How do you know it wasn't him?'

Dorothy shook her head. 'Love, I know my son. He wouldn't hurt a woman. The way he was with me, with his previous girlfriends . . . I know you're going to think the same as everyone else – I'm his mother. Right? I would say that. But I know my son. I've known him all his life, and it's not in his nature to do a thing like that.'

Bella gazed back at her, unable to speak, the uncertainty settling in the pit of her stomach.

'Here.' Dorothy opened the fridge and pulled out a carton of milk, placing it on the table. 'Help yourself to tea. I'll just . . .' She nodded towards the bags on the countertop.

'Of course.'

'So, what brings you here?' Dorothy asked, opening a cupboard.

'I came because I want to talk to him,' Bella found herself saying. 'I want to know if he did it, if he killed my mum. I want to hear him saying it.'

'He can't talk to you,' Dorothy said. 'He has conditions—'

'I won't tell anyone, I promise. If you could just ask him to phone me, it might help us both. I have to talk to him because I'm stuck. I'm stuck in limbo. I know I picked him out as the man I saw in the kitchen the night it happened, but now I just . . . I just can't be sure.'

Dorothy turned. 'What are you saying?'

'I've been having nightmares for years about a man in my hallway,' Bella said, 'and recently I've been having therapy and all sorts of memories are coming back and I just don't know what's real and what isn't. I can't be sure about anything.' Her legs were trembling, her knee jerking so hard she had to press a hand against it. 'But someone raped and killed my mother,' she continued, 'and I need to be sure that the police got the right person. A few days ago, I thought I was being followed, and if it's not Jamie, who can it be?'

Dorothy got up and tugged at a few sheets of kitchen roll, handing them to Bella, then sat back down and let Bella cry, her expression soft. Finally, she reached out a hand, patting Bella's gently, and said, 'I'll see what I can do.'

29

Four days later, on Wednesday evening, he called her. Bella was in the kitchen when an unknown number came up on her phone. She snatched it up. 'Hello?'

'It's Jamie,' he said simply. 'Jamie Clarke.'

Bella walked into the living room and sat down at a table by the window that looked onto the estate. All these years, she'd thought about him, imagined talking to him, imagined what his voice would sound like. In her head, she'd had hundreds of conversations with him, but now that he was here, on the other end of the phone, she didn't know what to say.

'You wanted to talk to me,' he reminded her.

'Yes. Yes, I did. I do.' Her voice sounded high-pitched and reedy. 'Thank you for calling.'

'I'm not supposed to,' he said.

'I know.' Bella swallowed, pulling herself together. 'And this isn't a trap. I promise you.'

'I could go back to prison if anyone found out.'

'They won't.' She cleared her throat. 'They won't. I swear

to God. I just . . . I just want to talk to you about my mum. I want to know the truth about what happened to her.'

A pause. 'I didn't do it. That's the truth. It wasn't me.'

Bella felt her heart flutter.

'I'm so sorry it happened,' he continued. 'I'm so sorry that you lost your mum in that . . . that *awful* way. I've wanted to say that to you for years, and I'm glad I can because it was such a horrible, despicable thing for you to have gone through . . .' His voice was thick with emotion. 'I can't begin to imagine what your life has been like because of it, but someone else did that to her, not me. I would never have hurt her. I could never do something like that.'

Bella closed her eyes, trying to make sense of what she was hearing from this stranger, this man with a South London accent just like her dad's, who sounded so very . . . *normal*. He was telling her that she had made a mistake when she identified him. But unlike in all the conversations she had imagined, there was no judgement of her in his tone.

'I thought the world of your mum,' he told her.

'Prove it,' she blurted back.

'How?'

'Tell me about her.'

He paused. 'What do you want to know?'

Bella felt her throat tighten. 'You said you were dating her. You said that to the court in your defence. So what was she like?'

Another pause. 'She was beautiful. She was funny. I mean, really funny. She had a great sense of humour. Do you remember that?'

'Sort of,' Bella said, tears springing to her eyes.

The Stranger on the Stairs

'And she was curious – interested in people. In philosophy. In the world. In everything. That's one of the things that drew me to her. She was inspiring to talk to. And she loved books. She loved stories.'

A flash to her mother teaching her to read. The word cards. The alphabet rhymes. The Jacqueline Wilson books she adored, which her mother would insist on reading first, to make sure they weren't too racy for her.

'She wanted to be a writer,' he continued. 'Do you remember that? She wanted to write children's books.'

'No,' Bella said, stunned. 'No one told me that.' Another flash to her mother making up stories on the way to school. One about a rabbit with a broken paw who became a world-class tennis player. A kangaroo who couldn't hop but then realised there were other things to be happy for. The disempowered overcoming life's challenges: *this* was what her mother cared about. She wiped her cheeks with her wrist. 'I want to meet you. I want to see you.'

'I can't,' he said, at last. 'The police. They're watching me. I can't.'

'We can meet somewhere.'

'They'll follow me.'

Bella thought about how she, too, sometimes felt she was being watched. Could it be the police? But she needed to see him. She needed to watch his face while he talked about her mother. She needed to look into his eyes.

'I'll come to you,' she said. 'I'll come in disguise. I'll think of a way so that even if they're watching, they won't know it's me.'

'They'll tell my probation officer anyway. And it could be grounds for putting me back in prison.'

'I don't know if I picked the right person,' Bella burst out.

The phone went silent. She could hear him breathing. Thinking.

'The identity parade,' she said. 'It was . . . confusing. I don't know if I made a mistake. So, if we could just meet, maybe I will remember. Maybe I will then be certain of who I really did see that day.'

Eventually, he spoke. 'I really want to. It's just that—'

'I'll check every car in the street and if there is anyone outside your house, I'll knock on someone else's door.'

He hesitated. She could tell he wasn't convinced, and why would he be? Why would he trust her?

'I will be so, so careful,' she said. 'I'll think it all through and I'll make a plan, and then I'll call you and make sure you're happy with it. Can I do that? Will you at least let me do that?'

'OK,' he said, at last.

30

Eve loaded an icebox into her car boot. It was Good Friday and the entire family was descending on Sascha and Graham, including Eve's parents, who were over from France. Sascha would be making roast lamb and potatoes, while Eve was on vegetables and had already prepared green beans and sprouts with chestnuts. Mackenzie and Simon were bringing dessert. Eve's parents would no doubt have brought plenty of wine with them. She hadn't seen them for over a year and was looking forward to everyone being together.

She pulled into Sascha's road just before twelve and was surprised to see Simon's car parked outside; she hadn't expected Mackenzie and Simon to arrive before her. Graham answered the door and gave her a quick hug, but he seemed a little distant and not his normal jovial self. She followed him down the hallway and into the kitchen, bracing herself for the possibility that he and Sascha had had a row. The table had been extended and covered with a chintzy blue tablecloth and was already set for nine. She smiled across at Mackenzie and

Simon, who were already seated at the far end, but before she could greet them properly, she caught sight of her mum, who got up, smiling, from the sofa in front of her, and then her dad was pushing away Pooh, the dog, and getting up too, and there were lots of warm hugs and welcomes.

Then Eve's nieces were there and Sascha was busy calling out orders to bring this and take that, chop this or pour that. Eve unpacked her vegetable dishes onto the island and Sascha said, 'Thank you,' somewhat curtly. Eve asked if she should heat them, but Sascha said no, she would do it, and asked her to open the wine instead. Mackenzie and Simon remained seated at the table and Eve flashed them another smile, which Simon returned. Mackenzie quickly became absorbed in something on her phone and Eve wondered if it was perhaps Simon and Mackenzie who had had the row.

It wasn't until they were halfway through lunch that Eve realised she was the problem. Eve's nieces and her parents and Graham and Simon were all chatting away as normal, but each time she spoke, Eve noticed Mackenzie and Sascha exchanging looks across the table, and it sank in that neither of them had made eye contact with her since she'd arrived. Immediately after dessert, Graham stood up and announced that Pooh needed a walk. Simon jumped up, a little too quickly, and said that he would come too, and then Sascha said that everyone should go and have a walk along the Thames Path towards Chiswick and give her a chance to clear up. Eve got up too, but Sascha hissed, her voice low, 'Not you!'

And then Graham had ushered everyone but her, Sascha and Mackenzie out of the door, and the house fell silent.

'What's going on?' Eve asked, looking from her sister to her daughter and back again.

'What's going on?' Sascha repeated. 'Now let me see.' She wiped her hands on a tea towel, looking as though she might cry.

Eve glanced at Mackenzie, who sighed, shaking her head from side to side and making a disbelieving face. 'We *know*, Mum,' she said. 'We know about your *boyfriend*.' She spat the word out.

'Oh, yes,' Sascha jumped in. 'That's it. You're sleeping with a convicted murderer and rapist. That's what's going on.'

For a brief moment, Eve felt as though she was going to faint. 'How did you find out?' she managed to say, sinking back into her former seat at the table.

'The police came,' Sascha said. 'A detective. He told us everything. He told us that your boyfriend's real name is Jamie Clarke and that—'

'—that he's not long come out of prison,' Mackenzie chimed in.

'And that he isn't rich and he doesn't own the house in Norham Gardens.'

'And that he's on the sex offenders register.'

'And that he tied a woman up and raped her – brutally raped and strangled her – in front of her seven-year-old daughter!'

'What! No! The police told you that?' Eve gasped.

'Mum, it's all over the internet!' Mackenzie challenged her, looking disgusted. 'Your boyfriend is *all over the internet*!'

'You told us he was famous!' Sascha said, letting out a strangled cry, a half sob, half laugh. 'But this . . .'

'The bit about her daughter seeing him – that's a lie,' Eve said. 'And they had no right talking to you.'

'Oh, so the police are wrong and you're right in this *fucked-up scenario*?'

'Yes, because he didn't do it!'

'Oh my God!' Mackenzie cried out. She looked incredulous for a second, then, placing her elbows on the table, she put her head in her hands.

Eve could see her daughter was upset and she wanted to go over and comfort her, but she knew she couldn't. Instead, she watched as Sascha went over and stroked Mackenzie's shoulders for a moment before sinking onto her own seat and picking up her wine glass.

'He's not my boyfriend,' Eve said weakly. 'I'm not sleeping with him.'

'Don't lie, Mum!' Mackenzie cried out, lifting her head. 'Why do you have to keep lying? You sat there at the wedding and you told us you were!'

'I didn't! That's not what I said.'

'How could you, Eve?' Sascha burst out. 'How could you even want to have sex with someone who tied up and beat and raped and strangled a woman and . . . and left her on the floor half-naked. Half-fucking-naked, and . . . and *dead*. And with her daughter right there,' she added, her voice shuddering. 'Her seven-year-old daughter!'

'He didn't do it.' Eve spoke more forcefully this time. 'It wasn't him!'

'Mum!' Mackenzie made a *wake-up* face. 'They all say that! How can you be so naive!'

Eve sighed. 'I can't believe you're judging him like this when you don't even know him.'

'And we can't believe you're defending him!' Mackenzie retorted.

Eve squeezed her eyes shut, blinking back her own tears, then took a deep breath. 'He's appealing his conviction. He has a lawyer and she believes him, and she's going to get his conviction overturned—'

'Of course she is. Lawyers are ambulance chasers. It's what they do.'

'She's doing it for free. Pro bono.'

Sascha curled her mouth dismissively, as if she didn't believe this for one minute.

Eve took a deep breath, deciding to keep the conversation on point. 'He's served his sentence,' she said. 'He's out on licence, which means he's done his time.'

'Oh my God. And that's what matters?' Mackenzie wailed. 'He's done his time? Is that all you care about?'

'Aren't you worried about what he could do to you?' Sascha asked, her eyes wide. 'He could kill you!'

'He's innocent,' Eve said. 'How many more times do I have to say that? He didn't do it!'

'You don't know that, Mum!'

'You don't,' Sascha agreed. 'How can you possibly know that?'

Eve took another deep breath. 'How can *anyone* possibly know unless they were there? How can anyone know for sure?' She paused. 'We learn how to trust people by the way they are towards us, towards others. And I've seen the way Joe is. I *know* him.'

'You've known him three weeks!' Sascha exclaimed.

'It's been longer than that.'

'A month, then.'

Eve glared at her sister. 'If he's exonerated, will you believe him then?'

Sascha and Mackenzie exchanged glances, but neither answered.

'Only, there have been quite a few other people locked up for rape or murder over the years,' Eve continued, 'and everyone called them monsters – right up until the moment when they found out they hadn't done what they were accused of.'

'Like who? Who has that happened to?'

'Peter Sullivan. Andrew Malkinson. Victor Nealon. Sam Hallam. Colin Stagg. The Birmingham Six. The Guildford Four. The Cardiff Three. Judith Ward. Timothy Evans . . . I could go on. So, if Joe gets his conviction overturned, too, will you still think he's guilty?'

'Joe's not even his name,' Sascha said, ignoring Eve's question. 'He's even lied about that.'

'No, he hasn't,' Eve said staunchly. 'That's his name now. That's one of the few freedoms he has left – to choose what he'd like people to call him.'

'So why didn't you tell us the truth?'

'Because of . . . *this* !' Eve spluttered.

Mackenzie's head shot up. 'You haven't given him any money, have you?'

Eve realised she couldn't take any more. She pushed back her chair and stood up. 'I'm going to leave now,' she said, 'before the others come back. Tell them what you like. Tell them I had a headache. I presume Simon and Graham know. Tell Mum and Dad I'll call them tomorrow. I'm sorry I didn't tell you. I had my reasons, but I doubt there's any point in explaining, or asking you to understand.'

31

He'd said yes. On Friday – which was, in fact, Good Friday – Bella drove west on the North Circular Road towards Oxford. She was going to Jamie Clarke's home. She was going to meet him. She was wired with anticipation, with the strangeness of it all. Each time the traffic stopped, she would angle the rear-view mirror towards her face and feel a surge of incredulity at the reflection gazing back at her. The make-up. The hair! She had often wondered what she would look like as a blonde, and now she knew.

She had found the wig online. It had lovely long wavy fair tresses and was so different from the sleek dark bob she'd worn since childhood. She had once worked with someone who had alopecia and knew she should have the wig professionally fitted, but when it arrived, it looked good enough. In fact, she barely recognised herself, and she was confident that no one else would either, not even Justin or her dad – not if she walked right past them in the street.

A stab of hurt came with the thought that both would

disapprove of the way she looked; in fact, her dad would hate it. He had never let her wear make-up when she was growing up. 'Get that muck off your face,' he would say if he ever caught her with it on. And now here she was, wearing lots of it – heavy eyeliner, deep red lipstick – and on the seat next to her was a pair of high-heeled work shoes, the kind she had never worn to work, ever, and which her dad would definitely think were slutty.

But she was playing a role, and she looked the part. She was dressed in a suit, which she had ordered from Boohoo along with a smart belted coat, and on the back seat were a clipboard and a fake ID and lanyard, all of which had come from an online office store. She had designed an impressive-looking badge and company logo to go inside them. Her art foundation year at Middlesex hadn't been wasted after all.

She was going to be a market researcher named Gemma Washington, who owned her own agency: GWS Research. Attached to the clipboard was an information sheet about the kind of work the agency did, along with a list of questions about people's online buying habits and a printout with a load of data that she'd got from ChatGPT. The whole thing – the new persona, the company, the questions – felt wildly creative. She felt alive in a way she couldn't remember ever feeling before, or at least not since early childhood, when the world had still been full of wonder and possibility.

Jamie had listened carefully to her plan and, after hesitating for just a moment, had agreed that she could come to his home in Oxford, where he was living while renovating a loft space for someone he knew. The owner was away and he had seemed worried about being alone with her, but Bella had reassured him about her intentions. He was, understandably, afraid. God, *she* was afraid. But they both wanted this meeting; they both knew it had to happen. And in some strange way, they seemed to have become united in their fear – of the police, of the outcome, of each other.

It was mid-afternoon when she arrived. The street was in an affluent part of Oxford and was impressive – broad, quiet and lined by huge mansion houses, all gothic in style but each one individual. Bella drove slowly, gazing at the ornate walls and arched doorways, until she found number twenty-one. The few parked cars in the road were empty. She made sure to check the driveways too, and then messaged Jamie to tell him she had arrived and that she thought the coast was clear. He replied to confirm that he hadn't seen anyone suspicious. Even so, they agreed that she would come to the door with her clipboard as planned, and when he answered, they would go through the pretence she'd outlined on the phone.

She got out of the car, her feet unsteady in her high heels, and then she was there at the front door, holding her clipboard, pressing the bell and lifting the heavy iron knocker. And then the door was opening and he was in front of her. She took him in: the short grey-brown hair, the dimple in his clean-shaven chin, the thin, unsmiling mouth, the metal-framed glasses, the intense blue eyes behind them – those famous eyes. *The eyes of a monster.*

'Hello,' she said, forcing herself to sound calm and confident. 'My name's Gemma Washington. I'm from an agency called GWS Research.' She lifted her lanyard to show him her ID. 'I wonder if you have the time to answer a few questions?'

'What kind of questions?' he asked, scratching his chin, playing his part well.

'Well, we're looking into the consumer habits of a series of different age groups and backgrounds to establish the impact of AI on market trends.'

He looked amused by this, as if trying not to smile.

'Could you spare me some of your time?' she asked, her own nervous energy rising.

'Sure,' he said. 'Why not? You'd better come in.'

He stood back to let her pass. She hesitated for just a second. He was around six feet tall and although not particularly intimidating, his chest was broad and she could see the muscles in his arms and shoulders. He could restrain her and hurt her, without a doubt, but she pushed the thought out of her mind and moved past him into the hallway, waiting while he closed the door.

'Not locked,' he said, demonstrating this for her by turning the latch easily and opening it again, very slightly. 'I mean, it's locked from the outside, obviously. But that's all you need to do to get out. You want to try it?'

Bella leaned forward and turned the handle. The door opened easily, and she closed it again.

He gestured for her to follow him to the kitchen, where he showed her to a seat at the table, nearest the door to the hallway. He offered her a cup of tea. She said she would just have water. She watched as he opened a cupboard and filled a glass at the sink, unable to believe that right here in the same room – padding around in his socks, dressed in jeans and a T-shirt with the name of a band on the front – was the man who had haunted her for the past twenty years.

'That was good,' he said, taking a seat opposite her. 'The market research thing. I almost feel like that's what you've come to ask me. Not that I'd have much to say. I don't do much online shopping.'

'I don't do much either,' she said nervously. 'Although this is new, obviously.' She tugged at her blonde tresses. 'And the clothes. And the shoes.' She paused. 'I actually have dark hair.'

'Like your mother.'

She nodded, swallowing.

'You remind me of her,' he said. 'You have the same eyes. The same smile.'

A lump rose in Bella's throat. 'My grandparents say that.'

'It's true.'

'I'm wearing too much make-up,' Bella said. 'It's part of the disguise. I wear barely any normally.'

'I can still see the likeness.' He took off his glasses and looked back at her, waiting, expectant.

'You met her in a shop,' she murmured.

He nodded. 'The corner shop on . . . Stamford Road, I think? It was the nearest one to your house.'

'I remember it. I know about the door. You came to fix it. I know all that. I read about it.' She paused, took a breath. 'I want to know why . . . why she let you into her life. If she did. If what you say is true, then why . . . ?'

The Stranger on the Stairs

He shook his head, his eyes questioning. 'Why . . .?'

'Why *you*? I mean . . . you said at your trial that you were seeing her, that you liked her and that she liked you back, so . . . why did she like you?'

'Well, that's a difficult question to answer.'

'I don't mean that she shouldn't have done,' Bella said, flushing. 'I just want to understand the attraction.'

'Well, like I said, she had a good sense of humour and so I suppose she must have thought I did too. We laughed a lot. And we had lots to talk about. I liked books too. We shared the same view of the world.'

'Which was?' Bella held her breath in anticipation.

The room was silent. Bella could hear the birds chirping in the garden, the rustling of the trees in the breeze.

'She didn't look down on me,' he said, 'even though she had a better education, a better job. She took people as she found them. She didn't judge. She thought anyone could achieve greatness, no matter where they came from. I felt more myself with her than with anyone I'd ever met before, and I knew that together we could be more than the sum of two people.' He paused and spots of colour appeared on his cheeks. 'That sounds a bit grandiose, but—'

'No. It doesn't,' Bella jumped in, wanting him to continue.

He cleared his throat.

'What did you talk about?'

He looked thoughtful. 'It was a long time ago, so it's hard to remember . . . It's like when you read a book and years later you can't remember much about it, except that you loved it.'

'You loved her?' Bella said, feeling her throat tighten.

'I was beginning to fall for her, yes. I wanted to be with her. I remember hoping that she wanted a future with me.'

She waited.

'She wanted to travel,' he said. 'I remember that.'

'Where?'

'Everywhere. Europe. America. Africa. I did, too. We talked about that quite a bit. Where we would go first.'

'Where?' Bella asked. 'Where would you have gone?'

He thought about this. 'Nepal. I think that was her first choice.'

'But she had me.'

'She thought it would be good for you. Educational.'

'She would have taken me too?' Bella felt the next wave of emotion rise inside her.

'Of course.'

'I was seven.'

'She wouldn't have left you behind.'

'How do you know?'

'Because you were her world.'

Bella swallowed back tears. 'Did she actually say that?'

'She didn't have to.'

'Did you know me?' she asked. 'Did I know you?'

'We only met a couple of times. But she talked about you a lot.'

'What did she say?'

'That you were the best adventure of her life.'

Bella looked at him, her heartbeat quickening. 'She actually said that?'

He nodded. 'More than once. She adored you. She talked about how – even though things hadn't worked out between them – she was glad she had met your father, because if she hadn't, she would never have had you.'

Bella closed her eyes.

'But I think she wanted to be sure about me – about us – before she let you get to know me. And . . .' He hesitated. 'She didn't want it getting back to your father that she had met someone.'

They looked at each other in silence.

'Did you know my dad?' she asked.

He shook his head.

'Go on,' Bella pressed him. 'You obviously know something about him.'

He sighed, looking uncomfortable. 'Well . . .'

'Please. There's nothing you can say that will hurt me. Or at least, if it does, it's a good thing. This is exactly what I came here for. Please. Tell me.'

'I never met him. I only knew about him through your mum.'

'What did she say?'

'Look, he's your dad, so I really don't—'

'We don't get on,' Bella said quickly. 'We never have. He was really hard on me. I moved out when I was seventeen and it was the best day of my life. I never wanted to live with him in the first place. I hated that I had to leave my home. My mum was the one I loved, but she was taken away from me, and if it wasn't you who took her from me, I need to know who did.'

'I wish I knew the answer to that,' he said.

She paused. 'But my dad wasn't nice to her, that's what you're saying?'

Jamie looked awkward for a moment. 'He gave her a bit of a hard time too.'

She lifted her eyes towards him. 'In what way?'

He swallowed. 'He didn't approve of the way she was bringing you up. She was . . . a free spirit. You know? And he didn't like that. He thought she should be more . . .'

'More what?'

'Restrained, I suppose. More . . . conservative. Less friendly with people.' He paused. 'He thought her clothes were too revealing. That she should cover herself up.'

Bella thought about this. What Jamie was saying rang true. 'He was the same with me,' she said. 'He wouldn't let me wear what I wanted. And he was strict with me. He had a whole bunch of rules about . . . well, everything. He wouldn't let me do half the stuff my friends were doing.'

He nodded.

'And you're right. He was critical of my mum. He rarely talked about her, but when he did, he never had anything good to say. It was always negative, and it really upset me. It was almost as if he thought she had brought what happened on herself by being the way she was. I didn't know then that this was victim shaming. I just knew it used to make me mad. He said she had let me "run riot", which wasn't true at all. I always did what I was told.'

'She was great with you,' Jamie said. 'She was a good mum. I could see how much she loved you.'

'How?'

'By the way you were. Happy. Relaxed. Bubbly. Yourself. You were just like her.'

'Tell me,' Bella blinked back tears. 'Tell me how I was like her.'

'Well,' he said, scratching his head. 'I mean, to look at, you were just like her. The same dark hair and olive skin. But it was the way you were. You did things together. You liked the same things.'

'Like . . . ?'

'Like . . . reading. Art. Writing stories.'

'Together?' Bella asked him, her heart rising in delight.

'Yes,' he said, his voice husky. 'She wrote the words and you drew the pictures.'

'Oh my God,' she said, blinking back tears. 'Yes. I remember. I drew the pictures for her stories.'

He smiled gently. 'I remember her showing them to me. She was very proud.'

Bella smiled back, and then it dawned on her, right at that moment, as she looked into his eyes: *this is all true*. Her mother had let Jamie Clarke into her life. Her mother had confided in him. Her mother had liked – maybe even loved – this gentle, kind man sitting opposite her, looking worn and injured. This wasn't the same person who had hurled her mother's phone across the room, who had violently broken her jaw and fingers, who had brutally raped her and ended her life.

She felt a rush of cold dread as the true force of this took hold of her, as the past twenty years began to take on a new shape and form in her mind. She gazed at the man sitting opposite her, at the anguish behind his smile, at the pain etched into his forehead, at the stoop of his shoulders, and a blade of horrible regret passed through her. She thought about what it would feel like to have your good name taken and tarnished, to have your reputation destroyed, to have the whole world hate you. She thought about what two decades in prison must have done to him and wondered where on earth he had found the strength to survive.

Fresh tears fell down her cheeks. 'I'm sorry. I'm sorry. I'm so, so sorry,' she whispered.

32

Eve picked up her handbag and walked straight down the hallway and out of her sister's front door, leaving behind her Tupperware, her icebox and her jacket. She had planned to stay the night, as she usually did when she came, and was relieved that her instincts had told her that something was wrong and she shouldn't drink more than one glass of wine. But her knees were trembling so hard that she could barely drive, and after she started the car, she drove past Kew Bridge to a road that backed onto the Thames, where she parked up and turned off the engine. It took her half an hour to stop shaking.

As she drove back along the M40 to Oxford, everything Sascha and Mackenzie had said began to replay on a loop in her mind. She was furious with herself for having talked about Joe to her family, for having kept up the pretence of the relationship after Joe had asked her not to, and for all the other silly things she'd said at the wedding that had only made everyone more curious about who she was seeing. She should have been more protective of Joe. All of this was her own stupid fault.

She knew she had to speak to him, if only to warn him that the police had been talking to her family. She switched on her Bluetooth and called him, but got no answer. As she approached Oxford, she called again. At the Headington roundabout, she left the A40 and turned onto the bypass, but found herself driving past the exit for Marston and heading towards North Oxford and Norham Gardens. It wasn't yet five, but Joe would have to be home by six because of his curfew, and if he wasn't there, she could sit and wait in the car.

A shiver of foreboding ran through her as she turned into the street. She knew she was overstepping the boundary between them, but if the police were now talking to her family about him, he needed to know that, didn't he? Detectives weren't called detectives for nothing. They'd have been able to tell by the looks on Mackenzie's and Sascha's faces that her relationship with Joe was more involved than he had let on to his probation officer.

She pulled into a bay across the road from number twenty-one and sat still for a few moments, soon feeling glad that she hadn't rushed in, upsetting Joe and putting even more pressure on him. Somehow or other, just being back in Oxford, and specifically here in this street, looking at these houses, had made everything return to its normal proportions. She was worrying about nothing, she decided. The police had been fishing for information, that's all, and Sascha and Mackenzie couldn't have had anything to tell them because they didn't know anything for sure, did they? So what could they have said? She would go home and wait for Joe to call her back.

She was just about to switch her engine on again when the

front door of 21 Norham Gardens opened and a woman stepped out onto the front path. Eve froze. Who was this? Someone from probation? Or a cop? She slunk down into her seat as the woman looked briefly to her left and right and then walked quickly out onto the pavement. It was still light and Eve could see her clearly: the woman was young and pretty – in her late twenties, perhaps, with long wavy fair hair. She was wearing a cream belted coat and high heels. She looked upset and her make-up had run, as if she had been crying.

Confused, Eve looked back towards the house, just in time to see Joe close the front door. Her eyes swivelled back to the woman, who was getting into a white Fiat Panda. Eve continued to watch for a moment as the woman pulled out and drove away along Norham Gardens.

And then, out of the corner of her eye, she saw movement in the bushes fronting the house next to her. A figure emerged and got into a car. The engine started and it turned out of the driveway and went quickly in the same direction as the Fiat Panda.

There wasn't enough time to note much about the car except that it was a Lexus, and it was black, and the windows were tinted so that she couldn't see who was driving.

But there was no doubt in Eve's mind that whoever the woman was, she was being followed.

PART TWO

33

Eve sat still for a moment or two, trying to make sense of what she had just seen. Was Joe being spied on from the house across the street? Why would Joe's neighbour be tailing his probation officer? And if the woman wasn't his probation officer, who was she – and why had she looked so upset? Eve turned to look back at the house the Lexus had just left. As she did so, a curtain moved in one of the upstairs windows.

The police. It had to be the police. They were watching him. But why? What possible risk did Joe present that they were going to this much trouble to track his movements?

Unless . . . was Joe in a relationship with the woman?

Eve switched on her engine and drove home fast. She walked into the living room, where she sank down into the armchair and closed her eyes, breathing in deeply and counting to ten as she attempted to untangle the knot of new information. Joe and another woman. Joe and an attractive young woman. So that was why he hadn't answered her calls – he had been with this woman. She could have been inside the house with him for hours.

Maybe all day. Maybe she had woken up there.

Eve felt ashamed of the tight ball of pain and jealousy that had begun to swell up inside her. She had no right to feel the way she did. Joe wasn't hers – he'd made that perfectly clear. But she had thought he wasn't going to be anybody else's either, and after everything else that had happened that day – after the huge bust-up with Sascha and Mackenzie over her supposed relationship with him – she couldn't help feeling hurt and used.

Mackenzie's voice came into her head. *'You haven't given him any money, have you?'* But she had. And now she felt foolish. Had that been all Joe wanted from her? Had *that* been her purpose, all along? It wouldn't have been hard to tell from her appearance that she wasn't short of a bob or two. And then . . . *Christ!* First, she had cried on his shoulder and told him she felt cut off from her family, and then she had told him she was renting her home until she could find somewhere to buy. She might as well have worn a T-shirt saying: *I'm desperate and I've got a few hundred thousand pounds in the bank.*

She squeezed her eyes shut as the shame and hurt intensified, then forced herself to breathe deeply. What she'd seen didn't make any sense. The woman was attractive, stylish and *young*, which might not be so surprising if Joe wasn't a convicted sex offender, if he actually owned a ten-million-pound house in one of the most prestigious streets in Oxford.

But then again, wasn't that the exact same way Eve had been lured in?

She could bear it no longer. She picked up her phone. *Joe. You need to talk to me*, she typed. Then she placed the handset in her lap and waited.

After a moment, there was a vibrating sound and a loud bleep. Eve jumped.

But it was her mum. *Just checking you got home safely? I hope you're feeling a little better?*

Yes, Eve typed. *Just the beginnings of a migraine. Under control now. Sorry to have left. I wanted to get home before it got too bad.*

Of course. What a shame. We miss you. Dad sends his love.

Eve flopped back in her chair and closed her eyes. She thought about what her family would be doing right now: her mum and dad, Mackenzie and Simon, Graham and Sascha. Ruby and Ella, Sascha's girls. She imagined them all huddled over a board game, laughing, the adults drinking wine. Happy. She could have stayed the whole weekend at Sascha's, as planned. She could have acted like a normal mother, a normal daughter, instead of the desperate mess that she seemed to have turned into.

She moved over to the sofa and curled up, pulling the throw around her, then closed her eyes again, shutting out the world.

34

Eve spent the following day – Easter Saturday – busying herself around the flat in an attempt to make good use of the spare hours that had suddenly presented themselves, hours she should have been spending with her family. But she was on tenterhooks, jumping at the slightest sound. By mid-afternoon, she felt sick with disappointment and regret. Joe still hadn't replied to her messages. She could have woken to a lazy, noisy breakfast in Sascha's bright, sunny kitchen, then gone for a walk along the river and a lovely pub lunch in Kew. Her fight with Sascha and Mackenzie now seemed meaningless, her stance in defence of Joe pointless. She had upset everyone in her life, and for what? So that she could spend the Easter weekend tired and alone, doing housework?

At around four, she felt hungry and realised she had barely any food in the flat, having planned to spend the weekend at Sascha's. She ate half a can of cold baked beans straight from the tin and had just finished making a shopping list when the door buzzer sounded in the kitchen. Her heart rose in anticipation as she hurried to answer it. She knew it was unrealistic to expect it to be Joe – who had never been to her flat – or Mackenzie, who would be nearing Dorset by now, but there was hope, at least.

'Eve, it's Iwan.'

For a moment, she couldn't place the voice or name.

'Iwan Raker,' he said. 'From work.'

Her head of department? What was he doing here – and during the holidays?

She buzzed him into the building and waited by the front door.

'I'm sorry to turn up out of the blue,' he said as she let him in, 'but I've just been finishing up some bits on campus and I knew you lived nearby, and . . .' He looked at her. 'Well, I didn't want to do this over the phone.'

'Do what?'

He took a step and peered round the doorway to the living room. 'Can I?'

'Of course.'

Eve closed the front door and followed him in. He circled the coffee table, then stopped next to the sofa, looking uncomfortable.

'We have a problem,' he said.

'What kind of a problem?'

He hesitated. 'We've had a visit from the police.'

Eve took a sharp breath. 'What about?'

'About the man you're seeing.' He glanced up at her.

She flushed. 'I see.'

'So, it's true?' He eyed her expectantly.

'I don't know,' she said stiffly. 'That depends on what you've been told.' She could hear the chill in her voice and she felt sorry for Iwan because he was just doing his job, but . . . the bloody police. Why were they doing this to her? They clearly weren't satisfied with coming between her and her family.

Iwan hovered next to the sofa for a moment, then sat down. Eve walked over to join him.

'Did they come to the college?' she asked.

He nodded.

'And what did they say?'

'That you're in a relationship with a . . .' he cleared his throat '. . . a sex offender. A convicted rapist and murderer. That he's just been released from prison. That he served twenty years.' He hesitated. 'That they're worried about the students.'

Eve sighed.

'As, of course, are we.'

'We?'

'Myself. Reena. Giles.' He shifted uncomfortably. 'And, of course, I've had to take this to the board of governors.'

Eve pictured this, the meeting in the boardroom on campus, the looks of concern on the faces of the dean and pro-vice-chancellor.

'So how did they do it?'

'How did . . .?'

'The police. Did they just turn up? Did they come to the Law Faculty?'

'Yes.'

'When? When did they come?'

'On Monday.'

'Monday? You mean . . . the Monday just gone?'

'Yes. I wanted to speak to you as quickly as possible, of course, but I'm sure you appreciate that I also needed time to talk with Reena and Giles, to look at the potential ramifications, and then to raise it with the board.'

Eve wasn't concerned about his delay in talking to her. She was furious with the police. What right did they have to keep talking to everyone she knew? She was pretty sure they were acting outside of their powers. Her mind spun back to some of the events of earlier that week. Everything now made sense: the tight smiles in the corridor, the clipped conversations, the way the staffroom had fallen unexpectedly quiet when she had entered after a mid-morning lecture. She gazed back at Iwan and knew without him having to tell her that the news was out. She was already being gossiped about within her department, and no doubt elsewhere in the university.

'Some of the students have got hold of it,' Iwan said, confirming her suspicions. 'And we've had a call from the women's officer at the SU. There have been requests to . . .' He paused. 'To ask you to stay away from campus.'

Her heart beat faster. 'You're suspending me?'

'No,' Iwan said, stretching out the word in way that said *not yet*. 'We're asking you not to go onto campus for the time being. Or through the student village.'

'Because . . .?'

'Because this is a potential safeguarding issue which needs looking into. The union has made the request and we feel it's a reasonable one. It's the Easter holidays anyway, and so there's no reason for you to go into the faculty building. If there is anything you need, we can get it for you.'

'For God's sake,' Eve said. 'What kind of a threat do you think I am?'

'It's just a precaution until we have had time to look into the issues the union has raised.' He hesitated. 'And it's for your own good. If you are seen in the student village or on campus, it could be damaging for you, as well as for us.'

'How?'

'Well, the board is concerned about the potential for any negative attention.'

'Wait,' Eve said. 'Like . . .?'

'Like photos of you being taken and posted on social media.'

'Photos of me? Why would there be?'

'Things can quickly escalate,' he said. 'If we don't respond appropriately, there could be protests and then—'

'Protests?' Eve looked at him despairingly.

'These things can quickly gather momentum.'

'Look, the police have got it wrong. I'm helping with a post-conviction appeal, that's all. I think it's a miscarriage of justice. The man concerned has got a lawyer and I'm helping her to establish the grounds we need to take it to the CCRC. Lots of law faculties have innocence projects.'

'Faculties do. But not individuals. The problem is that we weren't informed about this.'

'Well, now you know, so can't we just put out a statement through the comms team? We could ask for volunteers, make it official.'

He hesitated. 'Before I did that, I would need to know the truth about the nature of your relationship with this man.'

Eve tried to keep her expression neutral, but she realised

she couldn't lie, not to her head of department. This conversation would go back to the higher-ups and form part of the case against her, and – a thought that had come into her mind unbidden as she lay awake the previous night – the police could have evidence of their relationship. The idea made her feel sick with shame and fear, but if Joe was being watched by the police from across the street, it wasn't beyond the realms of possibility that someone could have been there in the garden that Sunday when she and Joe had begun to have sex in the kitchen, in full view of all of the windows. There could be photos.

'We . . . were intimate. Once,' she said, her skin hot. 'It was a one-off. Neither of us meant it to happen. He was hurt – badly hurt – by what the police had done to him, and I felt sorry for him and . . . well, it just happened. Once. But we agreed that it shouldn't happen again. We agreed that I wouldn't see him alone after that, not without his lawyer present. And so, now, I really am just a part of his legal team.'

He nodded. 'So when did you last see him?'

Eve flushed. 'On Monday,' she admitted. 'I went there to tell him that I was going to fund some of the costs of his case.'

'And you haven't seen him since?'

She shook her head. 'No.' She watched his expression. 'Why?'

'There have been reports that he's been seen on campus.'

'No!' Eve cried out in disbelief. 'That can't be true! When? When was he supposed to have been on campus?'

Iwan reached for his phone. He scrolled and tapped for a moment, then said, 'It was reported to have been on Wednesday.'

'Who reported it?' Eve demanded angrily.

Iwan shook his head. 'I'm afraid I can't tell you that.'

'OK, so where's the evidence?'

'I don't have any evidence as yet. Just the report.'

'It can't have happened,' Eve insisted. 'He would have no reason to come onto campus.'

'Except to meet you, perhaps?'

'Do you think I'm stupid?' Eve shook her head in disbelief. 'Why would I meet him there?'

'I don't know, Eve,' he said, sighing. 'But what I *do* know is that, as a faculty and as a college, we are responsible for ensuring the safety and well-being of our students, which means that when we receive a report like this, we need to put the building blocks in place for an effective prevention response.'

Jargon, Eve thought, feeling furious. Just jargon. She knew there was no way that Joe had been on campus, but she also knew that there was nothing more she could do at this stage. She would have to involve her own union, ask for a meeting, demand to see the evidence, and until then, she had no choice but to agree to what Iwan was asking.

When he had gone, she quickly snatched up her phone. There was another message from her mum, asking if she was feeling well enough for a visit. Eve wanted to weep at the kindness behind the offer, at the thought that her parents would cut short their time with Sascha's family to drive all the way to Oxford to see her, but she had no idea what they would think about her situation, and besides, it wasn't fair to take them away from their grandchildren.

The Stranger on the Stairs

She typed back: *I'm much better, Mum, and please don't do that. Let's talk in the morning.*

She put her phone on the table and stared at it, then picked it up again and opened her messaging app. Joe wasn't online. Come to think of it, he hadn't been online since . . . when? She selected his contact information, and then it hit her: he hadn't been online since she had seen the blonde-haired woman outside his house the previous day. With a sudden realisation, she leaped to her feet.

When she got to Norham Gardens, there was another car on the drive, a sleek-looking bottle-green Mercedes with 2023 plates. She hesitated, her heart beating faster as she stepped past it and pushed open the back gate. She could immediately see that something was wrong. There were shards of broken glass strewn across the path near the back door, which was boarded up as if it had been broken into. As she gazed at it, a man stepped out from the opposite corner of the house with a dustpan and brush. He looked up as he saw her. He had dark hair and a goatee beard and was tall, thin and angular, casually dressed in a T-shirt and cargo trousers.

'Don't come any closer,' he said, putting his hand up. 'There's glass everywhere.'

'I'm sorry,' she said. 'I'm looking for Joe.'

'He's not here.' He eyed her curiously. 'You must be Eve.'

'And you must be Chas.'

He nodded, looking sorry.

She swallowed hard. 'They've taken him back to prison, haven't they?'

35

It was Easter Sunday. Ben was at his dad's for the day and Sarah was in the kitchen at home, trying to trace Joe's whereabouts, which had been no mean feat on a bank holiday. She put down her phone.

'Well?' asked Will. 'Where has he gone?'

'Bullingdon,' she said.

'Oxfordshire?'

'Yes. It's a Cat C. It has a vulnerable prisoner wing.'

Will shook his head. 'Those aren't good places. They're full of . . . well, not the best kind of people.'

'The kind of people other prisoners want to kill.' Sarah sighed. 'God knows what he's going through. He was already in a bad place, mentally.'

'So, what happened? Why was he recalled?'

'Breach of licence. They're saying he met with a prosecution witness. He was also reported to have entered a university campus, which put him in breach of another of his conditions.'

Will frowned. 'Why would he do that?'

'I don't know.' Sarah shook her head. 'Chas doesn't know either. Joe called him from the police station, but he didn't get much out of him.'

'Can you get a visit this week?'

'I hope so. But I'm afraid I have more bad news to break to him.'

Will eyed her. 'What's that?'

'The police can't find Christy's clothing.'

'You're kidding?'

She shook her head. 'Which means that we can't instruct our own expert to do the testing.'

'They can't find any of it?'

'Nope.' Sarah shrugged. 'It's been destroyed, by the look of things.'

'But he's a lifer. They should have kept the clothes for at least thirty years.'

'Joe wrote to them, too,' Sarah said. 'Straight away, in 2003, asking them to preserve it. He got back all the reassurances they would do that.' She eyed him. 'It's starting to feel personal, if I'm honest, as if the police might have something to hide.'

'Hmm. It would be tempting to think that,' Will said. 'But you know this happens all the time, right? And not just in cold cases.'

'Yeah. I know,' she conceded.

'I believe I saw a study that showed something like twenty thousand trials collapsed between October 2018 and August 2021 due to missing and lost evidence – including evidence linked to a significant number of murders and sex offences.'

'Twenty thousand?' Sarah said. 'That's crazy.'

'How many police officers does it take to close a freezer?'

'It's not funny, Will.'

'I'm being serious,' he said. 'It's a big problem. The evidence freezers are literally overflowing. There was an article about it in *The Justice Gap*. The answer is three, by the way. One to push the door closed, one to hold it shut and one to secure the lock. Police staff are literally doing that. Which doesn't inspire you with confidence about the quality of the samples.'

Sarah sighed. 'It's a bloody mess. I'll try the forensic archives. Maybe they will have kept something – something that hasn't degraded. But I'm worried for Joe. This is another big door that's closed in his face, and I'm going to have to be honest with him that I'm running out of options for finding fresh grounds for appeal.'

36

Bella woke up feeling nervous. Last night, she had had the nightmare again, but this time it was different. In it, she had asked the man on the stairs if he was a policeman, upon which he had silently turned and left the house through the front door. She had spent the whole night trying to find him, or at least that's how it felt. Instead of waking up rigid and frightened as she usually did, she just felt worn out from the dream, which had taken her from the Blenheim Road house in Streatham to her dad's house two streets away, then to Dorothy Clarke's house in Woking, then to the kitchen at 21 Norham Gardens and back home to Blenheim Road again, where all she wanted to do was climb the stairs to her childhood bedroom and go to bed. But then she'd find herself back in Jamie Clarke's kitchen again, telling him how sorry she was that she had let the man get away.

She thought about the underlying atmosphere that had pervaded the dream, one of both regret at not having found the man on the stairs and fear about what might happen if she did.

She knew the reason. Until now, her brain hadn't allowed her to pick her dream apart, but as she thought back to the rest of the conversation she'd had with Jamie Clarke, it was all beginning to add up. She'd told him about her nightmare, about being woken by the sound of her mother being attacked, about the man on the stairs and how she had a strong feeling that this man was someone in authority. And now, as Jamie Clarke's words came back to her – '*You think it was a policeman who killed your mother?*' – she realised that this was the explanation that made the most sense.

The thought was terrifying, not least of all because she felt sure that she had seen the car with the blacked-out windows again as she left Oxford on Friday. It had been behind her more than once as she looked in her rear-view mirror on the motorway. She had stayed indoors all of yesterday, too scared to go out, too scared to call anyone. She had wanted to warn Jamie, but if it was the police who had been watching her, they could be tapping his phone, or hers, or both. She could be paranoid, but Adele had once told her that paranoia was just heightened awareness, and this new awareness was all the more terrifying because the police were who you trusted, who you ran to. Who could she run to now?

Jamie had asked her if she would speak to his lawyer. 'She'll know the names of everyone involved in the investigation,' he had told her. 'She might be able to find out who took your statement.'

But if she gave a statement to his lawyer, would this make her a witness in his appeal case? What would her VLO say? What would her dad say? And what if the press got wind of it? Even if it was true that she had made a mistake when she'd identified Jamie as her mother's killer, was she ready to announce that to the world?

She got out of bed, made tea and sat by the living-room window for a while, gazing out at the single tree – an oak – that stood, bordered by railings, on a scrap of grass in the middle of the estate. For twenty years, she had been a victim and the police had been her allies. How could she now go flinging around accusations against them? And what evidence did she have except for a bad dream and a flimsy memory that had resurfaced during a therapy session?

She sat for a moment longer, her fingers wrapped around the mug on the table in front of her, then got up, showered and dressed and fetched her car keys. She needed to talk to her dad again.

'I haven't got you an Easter egg,' her dad said, unapologetically, when she arrived.

'I haven't got you one either.' She sat down on the sofa.

'Do you want a cup of tea?'

She hesitated. 'OK. Thanks.'

Jenny, who was standing in the doorway, let out a small sigh, then disappeared into the kitchen.

Her dad eyed her over his glasses. 'So, go on, then. Spit it out.'

She took a deep breath. 'I came to talk about Mum.'

Her dad sighed and turned his eyes towards the TV.

'Can you turn that off, Dad,' she said crossly. 'I need to talk to you.'

'Here we go again,' he murmured.

'This is important,' Bella said, exasperated. 'Why won't you ever just listen to me?'

'I'm always listening to this.'

'But never hearing.'

Her dad picked up the remote and pointed it at the telly. 'Right,' he said, after the football snapped off and the room fell silent. 'What is it now?'

Bella took a deep breath, reminding herself not to jump straight into her questions about the police. 'I want to know where her things are,' she began. 'I want to know what happened to her clothes and books and—'

'What are you on about?' His brow knitted irritably. 'You've got everything. You or your grandparents. They got the house. You know that. Why are you asking about this now?'

'Because there are things I don't have. Things I've remembered. She wrote books. Stories. And she must have had diaries and photos and . . . clothes. She must have had whole rooms full of stuff. Things I made her. Things she made me. Things I should have had, and I don't believe Granny and Grandpa have them because if they did, they would have given them to me.'

'The police were all over the place,' her dad said, sniffing. 'They probably took most of it.'

'What for?'

'For evidence.' He shrugged. 'I don't know. But it isn't here.'

'Not even in the loft?'

'There's nothing of hers up there,' he said.

She licked her lips. 'So who was it who took her things?'

He frowned. 'Who was what?'

'The police,' she said. 'What were their names?'

'Their names?' He looked at her as if she was mad. 'What on earth are you asking that for? They were just police.'

'So you didn't take down their names?'

He shook his head, looking bewildered.

'Who took my statement?' she asked him.

He frowned. 'Who did what?'

'I want to know which police officer took a statement from me about what happened. It was a man. He came here.' Bella glanced around the living room, her eyes landing on the chair next to her father's. 'I was sitting over there.' She pointed. 'Next to you. On that chair.'

He gave the chair a sideways look. 'That's Jenny's chair, so you couldn't have been.'

Bella sighed. 'It was nobody's chair at the time, Dad, because Jenny didn't exist.'

'Didn't exist!' Her dad snorted.

'You weren't together yet,' Bella said, trying to be patient. 'There was only me. You and me. And that's where I was sitting when the policeman came to talk to me.'

Her dad stiffened. 'You can't remember that!'

'I do,' she countered. 'I remember a man with a notebook. He was sitting right next to me on that pouffe you used to have.'

Her dad shook his head in disbelief. 'This is rubbish. Utter rubbish.'

'Well, someone took a statement from me. They had to have done, because I made one.'

'You had to go into the police station,' said Jenny's voice from the doorway. 'You gave your statement there.'

They both turned to look at her.

'Not being rude, Jenny,' Bella said, 'but how do you know that? You weren't here.'

'Because that's what happens. My friend is in the police. When it's a child, they have to do it properly, in a room, with specially trained officers. It has to be recorded.'

'There.' Bella's dad slapped his knee.

'So, you actually remember that?' Bella asked, turning back to him.

'I do.'

Bella paused. 'So why do I remember talking to a policeman here, in this house?'

'It's that thing, isn't it?' her dad said. 'That false memory thing.'

Bella jumped up abruptly and walked over to the chair. 'A man came here. A detective. He showed me a photo.' She sat down and looked at the empty space next to her. 'He was just there, next to me, on the pouffe. He showed me a photo. And you looked at it too.' She paused, staring at her father. 'I know you remember this, Dad. I can see by your face.'

Her dad swallowed. 'Well, yes. I mean . . . I saw the photo. And it was definitely of him. The man who killed your mother. Jamie Clarke.'

Bella blinked. 'But why would anyone show me a picture of him?'

'I don't know. To remind you, I suppose.'

'And this was before I went to the police station? Before I identified him on the ID parade?'

'I . . . think so. Yeah.' He looked at Bella uncomprehendingly.

'Oh my God,' Bella said. 'Do you realise what you're saying?'

'No. What?'

'They're not supposed to do that, Dad!'

'Do what?'

'The police are not supposed to show you a photo prior to any form of identification!'

'Why not? They got him, didn't they? You picked the right one, so why does it matter?'

'It matters because that would have influenced me. I was supposed to go into that ID parade blind and look at a bunch of men in a line-up and not know which one I was looking for.'

'Well, I don't see what difference it makes,' her dad said. 'You knew what he looked like anyway. You'd seen him before.'

Bella's mouth was dry. She had met Jamie, but she still shouldn't have been shown a photo, she knew that much. 'What was his name, Dad?' she murmured.

'Whose name?'

'The detective. The policeman who came here.'

Her dad's jaw slackened and for a brief moment Bella thought he was going to tell her. Then he shook his head crossly. 'It was twenty years ago. How on earth am I supposed to remember that?'

Bella took a deep breath. 'You wouldn't have written it down?'

'Why would I have done that?'

'I don't know,' Bella said. 'Maybe because it was important?'

Her dad shot her an exasperated look and then gave her the

usual line when he wanted the conversation to be over. 'You told the police it was him. You made a statement. You can't go changing it now.'

'Who says, Dad?' Bella argued. 'You're always saying that, but why can't I?'

'Because it's . . .' He shrugged. 'Perjury?'

'What? No, it's not! It's just me remembering something I had forgotten.'

'Well, I don't see why it matters. It's all in the past, isn't it?'

'Not for Jamie Clarke,' Bella said. 'And not for me, either.'

Her dad eyed her suspiciously. 'I don't know why you have to keep dragging it up.'

'Because of . . . all of it, Dad! Losing Mum, losing my home, not being able to remember anything about my life when I was with her. And you . . . refusing to talk about her, or to say anything good about her. Can't you see what it's done to me? I'm your daughter! Why don't you care?'

Her father looked more uncomfortable than she'd ever seen him, and then he said, abruptly, 'I think you've outstayed your welcome.'

Bella felt the rebuke land hard against her chest. Apprehension rose inside her. Her father was all she had. For seventeen years, he had been all she had, but the truth was that their connection had always been fragile and superficial. She could never reach the real person behind the wall he had put up, and she saw with sudden clarity that this was never going to change. She had often wondered what Jenny saw in her father, how she got any kind of fulfilment from being with someone so shallow, but she realised now that he was shielding himself from *her*. Her father didn't want any kind of relationship with *her*. He never would. He had never really forgiven her for looking like her mother, for being like her mother.

Bella had never felt more alone.

37

Eve took a deep breath as she opened the email from her head of department.

Date: Tue, 3 April at 11.53

Dear Eve

Having considered the sensitive issues in this case and notwithstanding the fact that James Clarke has been recalled to prison by the probation service and no longer presents a direct threat to the students, the board of governors has expressed ongoing concerns regarding the negative publicity that your association with him has attracted, which, if it continues, is expected to bring both the faculty and the college into disrepute.

The board has therefore requested that you cease this relationship with immediate effect or face suspension. We invite you to consider your position in advance of a meeting to be arranged for the first day of the new term, the details of which will be confirmed with you and your union representative in due course.

Yours sincerely
Iwan Raker

Eve closed the email and sat back in the chair in her kitchen, feeling a lump form in the back of her throat. She stared into space for several moments, listening to the sound of the clock ticking on the wall in front of her, then opened a web page on her browser and typed in the name of her union. She was just about to get up to fetch her phone from the worktop, when it rang. She snatched it up, swiping the slider.

'This is a call from someone detained in custody,' said an automated voice. 'Hang up if you don't wish to receive this call.'

Eve waited, her heart hammering as the phone made a series of small clicks. A few seconds later, she heard the sound of a person at the other end. 'Joe?' she asked. 'Is that you?'

'Eve,' he said, in the simple way he did, as if her name was all he could manage.

'Are you OK?' she asked breathlessly.

There was a pause, and then he said, his voice low and flat, 'Not too great, if I'm honest.'

'I'm so sorry,' she said, suddenly feeling overwhelmed with emotion.

'It's good to hear your voice.'

'It's good to hear yours. I'm so pleased you called.'

'I wanted to call sooner,' he said, 'but I was only allowed one phone call and I needed to tell Chas. The police broke his door down. I wasn't sure if the house was secure. And then it has taken them until now to get me here and process me.'

'When did they arrest you?'

'Friday evening.'

Eve drew a breath. Right after she'd seen him from the street. All this time she had thought he was upset with her, that he was ignoring her, but this hadn't been the case at all. 'Why did this happen?'

A pause. 'They said I came to your college.'

She took a breath. 'And did you?'

'No,' he said staunchly. 'That part's a lie.'

'Then why . . .?'

Another pause. 'They're also saying that I met with a prosecution witness.'

Eve's heart fluttered. 'And did you?' When he didn't answer, she asked, 'Which one?'

'Not on the phone,' he said under his breath.

'Was it a woman?' she whispered. 'Did she come to the house?'

'Please, Eve. Not here. Not now.'

'OK,' she agreed reluctantly. She had so many questions.

'Come to see me,' he begged. 'Please?'

Her heart rose. 'Of course.'

'I've added you to my visitor list. You'll need my date of birth and prison number. Have you got a pen?'

She grabbed one, and a notepad, and sat down at the table while he gave her the details she needed.

'You can do it online,' he said. 'Or there's a phone number.'

'Don't worry. I'll work it out.'

He fell silent and Eve knew that he needed to know if she was still on his side. 'Just hang on in there, OK?' she said. 'I'm going to call Sarah. We're going to get this sorted out.'

'There's nothing you can do,' he told her. 'I don't even have an end date this time. It's all down to the parole board, and it will take months, probably a year, for me to even get a hearing.' The line went quiet. 'I just don't know if I can do this again,' he whispered.

Eve could hear the pain and hopelessness in his voice and tears sprang to her eyes. Whatever he had done, he must have had his reasons, and they must have been important for him to risk going back to prison. Right now, Joe needed her. He was desperate and alone in the world and she couldn't bear the thought of him in pain. She wiped her tears away and steadied her voice, forcing herself to sound commanding. 'Yes, you *can*, Joe. You *can* do this. This is just a setback, and this time it's different. You're not on your own any more. You have the best lawyer anyone could have, and . . . and you have me.' She swallowed. 'Someone who loves you.' She felt herself flushing. Should she have said that? But it was the truth. 'I don't care what you've been told,' she said, sounding as confident as she could manage. 'We're going to get you out of there.'

She waited. There was another long silence, and then he said, 'I'm going to get cut off in a minute.'

'I'll send you some money,' she said.

'You don't have to—' he began.

'Yes, I do. You'll need it to phone me and Sarah.'

'OK,' he murmured. 'Thank you.'

Eve held her breath, not wanting to begin a sentence only to get cut off, and there was silence on the line for a moment.

Then he said, in a small, choked voice, 'You will come, won't you?'

Eve felt her throat tighten. 'Of course I'll come. I'll come as soon as they let me. I'll book it the minute we get off the phone.'

'OK.'

'I'll see you very soon,' she said. 'I promise.'

'OK,' he said again, and then, just as the call ended, he said softly, 'I love you, too.'

38

Eve booked a visit for Thursday afternoon, then opened her laptop, feeling sure about her instincts that the prosecution witness Joe had met with was the same woman she had seen leaving his house on Friday. He hadn't wanted to talk about it over the phone, but he hadn't denied it either, and although Eve still couldn't understand why Joe would have taken this risk, there had to be a reason. The most obvious and important prosecution witness in the case against him was Christy's daughter, Bella. She had been just seven years old at the time of her mother's death, which would make her twenty-seven now, the same age as Mackenzie. This fitted with the woman Eve had seen. Eve was surprised she hadn't thought of this before.

She entered the words 'Christy Nicholls daughter' into the search engine and up came the Copilot summary and a series of news reports. *Bella Duncan is the daughter of Jeff Duncan and Christy Nicholls, who was murdered on 1st May 2003 in Streatham, South London*, she read. But it was the photographs that interested her. Bella Duncan had dark hair, cut in a short bob, but her features were the same as the woman she had seen, her stature the same. Eve was sure it was her.

So that's why the police were watching Joe. They must have been aware that he was meeting Bella. Eve couldn't deny they had grounds to be concerned, since Joe was prohibited from having any kind of contact with her. But a *stakeout*? At the house of the neighbour across the road? Tailing Bella out of the street, and presumably all the way home?

It seemed extreme, too extreme, if they were simply trying to protect her. And were their tactics even legal? Eve knew that under Clare's Law, the police were within their rights to come to her house and tell her about Joe, but she was pretty sure they had no right to contact her family members or her employers, not unless Joe really had been on campus. But Joe said he hadn't been, and Eve believed him.

She picked up the phone. 'Iwan?'

'Eve. You got the email?'

'Yes. But—'

'I don't think we should discuss it on the phone.'

'I'm not phoning to discuss it,' Eve said.

He paused. 'So how can I help?'

'I want to know who the police officers were who came to see you.'

Another pause.

'The names of the police officers,' she repeated. 'Do you have them?'

'There was just the one. A detective.'

Eve felt a lurch in her stomach. 'What did he look like? Can you describe him?'

'Why do you want to know this?'

'Because he's lying, Iwan! Joe was never on campus.'

'Eve, have you talked to the union yet?'

'Can you just tell me what car he drove?'

'I don't think this is an appropriate conversation for us to be having. I'll be in touch about the meeting.'

'Fine,' Eve said. 'But I want evidence. I want firm evidence that Joe has been on campus, not just spurious gossip or rumours. I will be there at your meeting, and yes, I'll have my union rep with me. And I'll look forward to seeing the evidence, because if you don't have it, then I'll be making a complaint about this officer and my rep will want to know who he is.'

When she got off the phone, Eve googled 'DI Jon Carver, Thames Valley Police'. She searched through news reports, and the Police Federation and IOPC websites, but nothing came up.

She was going to find him, one way or another.

39

On Thursday morning, Sarah was back at the kitchen table, typing a terse response to the data controller, expressing her dissatisfaction at the loss of Christy's clothing and asking for a referral to be made to the forensic archive service, which was where all the evidence was stored from any investigations undertaken by the forensic science labs before 2012. But she wasn't hopeful that they'd find any existing samples. There were more than four million items to look through relating to cold cases dating back to 1930, and it would take time to get permission to look through the boxes. Once again, it frustrated her that she had no direct route to the archives, that she first needed police approval, which seemed grossly unfair, since the police surely had a strong interest in keeping her away.

A blast of music emanated from the living room. It was gone twelve thirty. Time for Ben's lunch. She was flying solo again after the Easter weekend, the school holidays having started. Will had a pretrial hearing at the Old Bailey, and Andy, Ben's dad, was also working. But once again, Sarah reminded herself how different things had been before she'd gone freelance, before she'd got together with Will, and before Andy had come back to London from Australia and agreed to be part of Ben's life. People often asked her how she managed it all, but, like everyone with caring responsibilities, she coped because she had to.

And there was always someone whose life was harder. She remembered talking to the single mother of a child with Down's syndrome who had gone to Ben's after-school club and who rarely slept for more than four hours. Night after night, as the poor woman finally fell into bed at midnight, she had done so knowing that she would be woken again at four. It sounded like torture. The child's father had left her to cope on her own, and good respite care was hard to find, Sarah knew. Even if you could get the funding, there weren't enough care companies or carers with space for all the children and young people who needed their services, especially since the pandemic, when they had all abruptly stopped running, and many hadn't started up again. Meanwhile, these tired parents were holding down jobs while fighting for their child's education, as well as cooking, cleaning, bathing, dressing and feeding, staying awake, keeping on going.

She buttered bread and chopped up chunks of cheese and cucumber. Ben could feed himself food like this, but he had yet to fully understand that nobody was going to whip it away from him if he took his time, so you had to watch that he didn't stuff the whole lot into his mouth in one go. If left alone, he would fill his cheeks and keep on going until he looked like a hamster, a thought that made Sarah smile but also didn't, because on the rare occasion he had managed to do that without her getting to him quickly, she had been petrified he would choke.

She allowed Ben to have his iPad playing and sat next to him while he ate, then washed his hands and sat him at his computer. She would have to take him out soon. They wouldn't be able to get out of the car – it required two adults for Ben to be managed safely outdoors – but he enjoyed going for a drive, as long as he had his ever-present iPad on his lap, blasting out 'Five Little Monkeys'. Andy complained about the permanent noise that came hand in hand with Ben, but as long as Sarah wasn't trying to read at the same time, it didn't bother her. And Ben was happy; that was the main thing.

Back in the kitchen, she had begun to clear up Ben's lunch things and make herself a sandwich when a notification sounded on her phone. She stopped what she was doing and sat down at the table, pulling her laptop towards her and taking a deep breath of anticipation as she saw that it was from the police, and that there was a statement attached. It was from Louise Coulter, the burglary victim in Joe's case. At first glance, it seemed familiar, and as she began to read it, Sarah assumed the police had sent the same one she already had. But then she saw the date at the top: it had been made on 18 March 2003, six weeks before Christy had been raped and murdered.

It was the statement she had asked for numerous times and been refused. The one from the burglary file.

Criminal Procedure Rules r. 16.2; Criminal Justice Act 1967, S.9; Magistrates Court Act 1980, s.5B

STATEMENT OF: Louise Coulter

AGE IF UNDER 18: +18 yrs (if over 18 insert 'over 18')

OCCUPATION: Retail Manager . . . .

This statement (consisting of 2 pages signed by me) is true to the best of my knowledge and belief and I make it knowing that, if it is tendered in evidence, I shall be liable to prosecution if I have wilfully stated in it anything which I know to be false, or do not believe to be true.

Witness signature: L. Coulter . . . . **Date:** 12/12/2022

I am the above-named person and I live at 25 Blenheim Road, Streatham Hill, which is a semi-detached house. I make this statement in relation to a time my property was burgled.

On Tuesday, 18th March at around 06.00 I was asleep upstairs at my home address when I heard someone moving around downstairs. I live alone and was very frightened. I got out of bed and went onto the landing just in time to see someone at the foot of the stairs, running out of my front door, who appeared to be wearing a long puffer-style coat. I went into the front bedroom and looked out of the window. I could see the same person running out of the gate and turning to the right. I could see the person was carrying something, but I couldn't see what it was because they had their back to me and then my neighbour's hedge was in the way. I quickly got dressed and ran out of the house and into the street, but by the time I got there, the person was gone.

I called the police, who arrived a few minutes later and followed me back into the house, where I immediately noticed that my TV was missing. I went into the kitchen and found the back door ajar. I had definitely closed and locked it before I went to bed the previous night. I could see that the door had been forced open with some kind of tool, because the outer edge of the door was damaged and the lock broken. As well as my TV, I noticed a portable DVD player was missing. I later realised that my watch was also missing.

My TV was a 26" Philips flat screen. The DVD player was also a Philips and was 10.5 inches wide and black with a swivel screen. My watch was a Swatch with a platinum wristband and luminous pink face. It had sentimental value as my daughter and son-in-law gave it to me for my birthday last year.

I did not give anyone permission to enter my address and take any of my property. I fully support police action and am willing to attend court.

SIGNED: *L. Coulter* **DATE:** 18/03/2003

40

Sarah stared at the witness statement, then back at her inbox. She'd had numerous phone calls and several email exchanges, all of which had informed her that she'd already been given everything she was going to get from the police, and yet now here it was: Louise Coulter's original statement, made immediately after the burglary – the same day, in fact.

The burglar had left with jewellery and electrical items, all the usual things burglars came for, but there was no mention of any underwear having been taken. The burglar hadn't even gone upstairs. This new statement did nothing to support the case against Jamie Clarke and had almost certainly been deliberately withheld from her. Her instincts had been correct: the burglary file did hold secrets.

So who had decided to send it to her? And why?

She flicked back to the email that had come with the statement. There was no accompanying message. This was not particularly unusual for the police, or indeed for the CPS, if it was part of a series of ongoing disclosure, but this statement wasn't. It had arrived in isolation, with no explanation. She glanced down at the footer, which gave the sender's details: *DS Robyn Heaton, Major Investigation Unit, Farringdon Police Station.*

Sarah sat back in her seat, puzzled. The MIU wouldn't get involved post-conviction. It would be down to the data records people or the force's legal department. So why, all of a sudden, was this detective sending her the evidence she had been asking for?

She opened up the document she had prepared listing every witness in the case against Jamie and summarising the evidence each had provided. She ran through the names of the police officers who had dealt with the original investigation, but DS Robyn Heaton was not among them.

OK. So, word had got around, perhaps, that Jamie had got himself a lawyer and was looking into the merits of another appeal, and maybe this police sergeant – someone impartial – had time on their hands.

Sarah skimmed through the evidence provided by each of the Blenheim Road residents and sat back in her seat, feeling a renewed sense of anger and disbelief. It now seemed highly likely that the knickers allegedly stolen in the burglary were not discovered to be missing until *after* Jamie had been charged with Christy's murder. It was looking more and more likely that Louise Coulter's statement had been taken by the police to bolster their case, and if Louise Coulter had been manipulated into giving this evidence, then why not Benfield and Norris?

Sarah opened her inbox again and gazed at the email from Robyn Heaton, then clicked on REPLY and typed:

Thank you for your email and attachment, which I have now had the chance to consider and which I believe triggers further disclosure.

She paused again. All her instincts were telling her that this statement had been sent to her under the radar. Did she really want to set off a paper trail that could put Robyn Heaton in a difficult position?

She deleted the draft and looked at the phone number underneath DS Heaton's name. She could call the number instead. But should she?

Another sudden blast of loud music emanated from the living room. At the same time, Sarah heard the front door opening and Will's footsteps in the hallway. A second later, the volume was turned down and Will came into the kitchen.

'Have you been enjoying the background music?' He smiled.

'He hasn't been too bad,' Sarah said. 'But he's getting restless. I need to take him out.'

'Let me take him,' Will said, setting down his laptop bag.

'Are you sure? You've only just got home.'

'It's fine,' Will said. 'We'll take off for a bit. Go for a drive. Give you a break.'

After Will had gone upstairs, Sarah went back to her emails. She had been to Farringdon Police Station many times for other clients, but her name wouldn't be on Jamie's original police file. Had she met Robyn Heaton in some other capacity? Her name did sound familiar – and if she was in the MIU there, then . . . Wait. Wasn't Robyn Heaton one of the detectives on the Tate Kinsella case, the one she had worked on the previous year?

Sarah quickly found the file on her laptop, scrolled to the disclosure notice from the police, and there it was. Robyn Heaton had been the second interviewing officer. Sarah remembered her now. While the lead detective had been typically hard on Sarah's client, DS Heaton had been pleasant, fair and thoughtful. She had seemed honest, like someone you would have faith in, someone who would do the right thing – even if it was something that would hurt the police.

So, what was DS Heaton trying to tell her?

Whatever it was, she would expect Sarah to be discreet, which ruled out any more communication through the data controller. Sarah examined Louise Coulter's statement, going through it line by line to see exactly what it was that had made it so troubling to the police that it had been hidden from the defence. Was it simply the fact that there was no mention of any underwear being stolen? Or was it the fact that Louise Coulter – a lone, semi-dressed woman – had managed to frighten off the burglar? This hardly fitted with the burglar being the type of person to rape and kill a woman. At this, a sudden thought came to her. She stared at the statement again, and then she saw it: the repeated use of the word 'person'. *The person was carrying something . . . the same person . . . the person was gone.* At no point did Louise Coulter mention a 'he' or a 'him'.

This had happened in 2003, and Sarah very much doubted that Louise Coulter had been an early adopter of gender-neutral pronouns.

It seemed far more likely that she hadn't been at all sure her burglar was a man.

41

Sarah minimised Louise Coulter's witness statement on her screen, and then moved back to her summary of the evidence in Jamie's case. Was there anything there to suggest that the burglar had been male? If there was, she couldn't see it, and the only evidence against Jamie was that he had been seen fixing Christy's door with an electric tool three days earlier, which wasn't even evidence. It was circumstantial at best. The burglar couldn't have used a power tool, it would have made too much noise, and Sarah knew from experience that most levering-type burglaries were carried out with a simple screwdriver or crowbar because they were easily carried. The burglar could have been anyone, male or female.

As she got to the end of the residents' statements, she came across one from Brenda Barlow, which had been accepted into evidence by the defence. This meant it would have been read out in the courtroom. Brenda Barlow had been a key witness and Christy's next-door neighbour, on the other side from Kerry Munt, and yet she hadn't been called to give live evidence at Jamie's trial, which in turn meant that the defence hadn't disagreed with anything she had to say in her statement. Had they really had no questions to ask her?

Sarah opened Brenda's statement. It was entirely factual, she realised, and described only what had happened on the morning Bella had turned up on her doorstep. She had comforted the little girl, returned with her to the house next door, found Christy's body, called the emergency services – and that was it. It was markedly different from any of the other witness statements from the Blenheim Road residents. They had all had something to say about Jamie, and none of it good. Everyone had an opinion about him, about what kind of person he was – except Brenda. And yet Brenda had been the neighbour Bella had run to, so presumably the person she knew the best.

Sarah paused to absorb this fully, but as she did so, it made less and less sense. Brenda was a key witness. She ought to have given live evidence. Also, she had given her occupation as retired, meaning she was likely to have been home for much of the day. Of all the neighbours, Brenda would surely have seen the most of Jamie if he was a regular visitor to the house next door. So why was there nothing about him in her statement? Had she even been asked about him? It didn't look like it.

'OK,' Will said, coming back into the kitchen with Ben's water bottle and filling it at the tap. 'We're ready. We'll see you in an hour or so.'

Sarah glanced up at him, then back at the open document on her laptop screen. 'Wait,' she said, scribbling on a piece of paper and jumping to her feet. 'I'll come too.'

The Stranger on the Stairs

'Are you sure? I thought you'd appreciate the peace and quiet?'

'Site visit,' she said decisively, then shut down her laptop and unplugged it, tucking it under her arm. 'We're going to Streatham. Blenheim Road.'

42

Eve stood in line in the visitor centre at HMP Bullingdon, waiting with all the wives, mothers, girlfriends and children of the prisoners. She couldn't help but listen in on the conversations, which told her that these women had done this many times before, that the prison visit was as much a part of their weekly routine as the supermarket shop or the school run. They had long ago accepted whatever it was the men in their life had done and were resigned to shouldering the burden of child-rearing, finding enough money for food and paying the bills until he got out again. Many of the women seemed to know each other and Eve wondered if they could tell she was a rookie.

At half past one, the queue began to move. When it was her turn, she walked through the detector and held her arms in the air while a female officer patted her down. She then stood in her socks while her shoes were checked before she was finally able to collect her belongings from the trays on the belt in front of her and secure her bag in a locker. She walked through a gate into a sectioned-off area where some of the other women were waiting. Once a few of them were crammed in together, a prison officer joined them and pressed a button, which caused the big glass partition door to slide shut. The officer took her keys from her belt and unlocked a gate to her left. Everyone streamed out along a path, which crossed an outdoor section of well-tended grass and flower beds, and then into a building on the opposite side, where they waited once again while the officer unlocked a second gate and then a third, locking each one behind her before moving on to the next.

Finally, they walked up the stairs and along a corridor to the visitors' hall, where Eve saw Joe seated at a table near to the door, wearing a yellow prison sweatshirt under a burgundy visits bib. He looked thin and ashen, and her heart leaped as she walked towards him. She sat down in front of him and reached for his hand. He clasped hers tightly in his for a moment, squeezing it hard, then caught the eye of a prison guard and let go.

'It's good to see you,' she said.

'It's good to see you too.'

'How are you?'

He forced a weak smile. 'So-so. You know.'

'Are you on your own? In a cell, I mean?'

He nodded. 'I'm on the VPU.'

'Does that help?'

He hesitated and said, 'Well, I'm banged up with the lowest of the low, but I'm not the lowest because I didn't hurt a child, so it could be worse.'

She swallowed and bit her lip. 'What happened?' she whispered.

Joe gazed back at her, his shoulders stooped. He opened his mouth to speak and closed it again.

'Joe, the prosecution witness you met with . . . was it Bella? Christy Nicholls' daughter?'

He looked a little surprised but nodded.

'Why, Joe? Why would you risk it?'

He shifted in his seat, then looked over his shoulders. 'She contacted my mother, who gave me her phone number. She begged me to meet her.'

'But—'

'All those years ago, when she identified me . . . she said she wasn't sure if she picked the right man.'

Eve stared at him in shock. 'She said that?'

He nodded.

'Will she help you?'

'I don't know. I hope so.'

Eve's heart jumped. 'And that's why she wanted to talk to you?'

'She wanted to hear about her mother. I said no, at first. I knew it would be taking a huge risk, but . . .' He raised his eyes towards the prison officer standing guard. 'But she isn't sure it was me, Eve. All her life, she's been having these nightmares about a stranger being in her house, on the stairs. A man. She thinks it could have been a cop.'

'A cop?' DI Carver flashed into Eve's mind. DI Jon Carver – or whoever he really was. Was that why he was tailing Bella? Was that why he was talking to Eve's boss, her family, telling everyone that Joe was a rapist and a killer? Was this more than a police operation to keep tabs on someone believed to be dangerous? Did 'DI Carver' have some kind of vested interest in having Joe locked up again?

'But ... this is just a dream, right?' she asked. 'Bella doesn't have any solid evidence of any police officer being in her house that night, after her mother died?'

'No,' Joe admitted. 'But I think she now believes it wasn't me who killed her.'

'So what's she going to do about it?'

'I asked her if she would speak to Sarah and she said she needed to think about it, and then I got arrested. So now I don't know, and obviously I can't speak to her.'

Eve thought for a moment. 'OK. Well, Sarah probably won't be able to speak to her either.'

'Why not?' Joe's face fell.

'It could look as though you were communicating with her through your lawyer. Sarah will have to be careful, but, look, why don't I call her as soon as I leave here and we will work out the best thing to do?'

He nodded. 'I trust you, Eve. Whatever you can do.' He paused. 'How did you know? That it was Bella I spoke to?'

'I saw you together,' Eve admitted. 'I came to warn you ...' And then she told him about the argument with her daughter and sister, about the police going to talk to them and to her head of department at college, and about everything that had happened after that.

'I'm so sorry,' he said. 'For everything I've put you through.'

'I'm not worried about that, Joe. That's not why I'm telling you all this,' she said, lowering her voice to a whisper. 'But I think Bella was being followed after she left your house that night. I think there *is* someone within the force who is taking way too much of an interest in the two of you.'

Joe's eyes met hers.

'If you didn't kill Christy, then someone else did. And I'm going to help Sarah find out who he is,' she whispered. 'And then we're going to get you out of here.'

'I don't want you putting yourself in danger,' he said.

'I'll be careful.'

'God.' He put his head in his hands. 'I'm so sorry,' he murmured, flushing as he looked up again. 'For getting you into all of this.'

'Don't be silly.' She gave him an ironic smile. 'It's the most excitement I've had in ages.'

He smiled back weakly and put the tips of his fingers against hers.

43

'Sarah? It's Eve here. Can you speak?'

'Hold on a second. I'm just in the car. I need to step outside . . .' There was a pause and then Sarah said, 'OK, go ahead.'

'I've just been to visit Joe.'

'How was he?'

'Bearing up. Just about.'

'So what's going on? I haven't managed to get a legal visit yet. Frustratingly, it's often quicker to get socials.'

'Well, he told me what happened,' Eve said.

'And?'

'He talked to Bella. Christy's daughter.'

'What? How? And *why*?'

'She found him through his mother, apparently. Persuaded him to meet her. He was reluctant, but the upshot is that she isn't sure about the original evidence she gave.'

'Hang on a minute,' Sarah said. 'I'm standing in the middle of the street. I just need to get somewhere more private.' Eve could hear the sound of traffic and footsteps, and then Sarah was back. 'What do you mean when you say she isn't sure?'

'She's been having flashbacks. Nightmares. It's made her question the evidence she gave in Joe's original trial. She isn't sure she picked the right man.'

'So, let me get this right ... she wants to retract her statement?'

'I think so. I hope so. She seems to believe Joe didn't kill Christy. Joe thinks she was coerced.'

'OK. But now *he* could be accused of coercing her. That's why he had those conditions not to talk to her.'

'I know,' Eve said, 'and I told him that this presents a problem for us. But we wouldn't know any of this if he *hadn't* talked to her, would we?'

'Well, I suppose she ought to have gone to the police. But I can see why she wouldn't want to.'

Me too, Eve thought. 'I told him that you probably wouldn't be able to talk her. But someone needs to and—'

'No,' Sarah said sharply.

'I just meant that I could broker whatever needs to happen next?'

'No,' Sarah said again, then her voice softened. 'Not you, Eve. It can't be you. You're ... involved with Joe. And that's OK. It's fine for you to be in a relationship with him. But this makes you the last person who should be talking to Bella. We have to make sure her evidence will stand up in court.'

'OK, but, Sarah, someone needs to do this sooner rather than later, because ... because there's stuff going on.'

'What kind of stuff?'

'Bella thinks there was someone in her house the night her mum died – someone besides Joe. She thinks it might have been a cop.'

The line went quiet for a few seconds. 'Sarah?'

'Yes. Sorry. Just thinking about what you said.'

'Look, there's this DI who's been going around telling lies about Joe to my family and my boss, and probably anyone who will listen, and I'm pretty sure he's behind Joe's recall.'

'What's his name?'

'He says it's Carver. DI Jon Carver. He came to see me about Joe. Tried to warn me away from him, under Clare's Law, you know. But then he talked to my sister and my daughter and told them stuff that was untrue. And I'm pretty sure it's him who went to see my boss and told him Joe was seen on campus at the college where I work.'

'But he wasn't?'

'Joe says not, and I believe him – it would make no sense for him to have been there.'

'Which force is he from, this DI?'

'He said it was Thames Valley Police, which I guess would be the force to keep tabs on Joe as he's living in Oxford. But I've looked online for him and I can't find him. I've searched news reports and the Police Federation and IOPC websites, but nothing came up. I didn't want to call 101 and ask for him in case it gets back to him, but, Sarah, I think he's following Bella and trying to put the frighteners on her, and he probably knows where she lives by now, and . . . and if we want this retraction, we need to get to Bella before he does.'

44

Sarah walked to the end of the road, found a bus shelter and sat down, thinking hard about all the new information she had been given. When she had knocked at 19 Blenheim Road half an hour ago, she had been told by the woman who now lived there that she was the second person to have come looking for Brenda Barlow, and it had become clear from the subsequent conversation that Bella had been the first. Bella was very obviously troubled by the evidence she had given against Jamie and had gone to both Jamie and Brenda Barlow for answers. She clearly wanted to talk to someone. The question was, who was that someone going to be?

She opened up her phone contacts, gazed at them for a moment, then pressed SEARCH.

Robyn Heaton picked up on the first ring.

'It's Sarah. Sarah Kellerman.'

'Hi,' Robyn said simply, as if she had been expecting the call.

'Can we meet?'

The Stranger on the Stairs

'Yes.'
'Where?'
'Where are you now?'
'Streatham. Not far from the station.'
'Can you get to Brixton Hill?'

They met on the corner of a run-down housing estate just off the A23, a sprawling, brutalist maze of grey slate and PVC that looked incongruous, situated as it was at the end of a road full of white pillars and Edwardian charm. It hit Sarah how the distinction between the haves and the have-nots was so pronounced in parts of London. Some of these homes looked like the kind of portable cabins you saw on building sites.

'Here,' came a voice.

Sarah looked towards a large bin shed with a corrugated iron roof and metal bars. Next to it was a recycling container with the words SHOES AND TEXTILES on the front, along with a selection of graffiti. Robyn Heaton was behind the bins, and also behind the CCTV camera that faced them. She was dressed to match her environment in a dark hoody and baggy jeans, her red hair tied back in a tight ponytail.

Sarah joined her.

'Did you drive here?' Robyn Heaton asked.

'No. My partner dropped me off in Streatham and then I got the bus. He doesn't know I'm meeting you,' she added.

Robyn nodded. 'Might be best if we keep it to ourselves.'

'Of course.'

They both waited.

'Christy Nicholls,' Sarah prompted.

'Yes.'

'Were you part of the original investigation into her death?'

Robyn shook her head.

'But you know the case?'

'I know your man's back inside.'

Sarah hesitated. 'Do you know why?'

'He spoke to a witness.'

Sarah nodded. 'I've heard this witness wants to give new evidence.'

'A retraction?' Robyn's eyes widened.

'Not exactly a retraction. More like . . . an uncertainty. More like . . . someone having pressured her, perhaps.'

Robyn raised an eyebrow. 'But not your client?'

'I hope not. But that's why I can't talk to her.'

'Very sensible.' Robyn eyed her. 'Are you asking me to speak to her?'

Sarah eyed her back. 'I can find someone else to do it,' she said. 'It's fine. It doesn't have to be you.'

'Best not.'

'But thank you,' Sarah said. 'For . . . your help.'

Robyn looked down at her feet.

'Can I just ask why you're doing this?'

A pause. 'I was on the burglary team.'

'The one a few doors down from Christy?'

Robyn nodded. 'I was new on the beat. I was seconded to the team for a while.'

'Was there ever a suspect?'

Another pause. An incline of the head.

Sarah narrowed her eyes. 'A female?'

Robyn nodded again.

'Was she ever arrested?'

'No. The SIO on the case was convinced it was Jamie.'

Sarah felt her stomach turning. 'And that's the way things went, I suppose?'

'Yep.'

She paused. 'This SIO . . . is he still on the force?'

'Yep.' Robyn stretched out the word, imbuing it with meaning.

'Can you tell me who he is?'

'Check the witness list.'

'In Christy's case?'

She nodded. 'See who was first on the scene.'

Sarah raised her eyebrows. 'The SIO in a burglary was first on the scene in a murder investigation? How does that work?'

Robyn shrugged. 'Burglary in the same street. Could be linked. If the SIO's in the area and thinks he can help, there's every reason for him to be there.'

'But?'

'It's all there in his statement.'

'Right,' Sarah said, her heart racing in anticipation. She must have already read the statement in question and not seen anything in it. But then again, you don't know what you don't know. 'What happened to the female suspect in the burglary?'

'That's a very good question.'

'You don't know the answer?'

'I think I do. But she won't talk to me.'

'OK.' Sarah scratched her head. 'Well, then—'

'She might talk to you, though. Her name's Phillipa Price,'

Robyn continued. 'She frequents the night shelter on Acre Lane. There's a hostel up there, too.'

Sarah nodded. 'What does she look like?'

'White. Forties. Looks older. A lot older. Long-time user of class A. Stick-thin. Long brown hair. She lived in Streatham in 2003 and has never moved far away. Everyone round there knows her.'

'Thank you.' Sarah turned to leave.

'And Sarah?'

'Yes?'

'They've approved your request for a referral to the forensic archives.'

'Really?' Sarah turned back to face her.

Robyn shrugged. 'They can't in all conscience keep you out. I can tell you now, you'll find out that there was a single source of unknown male DNA found on Christy's top as far back as 2012.'

Sarah was too stunned to speak. 'You mean . . . it's not Jamie's?'

'It's not Jamie's,' Robyn agreed.

Sarah frowned. 'Is that why the clothing was destroyed?'

'I don't know. But the lab has retained some of the samples taken from her T-shirt and from under her fingernails. They are tiny extracts, but they can still be tested.'

Sarah felt a rush of optimism. 'Are you serious?'

'Yes, but don't get your hopes up just yet. There's no match on the PNC. There wasn't then, and there isn't now. I wouldn't get hung up on that for the moment. Find Phillipa Price instead. Get her to talk to you. If she's still alive, you'll find her.'

45

Sarah made her way back onto the main road, her mind turning over the conversation she had just had. What was she going to find in the burglary SIO's statement? Whatever it was, Robyn clearly suspected her former SIO of some kind of misconduct, in which case why had she not said anything for twenty years? Maybe she had insufficient evidence to back up her suspicions and didn't think she would be believed. Whistleblowers were supposedly protected by law, but Sarah knew what could happen in practice, and that Robyn could be victimised by her colleagues, especially if this SIO was being enabled or protected. You would have to be living under a rock not to know about the culture of sexism and misogyny that was baked into many forces, and into the decision-making processes.

Which brought her to Phillipa Price. She could understand why Phillipa wouldn't want to talk to a cop, but was she any more likely to talk to Sarah? If she had been allowed to get off with a burglary scot-free, she would hardly be likely to want to begin telling a complete stranger that she had done it after all. So what was her angle going to be?

It was gone four o'clock by the time she got to the night shelter, and a group of men and woman were hanging around outside the building, some sitting on the pavement, some standing, no doubt wanting to be sure to secure a place for the coming night. She scanned the group, but couldn't immediately see anyone who matched the description she had been given.

'Who are you looking for, love?' one of the men called out, then walked across the street to join her. He smelled strongly of alcohol and was unsteady on his feet.

'Phillipa,' Sarah said. 'Phillipa Price. Do you know her?'

The man turned back to the group and shouted out loudly, 'Anyone seen Phil?'

'She's up at the church,' someone replied.

'There you go,' the man said, turning back to Sarah. 'Do you know it?'

'No.'

'St Matthew's. Turn up that road there,' he said, pointing. 'When you get to the top, turn left and walk up the hill. It's on your right, past the lights.'

'Thank you.'

'Have you got a cigarette?' he asked her.

'No. I'm sorry.' Sarah's old boss Gareth used to get her to carry packets of them. Lighters, too. But she hadn't liked doing it. It had seemed wrong. Once again, she was glad she no longer had to follow the kinds of rules she didn't agree with.

The Stranger on the Stairs

She knew most of these people were down on their luck, but she would rather buy them a sandwich with her own money than flash Gareth's cigarettes around.

'Not to worry,' said the man, smiling broadly. 'You have a nice day now.'

She found Phillipa sitting on the church steps, arguing with a man in a puffer jacket with a towel over his shoulders.

'Well, you had better fucking find it, Phil!' the man shouted loudly as Sarah approached, before getting up and storming off.

'Phillipa?' Sarah asked.

The woman nodded.

'Are you OK?' Sarah asked her.

The woman sniffed and wiped her eyes with the back of her sleeve, then said, in a gravelly, South London voice, 'Just that a-hole. Says I owe him, and I don't.'

'Will he come back?'

She shrugged. 'Probably.'

'Well, for what it's worth, he does seem like an a-hole.'

The woman looked up and smiled a thin smile. Everything about her was thin. Her face. Her arms. Her legs. Her hair, which was lank, dark brown and hung loosely down her back. The sharp angles of her knees and elbows were visible under her jumper and trousers and her face was heavily lined. If Robyn was right and this woman was in her forties, the years hadn't been kind to her.

'Are you a fed?' Phillipa asked.

'No. A solicitor.'

'Wait. Oh fuck. Have I missed court?'

'No, no,' Sarah said quickly. 'Or, at least, not that I know of. That's not why I'm here.'

'Thought I was in trouble then.'

'I'm here about someone else who's in trouble.'

'Who?'

'A man called Jamie. Jamie Clarke.'

'I don't know him.' Phillipa pulled a pouch of tobacco out of her jacket pocket and began rolling a cigarette. 'Want one?' she offered, holding out the pack.

'No thanks. Mind if I sit down?'

Phillipa's response was to pull a lighter out of her pocket and hold the flame under her roll-up. Sarah put down her bag and slid onto the step next to her. She looked back at the tall arched doors of the church behind them, and then at the street ahead and the man with the towel, who was standing at the corner and was now on his phone. 'You lived around here long?'

'All my life,' Phillipa said, blowing out smoke. 'Grew up just down the road in Streatham.'

'Ah. Streatham,' Sarah said. 'I've just come from there. Blenheim Road.'

'Oh yeah.'

'You know it?'

Phillipa gave her a sideways look. 'It's where that murder happened. That woman. The one with the little girl.'

'That's right. Number seventeen.'

Phillipa turned. 'Oh. You're *his* solicitor.'

Sarah nodded. 'Yeah.'

'You don't think he did it?'

Sarah hesitated. 'Do you?'

'I asked first.'

Sarah smiled. 'Well, it's what I'm trying to find out.'

'So why are you talking to me?'

Sarah took a breath. 'I need to ask you about the burglary that happened a few weeks before that woman was killed. I think you know the one I'm talking about. The one at the house a few doors down.'

Phillipa stiffened. 'Are you sure you're not a fed?'

'I think you know I'm not. I think you know why I'm here, and I think you know what I'm talking about. I don't need you to tell me whether you did the burglary, Phil. I just need to know why you were let off.'

'What makes you think I would tell you that?'

'You seem like a good person.'

'Do I?' Phillipa looked at Sarah thoughtfully. 'Can you tell that to social services?'

'I don't know,' Sarah said, meeting her gaze. 'Can I?'

Phillipa blew out more smoke. 'You have kids?'

Sarah nodded.

'How many you got?'

'Just the one.'

'How old?'

'Nine. But he's disabled, so . . .'

'What's wrong with him?'

'He's autistic.'

'Ah,' she said. 'Two of mine are autistic.'

'Really?'

Phillipa nodded. 'And two of the others have ADHD.'

'How many children do you have?'

Phillipa held up all five fingers of one hand, then put her roll-up between her lips and held up another forefinger.

Sarah felt her eyes widen. 'You have six?'

'By four different baby fathers.'

'Where are they?'

'Three are with their baby fathers and the others got taken into care.'

'I'm sorry,' Sarah said. 'That's hard for you.'

'The youngest two . . . I'm trying to get them back. But I've got to clean up my act first. I'm trying. Which is why people like that effing a-hole . . .' she jabbed a finger towards the man with the towel '. . . ain't helping.'

'I bet.'

'I'm not even a smoker no more,' she said. 'I've been clean for weeks. I've got my script and I'm not topping up or nothing.'

Sarah realised that Phillipa was talking about crack. 'Well done. That's really good.' She thought quickly. 'Are you hungry? I'm buying.'

Phillipa looked surprised. 'I wouldn't say no to a KFC.'

'Where's the nearest?'

'Up on the main road. It's a five-minute walk.'

'Want to head that way?'

'With you?'

Sarah shrugged. 'Why not? And on our way, why don't I just pay the a-hole whatever it is he thinks you owe him?'

Phillipa stared at her for a moment. 'It's twenty. That's what he says.' She dropped the butt of her roll-up onto the ground, put her elbows on her knees and looked at her feet. Her expression was thoughtful for a moment, and then she said, 'OK. Come on, then.'

Sarah had enough cash to pay the man, who flashed a gold tooth at her and assured her that 'business was done'.

'He's having a fucking laugh,' Phillipa said, as they walked the short distance to Brixton Road. 'I didn't owe him nothing.'

'Have you ever thought of moving away?'

'Where would I go? I ain't been far from here all my life, but I know enough to know there's more like him on every street corner.'

Sarah nodded. This much was true.

At KFC, Phillipa chose a Boneless Banquet with beans and a Pepsi. Sarah ate some fries and messaged Will. *So, so sorry*, she typed. *I've been held up. I will be home as soon as I can. Can you give Ben his tea? Pasta and cheese will be fine. And there are some of those Quorn eggy things he likes in the fridge.*

Don't worry, already on it. All under control, came the reply. *Don't rush.*

Sarah let out a breath.

'Your kid?' Phillipa asked.

'My partner,' Sarah said. 'My son can't talk. He can't use a phone either. He's severely learning disabled as well as autistic.'

'Ah, love him,' Phillipa said. 'That must be hard for you.'

Sarah smiled. 'Being a parent's hard, isn't it? How old are yours?'

Phillipa held up one hand again, then added the forefinger,

counting them off. 'Oldest is nineteen – almost twenty, then they're eighteen, fifteen, twelve, six and four.'

'Do you see any of them?'

She nodded. 'I see the ones that are with their baby fathers. And I just started to see the two younger ones again.'

'What about the nineteen-year-old?' Sarah said.

'I don't see him.' Phillipa's face twisted and she suddenly looked even older. 'I don't know where he is.'

'He was adopted?'

She nodded. 'Taken off me when he was two months old. I couldn't handle him, to be honest.' Then, casually, as if she was talking about the weather, she said, 'His father's that piece-of-shit fed you're after.'

For a moment, Sarah couldn't speak. 'What are you saying?'

'I'm saying,' Phillipa said, 'that he fucked me twenty years ago and got me pregnant.'

'The lead detective on the burglary? He was your boyfriend?'

Phillipa laughed – a hollow laugh. 'You've got to be kidding. You think I went with him out of choice? I might be desperate, but I do have standards.'

'He raped you?'

Phillipa sighed and pushed away her food, took out her tobacco pouch and rolled another cigarette.

'OK, I'll tell you, but just you,' she said firmly. 'And I ain't making no statement.'

'That's fine,' Sarah said quickly. 'I won't ask you to do that.'

'Turn your phone off.'

The Stranger on the Stairs

Sarah took her phone out of her pocket and pointed it so that Phillipa could see there were no open apps. 'I can switch it off if you want me to, but I don't like doing that in case my partner calls. You mind if I put it on DND instead? He knows to call three times if it's urgent, then the call gets through. Ben used to have fits,' she explained. 'I had to rush him to hospital more than once.'

'It's OK,' Phillipa said gently. 'Leave it on.'

Sarah slid the phone across the table. Phillipa picked it up, inspected it, then slid it back.

'What's his name?' asked Sarah.

'We all knew him as Mitch. I honestly can't tell you his real name. We hated him. All of us. He was an arrogant piece of shit. He was known for smacking the girls about.'

'You mean . . . he used prostitutes?'

'Yeah.'

'And he hurt them?'

Phillipa nodded.

'And he hurt you?'

'Not me. Not then. Not like that.' There was a moment's silence while she studied her fingernails. 'But yes, I was on the game. At that time, I wasn't doing well. I was on the street for the first time and I was smoking a lot to deal with it and so I needed the money, but I never went with him, especially not after I heard about what he was into. I was only twenty-two at the time. I was the baby of us all, you could say. I was pretty then, too, believe it or not. I had the face, I had the figure, and there were better options for me.'

'Did he ask for you?'

'Oh yeah. All the time. But the other girls, they looked out for me. Geri ... she was this gorgeous woman. She always stepped in and told him I was unavailable, or that I was already taken. She was like a mum to me. They all were, all them girls, to be honest. We were like a family.' She looked wistful. 'Anyway, it was really late one night.' She glanced up at Sarah. 'Or early, depending on the hours you keep. About five, I think it was. I met with a punter who liked to do it before he went to work. Worked in the City or something, said it set him up for the day. Anyway, he took me somewhere near that road.'

'Blenheim Road?'

'Yeah. And then he refused to pay me. He gave some excuse, I can't remember what it was. All I remember is that I was in a state. I told him I needed my fix and we got into an argument, and he drove off. I started walking home. I was proper clucking. I had a screwdriver on me, which I used to take for protection and partly for ... well, you know. Just in case.'

'In case?'

'In case I needed money. Cars, mostly. That's what I did. You just looked to see what was there. A wallet or a pair of sunglasses or something you could sell. Sometimes the radio, if it was a good one.'

'So why that house?'

'Completely random,' she said. 'It was a nice street and they hadn't closed the curtains, and I got curious. I went down the path and looked in. I was on the eye out for a handbag or a wallet, but then I saw the TV. It was just a small one, a twenty-six-inch, not like the huge ones you get now, but it was a flat screen, so it was worth something and I knew it weren't going to be heavy. At the time, I knew a bloke who could shift them, so I went down the path and round the back and . . . well, you know the rest.'

'Except you got caught?'

Phillipa made a sorry face. 'It was the TV. Sold it to my mate, got my fix, next thing I know my mate got caught and they traced it back to me. It had my prints all over it, of course.'

'They had hard evidence it was you?' Sarah felt a jolt of pure shock.

'I was quick, but I weren't no professional. When you've got a habit, you're not thinking about what happens if you get caught. You're just hoping you can get your next fix before they catch up with you.'

'But you were never arrested?'

Phillipa took her tobacco pouch out of her pocket. 'Well, that depends on what you mean by being arrested.'

Sarah stared at her, confused.

'I bet he couldn't believe his luck when he found out whose prints he had,' Phillipa said.

'Mitch?'

'I bet he thought it was his lucky day. He'd been asking for weeks for me to go with him, and I'd always made an excuse.' Phillipa sighed. 'Anyway, he came and found me, made sure he got me on my own. I was outside the public toilets off Streatham High Road when he turned up, said he was going to have to arrest me. I asked him what for. He said, "You know what for." And then he reminded me that I was already on a suspended sentence, I think it was, or that this burglary was my third strike, or . . . I can't fully remember which, but then he said it was going to the Crown Court and I wasn't getting out for a couple of years, and I knew he was right. And I really didn't want to go back inside. But then he started smiling, and he leaned forward and said in my ear, "Of course, you could just play nice." He said he could make it all go away, "as long as we're friends", he said.'

She began to roll another cigarette and Sarah could see her hands were shaking.

'I couldn't speak at first. I didn't want to go back to prison, but I didn't want his hands on me neither. I'd heard the stories about him. I'd seen the bruises. I had heard he liked to choke you when he was doing it.'

Sarah felt her pulse quicken. 'So what did you do?'

'Well, I was too scared to say much. And then he said, "I'm being nice to you. You could at least thank me." And so I said, "Thank you," and he said, "Not like that."'

'So . . .?' Sarah prompted.

'So I told him I'd rather eat shit. And that's when his face turned like . . . like I'll never forget. Dark. Angry. Like . . . well, like he wanted to kill me. He said, in this horrible, nasty voice, "Well, that can be arranged." Then he took out his handcuffs and he grabbed hold of me and he put one cuff on and then he yanked me hard and smashed my face up against the wall of the toilets and then he handcuffed me from behind. And then he did the police caution and everything, like it was all official or something, and for a moment, I thought it was. I started to go with him, thinking we were going to his car, but then he suddenly turned and dragged me in the direction of the toilets and before I could even scream out, we were inside and he had locked us both in a cubicle. Then he pushed some kind of rag into my mouth and then he shoved my head down the toilet and flushed it until I was soaking and could hardly breathe, and then he yanked my trousers down and he raped me. And . . .' She paused, visibly shaking, and Sarah reached out a hand and touched her arm. 'And then . . . the rest,' she said. 'You don't want to know the rest. But suffice to say, it's what people do in toilets.'

Sarah closed her eyes.

'And then he made it all go away. Not sure how. Didn't ask. Didn't care, if I'm honest. By then, he'd hurt me so badly, it was all I could do to stay alive, to put one foot in front of the other.'

'And no one witnessed this?'

She shook her head. 'One or two of the smokers came in as we were coming out and he made it seem legit, like he was arresting me. He took me to his car, and then he looked over both shoulders and he took the cuffs off and said if I told anyone, he would come back and finish me off. He said he would make it look like an accident. He said that accidents happened to smackheads all the time. He said no one would believe me, anyway. He said I was just a dirty little junkie whore and who were people going to believe, me or him?'

'Did you tell the girls?'

Phillipa shook her head. 'I didn't tell a soul. I was petrified of him. They all saw the bruises on my forehead and I just said I'd picked a bad punter, and I think they wondered who it was, but my business was my business. That's how it was. As time went on, I realised that he'd had what he wanted and that as long as I kept my mouth shut, he wasn't going to bother me no more. It took a long time, though. For months, I couldn't sleep for more than a few hours at a time.'

Sarah swallowed. 'I understand that your word would mean nothing against his. I understand his power. I know how these things work. But the problem we've got is that twenty years on, he's still out there, and, Phil, you won't be the only person he's hurt.'

Phillipa heaved a long sigh. 'If there's other girls, then why haven't they come forward?'

'Same reason as you, I expect.'

'Well, there you go. And if you're looking for a statement, you'll have to find someone else, someone with more credibility, because you know as well as I do that he was right about one thing. No one is ever going to believe me.'

'I believe you,' Sarah said.

Phillipa shook her head. 'Thanks, but I'm not putting myself through that again.'

'I understand.'

'Do you?'

'I do. And I'm so, so sorry for what you went through. For what it's worth, I think you're incredible.' She reached out a hand and touched Phillipa's arm. 'I just wanted to tell you that. And I wanted to tell you how amazing it is that you've managed to get off the crack.'

'Got to admit,' Phillipa said. 'It ain't been easy. Especially at times like this.'

Sarah heaved a sigh. 'I know.'

Phillipa raised a brow. 'Do you?'

'Well, I know how much I want a glass of wine when I've had a hard day,' Sarah said. 'If I had your life, well . . . I think I'd want whatever it was that would make it all go away.'

'I bet it's hard with your kid,' Phillipa said.

'And that is what's special about you. Even in the middle of everything that's going on . . . even in the middle of what you've just been telling me, you can still imagine what it's like for me. That's why you're going to stay off it this time and fight for your kids.'

Phillipa shrugged. 'I'm trying. One day at a time, right?'

'Yeah. One day at a time.'

46

Sarah was still reeling from Phillipa's revelation as she walked through the shopping precinct in the direction of the tube station. As she looked around at the shoppers going about their everyday chores, it felt strange to be back in this world, the world where shopping got bought and food got eaten and ordinary things were busy happening to ordinary people, although, of course, what happened to Phillipa could and did happen to anyone. Sarah let out a long breath. So often, she lived through other people's trauma, and there was no way to offload the horror – she wasn't allowed to. She wondered how on earth Phillipa had survived such a horrific attack without telling a single person.

But now, more than ever, she was convinced that 'Mitch' was also Christy's attacker. It was too much of a coincidence. The choking. The violence. The degradation. The abuse of his power. The connection in time and place between the burglary and Christy's murder, not to mention his physical presence at the crime scene.

A surge of anger rose inside her at this, and she quickened her pace to expel some of her pent-up energy. How dare someone like him be first on the scene? How dare he get to see Christy's poor body like that? How *dare* he?

But he hadn't gone back to gloat. He had gone back to control the investigation. As she waited at the crossing for the lights to change, she realised that it was all beginning to make sense. Did Robyn think that could be his DNA on Christy's top, and was that why she had told Sarah to forget about the sample sitting in the lab? Robyn knew that Sarah's expert would be wasting time testing it. They would never get a match, because Christy's killer was never going to turn up on the Police National Computer, not if Christy's killer was a policeman. They would need some other evidence to link him first.

As she entered the tube station, she pulled out her phone to message Will. *On my way back*, she typed. Her finger hovered over the call button, but she knew she couldn't speak to him. He knew her too well. He would know she was upset, and although Phillipa wasn't her client, she felt the strong need to keep what she had been told to herself, at least for now, out of decorum and respect for Phillipa and because, first, she needed to get home to her laptop and see it. Know it. *Mitch*.

She needed to know his name.

Criminal Procedure Rules r. 16.2; Criminal Justice Act 1967, S.9; Magistrates Court Act 1980, s.5B

STATEMENT OF: Todd Andrew Mitchell

AGE IF UNDER 18: +18 yrs (if over 18 insert 'over 18')

OCCUPATION: Detective Sergeant . . . .

This statement (consisting of 3 pages signed by me) is true to the best of my knowledge and belief and I make it knowing that, if it is tendered in evidence, I shall be liable to prosecution if I have wilfully stated in it anything which I know to be false, or do not believe to be true.

WITNESS SIGNATURE: T. Mitchell . . . . **DATE:** 2/5/2003

On FRIDAY, 2nd MAY 2003 at 08.05 I was on duty in plain clothes in Streatham Hill, South London, single crewed under call sign X5TX, when information came in that a female had been assaulted with what appeared to be fatal injuries. The incident had taken place at 17 Blenheim Road. I was immediately alerted. Blenheim Road is very familiar to me as I am the SIO in a burglary investigation relating to a house four doors down. The burglary took place in March and my team have been carrying out extensive house-to-house inquiries at all addresses in the immediate vicinity, including number 17. I immediately suspected that the victim was CHRISTY NICHOLLS, who lived there with her seven-year-old daughter BELLA DUNCAN. I had met both NICHOLLS and DUNCAN more than once during the house-to-house. As I was in the area and believed that the offences could be linked and that I may have relevant information, I made my way to the address.

I was first on the scene and went through the open front door and living room to the rear of the property where I located the victim on the kitchen floor. I could immediately see that it was NICHOLLS and that she was deceased. This was then confirmed by the London Ambulance Service who arrived a few minutes later along with several uniformed crews. As I had known her, I made a formal identification of NICHOLLS, then left the crews to work.

I now turned my attention to the two key witnesses who were in the living room. I knew both witnesses as BRENDA BARLOW, who had made the 999 call, and DUNCAN, the deceased's daughter, who had found the deceased at around 07.30 hours that morning. I had met both witnesses previously and DUNCAN knew me well as she had been present in the house when I had talked to the deceased when canvassing the neighbourhood.

Both BARLOW and DUNCAN were sitting on the sofa together and were visibly upset. It was not appropriate for them to remain in the house at this time as it was a crime scene, and so I asked BARLOW if we could go to her house next door and she said we could. We went next door to number 19 and I sat with both witnesses in BARLOW'S living room. I told them that someone would be here to take a statement from each of them as soon as possible. While I was waiting with the witnesses, DUNCAN made a disclosure that she had seen a man in the house the previous evening. I informed her that specially trained officers would be here to talk to her soon and did not question her further.

Approximately half an hour later, victim support officers arrived and I returned to number 17, where I shared intelligence regarding the burglary with officers at the crime scene. I informed them that I was investigating a suspect for the burglary who was also known to have been visiting NICHOLLS in the weeks prior to her death. I gave the name and description to Detective Superintendent STEVE FULFORD, the SIO in the case.

At around 11.30 I became aware that the suspect was outside. When I got there he had already been pointed out by local residents as JAMES JOSEPH CLARKE, dob 21/6/1974. I am aware that CLARKE was then arrested for the offences of rape and murder and taken to Farringdon Police Station.

To assist the MIU officers, I took a statement from BARLOW and then remained at the scene to assist if needed until I went off shift at 15.30.

SIGNED: T. Mitchell   **DATE:** 2/5/2003

47

Sarah stared at the screen in front of her, her pulse beating fast at the injustice, at the audacity. It was all there, everything she hadn't been able to see the first time she had read DS Mitchell's statement – or, at least, it was what *hadn't* been said that now leaped out. The statement itself was impeccable, his justification for his presence entirely reasonable, his actions seemingly irreproachable. But she knew what he had done, and she had his name now. Detective Sergeant Todd Andrew Mitchell. *Mitch*. Phillipa's rapist. Christy's rapist. Christy's killer. She was sure of it.

At the edge of her consciousness, she could hear the music from the living room stop abruptly, then start up again in the hallway and move up the stairs. Ben often took himself up to chill out on his bed when he got overwhelmed, but it was gone seven and she suspected he was feeling sleepy. There was a handrail, so he could go up on his own, but it was a one-handed operation as he didn't go anywhere without his iPad. Sarah had never truly been able to move out of the phase you live through when you have a toddler, the one where you always need to know where they are and what they are doing. This was still how it was with Ben.

'Sarah?' She heard Will's voice calling her. 'The lark is ascending.'

'Is he OK?' she called back.

'Yeah. He's fine.'

She listened for Ben to reach the top of the stairs, then turned back to the screen in front of her.

'He's on his bed,' Will said, coming into the kitchen a moment later.

'That's OK. So long as he doesn't go to sleep. He needs a bath. I'll be there in a few minutes.'

'OK. I'm going up for a shave now, anyway. I'll give him a poke.'

'Thanks. Won't be long.'

Sarah knew she should go up to Ben, but she had so many thoughts to hold on to that she worried about losing something important. She grabbed a notepad and pen from the worktop nearby and began to jot them down quickly, her writing sprawling over the lines on the page as her hand tried to keep up with her brain.

1. First on the scene – opportunity to contaminate crime scene and justify later.
2. On his own next door with Bella and Brenda B for 30 minutes. Opportunity to contaminate Bella's evidence about who she'd seen.

3. Mentions numerous times how well Bella knew him. Paving the way to claim she's confused if point 2 fails and she ID's him.
4. Ideal opportunity to ensure Jamie arrested. Enough grounds for arrest with his intel and if J then turns up and appears to be last to see C alive.
5. Admits he took Brenda B's statement. Opportunity to control what goes into it.
6. Did he also take Benfield's and Norris's statements? And when?

She paused, put the tip of her pen between her teeth, then grabbed her mouse and scrolled back to the beginning of the statement, cross-referencing with the points she had listed on the sheet of paper next to her. Was there anything else she had thought of before Ben took flight? She found herself smiling as she was reminded of Will's reference to the George Meredith poem 'The Lark Ascending', which she knew was about a skylark soaring to freedom. Dear Ben. She knew, by now, that he would always need to be looked after, that he would never work, or marry, or have children, or have any big ambitions. He was never going to soar very high.

But Jamie could be free. He *should* be free.

She let out a breath. OK, well, she had enough to work with. She placed a large asterisk beside item 6 on her list, then put down her pen and pushed back her chair. Once Ben was in bed, she would go through the first-responder statements again, although she was beginning to see just how much could be left unsaid. If she could only get access to the CID and murder team office diary and officer notebooks, she would be able to see all the updates for herself – find out what evidence came in, and at what time. See who was where, and when and . . . *Christ!* she thought, as she went into the living room to gather up Ben's things and switch off his computer. It all seemed so bloody obvious, in hindsight. Of course Todd Mitchell was just a street away when the call came in from the force control room. He had probably been sitting out there in his car for hours, ready to push his foot to the floor and race to the house, ready to offer up his *relevant information* and *share his intelligence* and pollute the whole bloody crime scene with his lies.

But whether she could prove any of this was another matter.

48

Once Sarah had bathed Ben and got him to bed, she sat back down at her laptop and pulled up the police report, known as an 'MG5', which summarised the police case in the investigation into Christy's death. She skimmed quickly to the relevant section, picking through it line by line:

Area intelligence revealed that a burglary had taken place in the same street six weeks previously and that officers who had conducted house-to-house inquiries had taken statements from witnesses who had seen a man entering 17 Blenheim Road on more than one occasion during this time. They described the man as being of medium build, approximately 6 feet tall, in his late 20s to early 30s, with mousy brown hair and piercing blue eyes. The description matched that of the defendant, who arrived in Blenheim Road while police were present and was pointed out by local residents. Two of these witnesses told police they had seen this same man emerge from the back of 17 Blenheim Road the previous evening at around 9.45.

Sarah frowned at the screen. Broken down, *area intelligence* was clearly Todd Mitchell, and *officers who had conducted house-to-house inquiries* was also Todd Mitchell, or, at least, there was every reason to believe he'd had a pretty big hand in taking the residents' statements and making sure that Jamie's name came up. And what exactly did *pointed out by local residents* mean? What had they actually said at that time? *When* exactly had Benfield and Norris become eyewitnesses? Mitchell had taken Brenda Barlow's statement, by his own admission. Had he managed to get to them, too?

She sat back in her chair, thinking it through, casting her mind back to the events that had sealed Christy's fate. Her meeting Jamie in the corner shop that day in March might well have been the catalyst, along with the – completely coincidental, as Sarah now knew – burglary at Louise Coulter's house. But not for the reasons the jury had been given. Not because Jamie had meant Christy any harm, but . . .

But because Todd Mitchell had wanted Christy and couldn't have her. That had to be it. And he couldn't handle the rejection. After all, Phillipa had rejected him, and look what he had done to her. So, Mitchell had met Christy during the house-to-house and taken a shine to her. He had been rebuffed by her, then gone back to take what he couldn't have. Jamie was in the way. Jamie already had what Mitchell wanted. Mitchell had been jealous of Jamie. And once he had decided what he was going to do, Jamie had been the perfect candidate to take the fall.

Sarah felt a shiver run down her spine. Christy's rape had been premeditated – this was clear from the duct tape gag and the binding that had come with the rapist to the crime scene – but just how carefully, and for how long? Had Mitchell always planned to let Phillipa off the burglary in order to point the finger at Jamie? Or had he simply realised, after he'd raped Phillipa, that he needed a new suspect for the burglary and that Jamie would fit the bill?

She looked up gratefully as Will placed a large bowl of pasta and a glass of wine next to her laptop.

'Mind if I join you?' he asked, bringing over his own bowl and glass.

She smiled. 'Of course not.'

He sat down and tucked his knees under the table. 'You want to run it by me?' he asked, raising a brow.

'Christ, Will,' she said. 'I don't even know where to begin.'

He looked at her sympathetically, then nudged her pasta bowl towards her. She picked up her fork. As she ate, she could feel the glucose refuelling her brain and she was soon able to begin putting her thoughts into some kind of order.

'OK,' she began. 'So, I think Jamie was framed by a cop.'

'By . . . a cop?' Will stared at her.

She nodded. 'I know it sounds incredible, but—'

'Which cop?' Will's eyes narrowed.

'Todd Mitchell. The burglary SIO.'

'How? Why?' He leaned forward.

'Because he wanted Christy Nicholls and she rejected him.'

He put down his fork. 'And so he killed her?'

'Raped her first, then killed her to shut her up.'

'How sure are you?'

'Pretty sure.'

'Can you prove it?'

She hesitated. 'No,' she said. 'Not yet.'

His forehead creased. 'Then you need to be careful.'

At that moment, her phone rang. She picked it up. It was a number she didn't recognise.

'Hello?'

A female voice said, 'Hello. Is that Sarah?'

'Speaking.'

'My name's Sandra Robbins,' said the voice. 'I think you wanted to talk to me?'

For a moment, Sarah couldn't place her.

'About my aunt,' the woman said. 'Brenda Barlow.'

Sarah turned back to Will and made an excited face. 'Yes,' she said quickly. 'I do want to talk to you. Very much.' She pulled her pen and pad towards her and turned up the volume on her phone.

'It was the woman we sold the house to who gave me your number. She said you're a solicitor? Is that right?' Sandra Robbins was saying. 'Only, I wasn't there when it happened. I wasn't an actual witness.'

'That's fine,' Sarah said quickly. 'I'm really just looking for any information you can give me . . . and to see if you can shed any light on one or two things for me. And then maybe you could put me in touch with your aunt?'

'I'm afraid not. She died the year before the house was sold. That's why we had to deal with the sale.'

Sarah hesitated, disappointed. 'I'm sorry,' she said. 'Were you close?'

'I was her only relative,' Sandra said. 'So, yes, we were pretty close. My mum and Brenda were sisters and all of the rest of her family had passed on, so I was all she had, really.'

'And did she talk to you about what had happened to her next-door neighbour?'

'Well . . . yes. Of course. She was really upset. She called me and I went straight over.'

'You went to the house?' Sarah asked surprised. 'That day?'

'Yeah.'

'What time was that?'

She hesitated. 'Gosh. It's hard to remember now.'

'OK. Well . . . were the police still there?'

'They were still there next door, yes. It was all taped up outside. And someone was with my aunt when I got there. A witness support lady, I think it was.'

'A female officer?'

'Yes. She asked if I could stay with my aunt and I said I could, so she left. My aunt was very quiet and I even thought about calling the doctor. She was in shock, as you would imagine. It was pretty awful for her, seeing the woman's body, and . . . well, it was terrible, wasn't it? What he did to her?'

Sarah paused. 'Sandra, I need to tell you . . . I'm Jamie Clarke's solicitor.'

'The guy they convicted?'

'Yes. The guy they convicted. I've been working on lodging an appeal.'

Sandra didn't speak for a moment and Sarah felt the tension creep into her neck.

'So you don't think he did it?'

'Well, that's what I'm trying to find out and I'd really appreciate your help. Anything you can think of. Anything you can remember, no matter how irrelevant it might seem.'

Sandra breathed heavily into the phone. 'You know, I did always wonder about the fact that he could have been out so much sooner if he had just admitted it.'

'Right,' Sarah agreed.

'And the way he looked.'

'The way he looked? You mean on the news?'

'No. I mean . . . in real life.'

'You met him?'

'Well, just over the fence. You know, when me and Aunt Bee were in the garden.'

'You saw him in Christy's garden?'

'A couple of times, yes.'

'Did you speak to him?'

'Once or twice.'

'What did you say?'

'Oh, just pleasantries, you know, about the weather or the garden. He seemed to be a bit handy with the plants.'

'You saw him . . . gardening?'

'Well, not exactly, but they were stood by the flower bed one time and they were talking and he seemed fairly knowledgeable.'

'You saw them together?' Sarah breathed in sharply.

'Well, yes. Once or twice.'

'What were they like? Together, I mean.'

'They seemed happy.'

'What makes you say that?'

'Well, you know the way it is with a new couple,' she said. 'You can kind of tell it's new. They have a kind of energy around them.'

'They seemed like a couple?'

'Well . . . yeah. They did.'

Sarah knew she had to ask open questions and not lead the witness. 'Could that energy have been because she was afraid of him?'

'It's hard to say, but I don't think so.' Sandra paused. 'We heard them laughing a lot.'

'Laughing?' Sarah repeated.

'Well. Yes. She often had her back door open and you could hear them inside the house. Whenever he was there, she seemed happy. There was nothing that made me think otherwise and I remember being shocked when I found out who they had arrested. I didn't realise until later that day that it was him. A couple of days afterwards, when they'd charged him, the news came on and his face flashed up and I turned to my aunt and made a face, as if to say that I couldn't believe it, and she looked back at me and then she shook her head and tutted. I couldn't believe he could do that to a woman, and neither could she.'

'Did you tell the police any of this?'

'My aunt did.'

'When? What did she say?'

'Just that she didn't believe he'd done it,' Sandra said. 'And that she didn't think it was in his character.'

'So why was there nothing about that in her statement? Your aunt was a key witness. Why didn't she mention this? Why wasn't she called to give live evidence at Jamie's trial?'

The line fell quiet and then Sandra said, 'I did wonder about that.'

'Did you ask her?'

A sigh. 'She clammed up when I tried. I wasn't there when the police took her statement and it was a month or so later when she said she didn't have to go to court, and that was that.'

'So, she never discussed it with you again?'

'No,' Sandra paused. 'But she seemed frightened. At the time, I assumed it was because of what had happened to the woman next door. I kept saying to her, "Bee, it's OK. They arrested him. He's in prison." But she didn't seem to be comforted by this.'

Sarah closed her eyes. 'And now?' she asked. 'What do you think about that now?'

'Well, like I said, I have wondered over the years, especially after he served his sentence and could have been let out. But . . . you don't know someone just by meeting them in the garden, do you? You hear about it all the time, about somebody seeming normal and then people finding out they've been living next to a psychopath. Even the wives and families of murderers say they had no idea.'

'Did you go to the trial?'

'I did, yes.'

'Did your aunt?'

'She didn't want to. She didn't want to be upset by the evidence.'

Sarah hesitated. 'Was that the only reason?'

'What do you mean?'

'Had someone pressured her not to go, do you think?'

There was a long pause, and then Sandra said, 'I'd never really thought about that, but I suppose it would explain a lot.'

Sarah put her phone down on the table and typed up the notes from the conversation she had just had, then closed her laptop and walked along the hallway to the living room and looked through the door. Will was on the sofa, wine glass in front of him, watching reruns of *QI* and laughing his head off. She smiled, then went softly upstairs and put her head round Ben's door. As she did so, he flipped over from one side to the other, his limbs heavy with sleep, his mouth ajar. She closed the door again and crept back downstairs to the kitchen. As she went, she ran through everything she had been told that day: Joe and Christy had been happy. Brenda had been frightened. Bella had been unsure. Phillipa had been raped.

And there was one man – one man – at the centre of it all.

49

The college campus was quiet as Eve drove in with Jake Stone, her union representative, whom she had invited over to her flat for a final conference before the meeting that morning with Iwan, Reena and Giles. For Eve's sake, and for the sake of the college, they'd decided to hold it before the students came back and Eve felt relieved that she'd managed to fly under the radar. But as she and Jake pulled into the car park outside the Law Faculty, she was surprised to see Iwan there, waiting for her.

'Hmm. Looks like we've got an escort,' she said.

'Really?' Jake frowned. 'That's a bit unnecessary. And anyway, I thought they were trying to keep this thing under wraps.'

But as they got closer, Eve could see by the expression on Iwan's face that there had been a development. He looked anxious, raising a limp hand in an approximation of a wave and then dropping it again.

Eve got out of the car first and walked over to meet him.

'Can you get rid of your rep?' he said under his breath.

'Why?' Eve said. 'What's going on?'

'I need to talk to you alone.'

'I thought we weren't supposed to do that?'

'I know, but . . .'

'Where are Giles and Reena?'

'They've gone. They left fifteen minutes ago.'

'Why?'

'I told them you couldn't make it.'

Eve looked hard at Iwan for a moment, then turned back to her rep, who was taking a briefcase out of the boot of his car. 'Jake, the meeting's been cancelled,' she called out. 'I'm so sorry to have wasted your time.'

'Yes. Really sorry,' Iwan echoed.

'No worries.' Jake shrugged. 'Do you want a lift home?'

'I'm fine,' Eve said. 'I'll walk.'

As soon as Jake had gone, she turned back to Iwan. 'What's going on?'

Iwan looked over his shoulder. 'Let's go inside.'

Eve followed him into the faculty building and into a conference room, where he shut the door and waved at a seat. Eve sat down.

Iwan pulled out the chair opposite and sank down onto it. 'I had another visit yesterday from the same detective—'

'DI Carver?' Eve interrupted.

He eyed her. 'Yeah.'

'Go on.'

'Well, the whole thing made me uncomfortable. He was supposed to have sent me the paperwork in time for this meeting, but – long story short – he had given me nothing and he was leaning on me to agree certain things as fact. I told him I would go where the evidence led me and I asked again for the statement from the student who had reported seeing Clarke on campus. He got stroppy, said he couldn't give it to me. I asked for her name and he wouldn't tell me, and then he said I was obstructing his investigation, so I asked to see his warrant card again.'

Eve felt a surge of adrenaline. 'Did he show you?'

He shook his head. 'Point-blank refused. Then he left.'

'And so?'

'And so . . . what?'

'What do you think?' Eve asked. 'About the so-called complaint. Joe being on campus. The bogus cop?'

Iwan sighed loudly and looked at the ceiling. 'Well, something's off, isn't it?'

'Yeah,' Eve agreed. 'Something's very off.'

'I'm sorry,' Iwan said. 'For not believing you. For not supporting you. But . . . here.' He fished in his pocket and pulled out a folded-up piece of paper. 'I took down his registration number.'

Eve took the piece of paper and opened it up. 'A black Lexus?'

Iwan nodded.

'With tinted windows?'

'Yeah.'

'Thank you. I'll give it to Joe's solicitor. She may know someone who can run a check.' Eve thought for a second. 'You're a solicitor, aren't you?'

'Yeah.'

'Do you have a practising certificate?'

'Yeah.' He nodded. 'I still do a bit of—'

'Could you help us?'

'How?'

'We have a witness who needs proofing.'

Iwan thought about this. 'Who?'

'Her name's Bella Duncan. I'm not going to lie to you, Iwan. She's the victim's daughter and she gave evidence against Joe originally. She's the only eyewitness to her mother's murder, but she now thinks she made a mistake.'

'You've spoken to her?'

'No,' Eve said quickly. 'No. We need someone independent to do that for all the reasons you're thinking . . .'

'Witness intimidation,' Iwan mused. 'Or perverting the course of justice.'

'Yes. And it especially shouldn't be me.' Eve flushed. 'But you're independent. You're the perfect person.'

'Shouldn't she be talking to the police?'

Eve raised an eyebrow. 'Look, Iwan. I don't know who this DI Carver really is, but I know you're wary too, or you wouldn't have taken down his reg. If you want to call 101 and check with Thames Valley Police, then be my guest, but I'll bet you a hundred quid they've never heard of him.'

Iwan swallowed and Eve could see she was getting through to him.

'If you don't talk to Bella Duncan,' she said, 'then Carver will, and he will definitely influence her. We need to get there first.'

50

Bella was in bed when her phone rang. It was a number she didn't recognise and she immediately felt her pulse quicken. Twice this week she had got a call from a withheld number where the person at the other end would say nothing, then just hang up. And then yesterday, she had seen that same black car again. It was parked outside the flats, just at the top of Pleshey Road, as she had come past on her way back from the shop. She had felt as though she was having a panic attack. She couldn't catch her breath and her heart was racing so fast she thought she was going to pass out.

She was supposed to have been at therapy this morning, but she had cancelled. She was too frightened to go out, and there was literally no one she could talk to. She and her dad weren't speaking, and Justin would just tell her she was imagining things. He would be angry that she hadn't gone to therapy and would accuse her of making excuses not to move on with her life.

As she pulled the covers up around her, a loud bleep sounded from her phone and the adrenaline soared through her, but then she realised that whoever had called had left a message. She picked up her phone with trembling fingers and dialled in to her voicemail. It was Dorothy, Jamie Clarke's mum. Bella almost cried with relief at the sound of her voice. 'Bella, love?' her voice said. 'I'm phoning to ask if I can give your phone number to a solicitor who is helping Jamie. I'm not sure if you are aware, but the police found out about you and him talking and unfortunately he has been sent back to prison. I know we shouldn't be speaking, but I wasn't sure if you knew this and anyway, the damage is already done and I need your help. Please can you call me when you get this message?'

Bella listened, feeling sick at the thought that Jamie had gone back to prison because of her. She couldn't believe how selfish she had been. Not only had she ruined his life twenty years ago, but now she had done it again.

She called Dorothy straight away.

'Of course,' she said. 'Please give the solicitor my number. And I'm so, so sorry.'

A moment later, her phone rang again. This time she picked up.

'Hello, Bella,' said a man's voice. 'My name's Iwan Raker. I work with Eve Shotton, who is Jamie Clarke's ... erm ... friend. We wondered if it would be possible for me to meet with you? I'm completely independent of the police and of Jamie himself and I won't try to influence you in any way, but I understand that you may have some information that would help Jamie's case. I could come to you today, if you like? Eve will come too and wait in the car while we talk.'

Bella felt overwhelmed with relief at the thought of

having a solicitor here in her flat, today, as well as a friend of Jamie's sitting outside in the car, keeping watch. She would tell the solicitor everything. He would know what to do. She agreed that they should drive up straight away. She immediately felt energised. She got out of bed and cleaned and hoovered the entire flat, then went to the bathroom and got undressed. She was still wet from the shower when there was a tapping sound at the front door. She was a little taken aback. The solicitor was early, she thought, but she didn't have her phone and couldn't see what time it was. She towelled herself off quicky and pulled on her dressing gown, then ran to answer it.

'Hi,' she said, opening the door a crack and peering through.

'Hello, Bella.' The man on the doorstep flashed a police warrant card at her. 'My name's Jon. I'm a detective from CID. I need to have a quick word with you. Can I come in?'

'Erm. Sure,' Bella said, wondering what this could be about. 'I just need to get dressed. Can you hold on a minute?'

'Don't worry about that,' he said, stepping towards her. 'This won't take long.'

Bella hesitated, then opened the door a little wider. Something didn't feel right, but she couldn't put a finger on it, so she stood back and let him in. He closed the door behind him, then scanned her face, her body, her legs. Bella pulled the cord of her dressing gown tight around her waist. His eyes came back up and met hers. 'OK, Bella. We need to talk.'

'I need to get dressed,' Bella said again.

'Like I said, this won't take long.' He held out a hand towards the living room. 'After you.'

Bella stood her ground, a knot of fear tightening inside her. 'I just want to get dressed first,' she said, trying to sound casual.

The detective peered past her down the hallway. Bella could see his eyes darting around. 'Sure,' he said, his gaze snapping back towards her. 'Go ahead. Get dressed.'

He didn't move. The bedroom was only a few short steps away and Bella didn't feel comfortable taking her clothes off with him standing almost outside. She knew this wasn't paranoia. She could feel her legs beginning to tremble the same way they did in her dreams.

'The living room is just in there,' she said, pointing. 'You can take a seat.'

'That's OK,' he said. 'I'm good here. I'll wait for you.'

'I don't feel—'

'Bella. Come on now. Stop messing around.' He took hold of one arm, steered her into the lounge and lowered her onto the sofa. 'Nice place you've got here,' he said, pacing around the room and peering out of the window. 'Where's your phone?'

'In the bedroom.'

He nodded, walked over and closed the door.

'Now,' he said softly. 'I want to make a few things clear to you. Jamie Clarke's in prison. He killed your mother. He needs to stay there, and you, Bella . . . you need to keep your mouth shut. Have you got that?'

Bella stared at him, unable to speak. Everything was starting to feel distant, as if she was trapped in one of her nightmares.

'Are we clear?' he said.

Bella gazed back at him, taking in his jawline, his beady black eyes, the curl of his lip. 'I know you,' she said, finally.

He frowned and waited, arms crossed.

'It's you,' she gasped. 'You're the man on the stairs.'

A slow, mocking smile.

'You're the man in the kitchen,' she whispered. 'You killed my mum.'

'Oh, Bella.' He rolled his eyes in a cartoonish way, as if he thought she had made a bad joke.

Bella looked at the door, feeling a punch of adrenaline rising up inside her.

'Go on,' he said. 'If you think it's me, then run.'

She started to get up, but then he was there, grabbing her by the throat and throwing her back down onto the sofa. A second later, he had got her into a headlock and dragged her to the floor.

Bella grabbed hold of his hands, tugging hard at them and trying to release his grip. It was then that she felt the blow to the side of her head, followed swiftly by a second one to the face. Stunned, she dropped back onto the ground. She could feel blood streaming from her nose. She lifted a hand to touch it, and then felt the cord of her dressing gown being untied.

'No!' she screamed, kicking out wildly.

And then he was on top of her, grabbing her hands and pinning her to the ground. He had hold of her dressing-gown cord and, in one swift movement, had looped it under her head and tightened it around her neck. A cloth was forced into her mouth.

'Are you going to behave yourself, Bella?' he asked her, unbuckling his belt.

The Stranger on the Stairs

Bella screamed the silent scream that haunted her nightmares, and then his weight was pressing her to the ground, and she was stuck and everything was dark, and Bella knew without a shadow of a doubt that what had happened to her mother was going to happen to her.

51

Eve and Iwan pulled into Bella's estate and parked next to a block of flats. The satnav told them they had reached their destination and they made their way to the entrance, where they could see they had the right block. The door to the building was open, and so they went in. As they made their way up the stairs, one of the residents opened their door.

'There's something going on up there,' she said, looking frightened. 'The flat above me. There's been loud banging for a few minutes now. It sounds as if there's a fight going on.'

'Who lives there?' Eve said, sharply.

'It's young Bella, my neighbour. Sounds like her fella's hitting on her, but he's not the type and I've never heard it before, so I didn't know whether to call the police—'

'Call them!' Eve hissed, then she grabbed the handrail and raced up the stairs, with Iwan hot on her heels.

There were only two flats on the first floor and Eve could hear sounds coming from the nearest one. She banged on the door, then peered through the frosted glass, but all she could see was a hallway that ran into darkness. She banged again, and then Iwan took her arm and moved her aside. He lifted his leg and kicked hard with the flat of his foot. The door rattled. He did it again and again, and then to Eve's surprise, the door flew open and a man lunged past them. In a flash, Iwan caught hold of him in a bear grip while Eve moved in from the side. The three of them grappled for a moment, and as she clung on, Eve could see that the man was DI Carver.

'Hold on to him, Iwan!' she cried out. 'Keep hold of him, just for a moment longer.' And then she let go, pushed Carver's head back, grabbed hold of his face and scraped her fingernails down his cheeks as hard as she could.

'Bitch!' he screamed out. He grabbed Eve by the arms and threw her hard against the handrail, then shook free from Iwan's grasp and flew – almost fell – down the stairs in his race to get away. Iwan sprinted after him.

Eve, meanwhile, ran into the flat and along the hallway to the living room, where a woman in a dressing gown was on the floor, curled up into a ball, crying, her hands taped together and a piece of rag in her mouth.

'Bella?' Eve said.

The woman turned her head and nodded. Eve sank down beside her and took the piece of cloth from her mouth, then said, 'You're safe now, my love. You're safe. I'm Eve. I'm Joe's girlfriend. The police are on their way.'

'Where is he?' Bella sobbed. 'Has he gone?'

Eve nodded. 'Yes. He's gone. He's not in your flat any more, I promise. Is that cord round your throat hurting you?'

'No.'

'The tape round your wrists?'

'No.'

'Then leave everything just as it is for now, if you can, just until the police get here.'

'OK,' Bella agreed.

Eve helped Bella up and walked her to the sofa. Iwan came back a few minutes later with the police. The room was filling up. A paramedic sat down next to Bella.

Eve stood up. 'My name's Eve Shotton,' she said to an officer. 'I scratched the man who did this. I need you to bag my hands.'

The police took her to one side and began to do as she had asked.

She turned to Iwan. 'Did he get away?'

He nodded. 'Unfortunately. His car was outside.'

'The black Lexus?'

'Yes.'

'He can't get far, surely?'

'I hope not.'

Eve heaved a sigh. 'I think we got our evidence, Iwan.'

52

Sarah stared at the ceiling for a moment, then lifted the phone to her ear.

'Are you still there?' Robyn asked.

'Yes. Yes, I'm still here,' Sarah said, her voice a whisper. 'OK, so he's done a runner, but this is good, right? Once they get him into custody, they'll be able to take his DNA and match it – not only to the samples from Eve's hands, but also to the samples from Christy's clothing.'

A pause. 'That's the hope.'

'So how close are they to finding him?'

'I don't know.' Robyn sighed. 'They've run a check on the Lexus. It's a hire car, paid for in cash. The likelihood is that he will have got a different one by now and—'

Sarah's heart sank again. 'You think he's left the country?'

'I just don't know. It all depends on—'

'On who is protecting him?'

'Or protecting themselves. Let's face it, he's an embarrassment. And mistakes were made in Christy's case. Regardless of whether the evidence was deliberately lost or not, there has to be a strong interest in shutting him up.'

Sarah thought about this. 'And if he helped to convict the wrong man, they won't want the truth to emerge. They will be doing whatever they can to cover it up.' She paused, thinking. 'Maybe he'll just end his own life. A bent copper in prison – that's not going to be an easy prospect to face.'

Robyn didn't argue.

'And meanwhile,' Sarah continued, sighing, 'we have samples but no DNA profile to match them with, and Joe is still in prison.'

'You might have enough for your application to the CCRC.'

'I'm not sure. I think the CCRC are going to want more than Bella's new evidence, and the attack on her doesn't automatically take us to the attack on Christy. Everything points to Mitchell, but it's all circumstantial. We need that forensic connection.'

'So, what do you suggest?'

Sarah closed her eyes. 'There's a way,' she murmured. 'A way to find out.'

'Find out what?'

'If any of the samples in the lab came from Todd Mitchell.'

Sarah heard a pause. 'How?'

'Phillipa has a son. She said he's Todd's.'

Silence. 'You're kidding.'

'So, if that's true, they're going to share half their DNA.'

53

It was quiet on the legal visits wing at Bullingdon prison and Sarah could feel the stillness in the air as she sat at the table, opposite Joe.

'So, what do you think?' she pressed him.

'Why do you need my permission?' he asked.

'Because you're my client and it's up to you how I run your case.'

He heaved a sigh. 'You want *me* to decide whether we should blow up the life of a nineteen-year-old kid?'

'I know. It's a tough one. And what we have already may be enough to cast doubt on your conviction – which is all we have to do, of course. We have Bella's evidence that Mitchell attacked her in order to shut her up, and Eve and Iwan's evidence that they arrived just in the nick of time to stop him from raping her, which may be enough to convince the Court of Appeal that this was connected to her mother's rape and murder . . . but it still won't be enough to get you into that "for sure" territory that's needed.'

'For what?'

'To clear your name. To fully clear your name. And to get you compensation for everything you've been through.' She hesitated and Joe's eyes flickered to meet hers. 'The burden of proof in a criminal case is on the prosecution to prove you're guilty,' she explained, 'and if there's any doubt, that has to be exercised in your favour. But, in 2014, the Lord Chancellor of the day decided to switch that burden around for anyone trying to claim compensation for a wrongful conviction, and so it will be for us to show that it definitely *wasn't* you who killed Christy – and we won't be able to do that without the forensic link. But it's not just about getting compensation, Joe. What we have amounts to speculation, and unless Mitchell pitches up in custody and they take his DNA and we get a match, we won't legitimately be able to point the finger at him or anyone else. We will only be able to tell the judges – and the rest of the world – that they can't be sure it was you.'

Joe nodded, then sat back in his chair and raised his arms, linking his fingers and putting them behind his head. Sarah could see him thinking hard.

'And it's a legitimate method, this . . .?'

'Familial DNA searching.'

'It will stand up in court?'

'If Robyn takes the sample, yes. It will have to be done by the police. Robyn's contact at the police lab says they can do it, and if we do get a match, I think the CCRC would have to listen.'

Joe thought about this. 'Could he have contaminated the

evidence somehow? Left his DNA on Christy's body when he got to the crime scene?'

Sarah shook her head. 'The forensics people say not. He would have had to leave blood or saliva.'

'What if he says he tried to resuscitate her?'

'It doesn't provide the same kind of cellular material. And besides, they ran some tests. The first set of results confirmed the finding that there was this unknown male profile on her top, but they also found a hair root under her right-hand middle fingernail.'

'Christy grabbed him by the back of the head?'

'That's what we're thinking.'

'And that explains the three broken fingers.'

Sarah nodded. 'It all fits.'

'So what does he know?' he asked. 'This kid?'

'Harley. His name's Harley.'

'Harley,' he repeated, nodding.

'He knows his mum was a drug user and that she couldn't look after him. He knows he was taken into care when he was two months old and adopted four months later.'

'And he has no idea who his dad is?'

'No. When she signed the adoption papers, Phillipa claimed not to know. With good reason, of course.'

'Has he ever tried to find out?'

'I don't know. But Robyn has located the adoptive parents and she will ask all of these questions. They will be carefully prepped, as will Harley.'

'They'll have to tell him his dad is a rapist,' he murmured.

'I know.'

Joe looked up, his face flushed. 'Is this right? For us to do this to him? He's going to be traumatised.'

Sarah swallowed. 'OK. Let's take you out of the equation for a minute. What about Bella? Doesn't she deserve to know the truth about who killed her mother?'

He nodded. 'Of course she does.'

'And doesn't Christy deserve justice?'

He nodded again.

'Harley may even want to know his father.'

Joe's head shot up. 'Are you serious?'

Sarah shrugged. 'He will have a very big decision to make, and it will have to be *his* decision. And if he chooses *not* to help and not to know the answer, we will respect that. I'm not saying this isn't going to hurt other people, but at the very least, Harley will have a clearer picture of who he is and where he came from, and he will still have two adoptive parents who love him. But if we can get that forensic link to Christy, then not only will it be enough to take to the CCRC, but Robyn can jump above heads and take it to the chief of police, get extra resources into the manhunt for Mitch and, if he's still alive, get him safely behind bars.'

Joe thought about this. 'What's Harley doing? Is he at uni?'

'No. He's taken a gap year. He's just come back from travelling with friends and he's trying to decide what to do next. It's a good time.'

'A good time,' Joe repeated, then let out a heavy sigh.

'I understand,' Sarah said. 'I understand how you feel.'

Joe looked at her. 'Sarah, I had my life destroyed by the police, and I know how that's made me feel. I'm not going to tread on someone else to get what I need, especially not a young lad. I can't make this decision.'

Sarah nodded. 'OK.'

'But,' he said, 'I don't want to be responsible either for all the other people Mitchell has hurt, including Bella and Christy, and for the people he could go on to hurt. So you have my authority to run my case in whichever way you think is right.'

54

Harley's parents were called John and Elaine Truscott and they lived in Lyndhurst, in the New Forest. It was an hour's drive to their home from the Fleet services just off the M3, where Sarah and Robyn met the following Saturday. Sarah got out of her car and into Robyn's. It was a little sports car, an M3. It had been a hot afternoon and as they left the motorway, Robyn rolled the top down. The breeze was pleasant, the air filled with the scent of dank wood and grass. Sunlight glinted through the ancient oaks and pines that bordered the road. Beyond was mile upon mile of open heathland full of grazing wild ponies. Sarah's heart lifted as she thought about how much Ben would love to watch them. When this case was over, she would bring him here.

The Truscott family lived in a three-storey terraced townhouse just outside the town centre. John Truscott opened the door and stepped aside for them to enter, then held out his hand and shook theirs politely. Sarah couldn't help feeling her stomach twist as she noticed the pained but resolute look on his face. He pulled the door closed and led them up the stairs, past a small kitchen and into a living room, where his wife was waiting in an armchair. Sitting awkwardly on the sofa in the middle of the room was a young man in a blue football shirt and grey joggers. Next to him was an equally young girl with long brown hair.

Elaine Truscott leaped up quickly when they entered. 'Come in, come in,' she said, waving them through, then she nodded at the young man on the sofa and said, 'This is Harley.' She nodded at the young girl next to him. 'And this is his girlfriend, Grace.'

The pair on the sofa stood up and looked nervously at Robyn and Sarah, who moved further into the room at Elaine's request. 'Please have a seat,' she said. 'I'll put the kettle on.'

Everyone sat down, and Sarah smiled at Harley and Grace and looked around the room. There was some nice art on the walls, a pine dining table in the corner, a floor-to-ceiling window with a Juliet balcony visible outside. But her eyes soon fell back onto Harley. She could see Phillipa in him: the long dark lashes, the curly dark hair, the wide brown eyes and olive skin.

'OK,' Elaine said brightly, coming in with a tray of drinks. She placed it on the coffee table, nudging away a pile of magazines. She began to hand mugs to Harley, who got up and passed them around. Then she looked across the room at her husband, who nodded. She turned to her son. 'Over to you, love,' she said gently.

Harley sank back down onto the sofa, his knuckles white as

he clutched his girlfriend's hand. Sarah steeled herself for what was coming next.

'I don't want to do the test to find out if he's my dad,' he said, after a moment or two. 'I don't want to know him. Not if he did what you're saying. And if he didn't do it, then . . . well, I'm still not sure I want to know him, because he doesn't sound like a very nice person. But me and Grace . . .' He paused and looked at his girlfriend, who gave him a gentle smile. 'We think that if it helps other people, then I should do it. So, I've decided to take the test.'

He sounded decisive and the room fell still. Sarah felt for John and Elaine. This must be so hard for them. For almost all of his life, they had been Harley's parents – his only parents.

She waited for a moment, then leaned forward. 'Are you sure?' she asked, looking Harley in the eye.

Harley nodded and Sarah saw the look Grace gave him, one of pure love and adoration. It was a very sweet sight, and Sarah swallowed hard as it struck her, in one small moment of sadness, that as Ben's mother she was undoubtedly the only woman who would ever look at Ben that way. But she was very glad that this lovely girl was there on the sofa next to Harley, and that he had someone special to be there for him.

'Thank you,' she said to them both, as Robyn took the test kit out of her bag and began to take off the cellophane wrapper.

Harley turned to Sarah. 'I'd like to meet Phillipa, though,' he said. 'If she wants to meet me, that is.' He glanced at Elaine and shot her a warm smile. 'Not to replace my mum or anything, because that could never happen, but . . . just to know who she is. And because she doesn't deserve any of this. And just to help her. If it does. Help her, that is.'

Sarah inhaled deeply and thought to herself that she had no idea how Phillipa was going to react, but she knew that if Harley was her son, she would want to meet him. She said, 'I think it *will* help. And I think it's a great idea.'

55

The lab result came back on Monday morning. Robyn rang to tell Sarah the good news: the buccal swab taken from Harley had provided a partial match to the hair root underneath Christy's fingernail as well as to a bloodstain on her top. Robyn was now as sure as she needed to be to take this to the chief of police, and Sarah could make her application to the CCRC. But they both needed just one more thing.

Sarah went downstairs to find Will in the kitchen. Her heart was in knots, the energy inside her sitting tight as a ball of string.

'Will,' she breathed. 'Will. It's him. It's Mitchell. It's him.'

'They've arrested him?' Will dropped his piece of toast and jam onto his plate.

'No. Not yet. No,' Sarah said. 'But we've got the evidence we need to prove that he did it. He killed Christy. They took the swab from Harley and built a profile, then they uploaded it to the database and it was a partial match to the hair follicle and . . . and I need to get to Brixton.'

'Jesus, Sarah,' Will said, alarmed. 'I'm in Snaresbrook this morning. What about Ben?'

'It's fine,' Sarah said, kissing the top of his head. 'Don't worry. I'll drop him off at school on my way.'

Will thought for a minute. 'No. Go,' he said. 'Go now. Do what you need to do.' He grinned at Sarah, who was still hovering in the doorway. 'Go!'

'Thank you!' Sarah ran into the living room, where she hugged Ben and kissed him on the cheek. Ben gave her a shove, because that's what Ben did when people were too excited around him, and Sarah laughed and ran for the door.

She found Phillipa in the hostel. She was in the kitchen with another resident and a warden. Everyone turned to look at Sarah as she came in.

'Guess what?' Sarah grinned at her.

'No!' Phillipa said, stretching out the word and sliding back her chair. 'They haven't . . .?' She stopped short, glanced at the curious faces next to her, then stood up and ushered Sarah towards the door. 'Have they arrested him?' she whispered.

'No,' Sarah said. 'They're still looking for him. But . . .' She took a long, deep breath.

Phillipa was mad at first. She was mad that Sarah had talked to Robyn about her, and she was mad that Sarah and Robyn had gone together to meet Harley behind her back and had told him the truth about his father, and she was upset and angry about the possibility that Harley might want to meet him. Sarah understood. She understood it all. She walked, almost ran, trying to keep up with Phillipa as she marched staunchly through the backstreets north of Acre Lane. They passed through a housing estate, past a basketball court and some tennis courts and into a small playground, where Phillipa stopped on the grass by the swings, seemingly unsure where to go and what to do next. She began pacing back and forth for a moment, and then she stopped shouting at Sarah and fell quiet. She walked over to the swings and sat down on one of them, and Sarah sat on the swing beside her and Phillipa listened. She listened to the whole story and when Sarah told her that Harley had wanted to help put his father behind bars, and that he also wanted to meet her, she became tearful and said, 'He's a good lad. What a good lad.'

'He's your son,' Sarah said. 'He takes after you.'

Not him. The words hung silently in the air between them, and Sarah left them there.

'So,' Phillipa said, after a while. 'How do I go about it?'

Sarah felt her heart leap. 'You mean . . . ?'

'How do I make this statement? Do I have to walk into a police station, or what? Because I don't want no one seeing me and thinking I'm some kind of snitch.'

'No,' Sarah said quickly. 'No. Nothing like that. You don't need to do anything. Robyn will come to you. She'll meet you wherever you want. Just tell me where.'

Phillipa nodded, then said, 'Does he really want to see me?'

Sarah nodded. 'Yes. He really does.'

Phillipa looked doubtful. 'Did someone tell him he had to?'

'No,' Sarah insisted. 'No, of course not. It was all him. I could tell. He wants to get to know you.'

'They kept his name,' she said. She pushed the swing back and let it fall forward. 'Harley. I gave him that name.'

'I like it,' Sarah said.

'I hope his surname ain't Davidson,' Phillipa said with a small smile.

'No.' Sarah smiled back. 'It's Truscott.'

'Truscott,' Phillipa repeated. 'Harley Truscott.' She pursed her lips and nodded, as if she approved. Then she glanced at Sarah. 'What does he look like?'

'He's gorgeous,' Sarah said. 'He's the spit of you.'

'Really?'

Sarah nodded. 'Tall. Thin. Dark hair, like yours. Big brown eyes. A little tash.' Sarah drew a line underneath her nose.

'No!' Phillipa said, with a grin. 'Not a tash.'

'It's just a little one,' Sarah said. 'And he has a girlfriend,' she added.

'Aww. What's she like?'

'Lovely. They're very sweet together. I think they're in love.'

'Aww,' Phillipa said again.

'So, you want to meet him?'

She nodded. 'Yeah. I do.'

'Good. I think he'll like you.'

'You think?' Phillipa looked pleased.

'Of course.'

They swung in silence for a few minutes. Then Phillipa looked round at Sarah and said, 'Go on, then. Set it up.'

'The meeting?' Sarah asked. 'With Harley?'

Phillipa inhaled deeply, then said, 'And with Robyn. I get it. Continuity, I think you people call it.'

Sarah smiled. 'More like explanatory evidence. How Harley came to be Mitch's son. But justice for you, too, if you want it.'

Phillipa thought about this. 'Yeah,' she said finally. 'I think I do.'

56

Three weeks later

Bella was in the car, skirting Regent's Park along Albany Street, towards Camden, when she got the message.

They've got him!!!

She shot a glance at the screen of her phone, then swung a left at the lights and into the outer circle of the park at Gloucester Gate, heading towards the zoo. It was early evening, just getting dark, and the roads were emptying, but she wouldn't be able to process what she had read until she had stopped the car, and she knew there was a car park there. She found it, pulled in and turned off the ignition, then called Eve straight back.

'Todd Mitchell?' she asked. 'They've got him?'

'Yep!'

'Are you sure?'

'I'm positive. Sarah just called me.'

'How?' she asked. 'How did they catch him?'

'He turned up in a dumpster.'

'A *dumpster*?' Bella gasped. 'You mean . . . alive?'

'Alive but tied up and gagged and dumped out with the rubbish outside a factory in Maidstone.'

'Oh my God.' Bella drew a sharp intake of breath. 'Who did that to him?'

'The police think it was an organised crime group. They think he called in a favour or had something on them or . . . something. Anyway, the theory is that he went to them for help getting out of the country and they gave him shelter for a while and then turned on him.'

'Did they want him dead?'

'Maybe. Except that his phone went off grid soon after the attack on you, and then suddenly came back on. It was lying on a pile of rubbish next to him in the dumpster. So whoever did this was most probably having fun and games with him. He would have known he had until the battery died to be found alive.'

'Jesus.' Bella shuddered. 'He got lucky.'

'In a way. He might have been better off dead. Prison isn't going to be a whole lot of fun for him either. Prisoners don't like cops, and especially not bent cops who are rapists.'

'So where is he now?'

'He's in police custody. He'll go to court in the morning and from there to Wandsworth prison, Sarah thinks, where he will stay until his trial.'

'There'll be a trial?'

'Well, they'll have plenty of evidence against him.'

'Unless it gets lost again.'

'I don't think there's much chance of that this time. The chief of police, the press . . . the eyes of the world are on this now. And Sarah has the DNA match to Harley as insurance. I think we can safely say that Todd Mitchell will never hurt another woman again.'

They ended the call and Bella sat gazing into the distance for a few moments. Todd Mitchell had been found. He had been found alive and had been taken into police custody. She had never felt relief like it. She could finally breathe again. But as she switched her engine on and drove back home, she knew it wasn't over for her yet. She still had to come to terms with the colossal mistake she had made.

She was doing whatever she could to put it right. There were officers already being held accountable in Mitchell's absence. The force had already referred itself to the Independent Office of Police Complaints. There would be an inquiry into Mitchell's misconduct and into how he had managed to get away with what he had. Bella knew this, because the chief of police had asked her to be there, to give evidence. She would, of course.

The Blenheim Road witnesses would have to give evidence too, she had been told. Benfield and Norris would have to explain why they had lied about seeing Jamie on the evening of Christy's murder. They, too, would have been pressured or cajoled by Mitchell, no doubt. Eve had been confident that it would all come out.

Bella felt a strange combination of pain and elation at the thought of this. There would be justice for her mum. There would be justice for her. But there would also be justice for Jamie Clarke, who, right now, needed it the most.

57

The sun was high in the sky as Eve drove with Dorothy towards the prison. Eve had risen at five thirty, collected her from her house in Woking at seven thirty, and had then driven her all the way back to Oxfordshire – a three-and-a-half-hour round trip. It was already feeling like mid-afternoon instead of mid-morning, but Eve didn't mind. She hadn't wanted Dorothy to miss this moment. It was going to be a lovely surprise for Joe.

The traffic freed up as they left the M40 and headed into the countryside. The road to the prison was winding and quiet, the landscape flat. The hedgerows were uneven, one minute enclosing them in a corridor of trees, the next falling away and opening up onto fields full of sheep. Eve glanced across at Dorothy's bowed head and thought she was nodding off, but realised that instead she was lost in thought.

She turned back to the road, not wanting to intrude on the older woman's quiet contemplation, but she felt a lump in her throat as she thought about all this woman had been through. Her excitement at seeing her son walk free must be tinged with sadness, and anger, too, when she thought about all the years she had lost, all the pain and heartache she had endured. For Eve, it had been a matter of months. For this woman beside her, it had been twenty long years.

They met Sarah in the car park and walked towards the prison gates, waiting outside a block near the back of the prison for Joe to be processed. After several minutes, the door opened and he came out, holding a rucksack and a wad of papers in a plastic bag. He looked tired and slightly bewildered and overwhelmed, but his face lit up as he spotted his mother. He reached out and put his arms around her. He shook Sarah's hand before hugging her, too, then finally turned to Eve, took hold of her and folded her into his arms, holding her tight for several seconds, and Eve could tell he was unable to speak.

Eventually they broke away and he kissed the top of her head. 'Are you OK?' he asked her.

She nodded, trying not to cry. 'I'm OK,' she said. 'But there's someone who isn't, someone who wants to see you.'

Bella waited in the kitchen at 21 Norham Gardens. She had arrived early, but Chas had made her a cup of tea and was being kind to her, asking about her life and her plans. She answered his questions as best she could, all the while feeling anxious inside and peering up at the clock.

Finally, the back door opened and Eve and Joe were there

with Dorothy, the kitchen suddenly feeling full and busy with people. Bella looked on as Chas gave Joe a warm hug and told him he could stay as long as he needed. Joe thanked him and Chas grinned and said, 'Well, you haven't finished up on the loft yet, have you, mate?'

'Sorry—' Joe began, instinctively, and Chas shook his head and said jokingly, 'I don't know, going off the job and leaving it half finished.'

Eve, Joe and Chas laughed, and then they started to chatter all at once, about who wanted what to drink and eat and where all of Joe's things were.

Bella took a deep breath as she watched them together and wondered if she was already outstaying her welcome. She couldn't help thinking, suddenly, that she didn't belong here, that she shouldn't have come. But then Dorothy came over and put an arm around her, seeing she was upset, and Joe sat down opposite her and said, 'Hey, Bella. Good to see you. Are you OK?'

She shook her head, feeling the tears coming. 'I wanted to say how sorry I am,' she said. 'For what I did to you.'

'Hey,' he said gently, reaching out across the table but not quite touching her. 'I don't blame you.'

'How can you not?' she sobbed, her voice cracking and the words falling apart. She looked up as Eve passed her a piece of kitchen roll and she took it. 'I ruined your life,' she continued. '*I* would hate me.'

'I don't hate you,' he insisted. 'I never have. You were just a child. I knew someone had influenced you. It's what I've always believed.'

Bella wiped her eyes and gazed at him. 'I thought it was just a nightmare. The stranger on the stairs. If I had only faced up to it sooner—'

'Bella. Love,' he reassured her. 'You were just as much a pawn in all of it as me.'

'Except that I didn't spend the past twenty years in prison.'

This was unarguable, and he didn't try to minimise it.

'What was it like?' she asked, uncertainly.

His gaze held hers. 'Have you ever been sat on a bus and someone sits down next to you and you know instantly that they're not quite right, mentally?'

'Yes.' Bella nodded.

'Do you think up some reason why you need to change seats? Or do you get off at the next stop?'

'Probably just get off the bus.'

He nodded. 'Well, in prison, the majority of people are the scary person sitting next to you, except you can't change seats or get off the bus. Every day, you're on high alert, never knowing if you're going to look at someone the wrong way and have them come up behind you and slit your throat with a razor blade hidden inside a toothbrush.'

Bella nodded.

His mouth tightened. 'I somehow managed to dodge the razor blade, but nobody talks about the mental scars you're left with, the ones that accumulate after you're shut up in your cell each evening, having survived another day. Before it happened to me, I used to hear people talk about prison as if it's no great hardship because you get to have a TV in your cell, because you get three square meals and a roof over your head. But it's indescribable unless you've lived it. The horror, the fear . . . and the boredom. It's hard to imagine, I know, being bored and hypervigilant at the same time. It's not a good combination. It takes its toll over time.'

'I'm sorry,' Bella said, swallowing hard to control her tears. 'I'm so, so sorry. I can't begin to tell you—'

'It's not your fault,' he reassured her again. 'And if you hadn't listened to your instincts and found me, then Mitch would never have attacked you and he would never have gone on the run. You played your part in getting me out of there, Bella. For that, I will always be grateful.'

Bella really wasn't sure she had done very much. But as she drove home, she felt a wave of relief and lightness pass through her. She was definitely feeling better within herself.

It was a few more months before she realised that her nightmares had gone, or at least that she hadn't had one in months. She occasionally dreamed about coming down the stairs, but the dream was different now. It felt sad but not frightening, and when she woke up, she no longer felt rigid and petrified.

She talked about everything with Adele and realised that she had started to feel excited about the future. She planned to go abroad – the first stop would be Nepal – and when she got back she was thinking of returning to art college to study illustration. When she had told her dad, he had offered to support her financially – he had some money put aside, he said. With Adele's help, Bella had come to realise that there was more than one way to love someone and that he was doing his best. She realised that it was time to forgive him and accept him for the person he was.

She left on a sunny afternoon in mid-August. Justin took her to the airport. He told her he would wait for her, and Bella said that they shouldn't make each other any promises. It was time for everyone to live their own, authentic life.

58

One year later

The cameras flashed and clicked as Joe, flanked by Eve and Sarah, crossed the Strand towards the entrance to the Royal Courts of Justice. There were crews everywhere, hundreds of them spread across the pavements, some standing, some sitting cross-legged, holding out sound equipment. Eve felt Joe's hand reach for hers and grip it tightly. She knew the significance of this moment, but she also knew how hard he would find it to be in the spotlight like this. She, too, was a little wary at the thought of being tomorrow's front-page news.

Inside, they filed into their seats in the public gallery and were soon joined by Bella – who was just back from travelling – and Phillipa and Dorothy. Sarah pointed out Harley and Grace, who were sitting in the row behind, and they exchanged smiles. Eve noticed how Phillipa's face lit up as she looked at her son. The barristers stood together and spoke in hushed tones for a few moments, and then the judges came in.

The hearing began. Joe's barrister stood up and opened the case. Eve had met him and knew he was Sarah's partner. He spoke eloquently about the historic injustice, the unsafe conviction, the deplorable disclosure failures by the police, which had undermined any prospect of a fair trial. The barrister for the police had little to say and Joe was told by the judge that his appeal was allowed, that he was finally a free man, no longer subject to the conditions of his licence. His conviction had been overturned.

Eve turned to Joe, who flung his arms around her. Outside on the steps, the cameras clicked and flashed a second time as Joe spoke briefly to the press and the world to tell them what it was like to have spent twenty years being ignored and overlooked by the very institutions that were meant to have searched for the truth.

'The police did this to me,' he said. 'The CCRC did this to me. And I'm here to say to them: you need to do better. Because I'm not the only one this has happened to.'

And then he turned to Bella, seeking her out and asking her to come and stand next to him. Hundreds of faces all turned towards her as she smiled shyly and stepped forward.

'It was not just me who was denied justice,' Joe told her as more flashbulbs went off. 'And what happened to me was not your fault. You are a courageous young woman who was manipulated by the police when you were just a child. But you saw a glimpse of the truth and you looked hard to find it. Your mother would be proud of you, as am I.'

There was a lot of clapping and cheering. Eve felt as if she could burst with pride. The wheels of justice had certainly turned slowly, she thought. But history had been made. It was a day they would never forget.

She turned and took Joe's hand, and they walked across the street and headed south towards Will's chambers to drink champagne and celebrate the start of their new life together.

BBC NEWS

England | Local News | London

Christy Nicholls murder: Todd Mitchell given whole life sentence

30 January 2025

A police officer who raped and murdered young mother Christy Nicholls in her home in 2003 has been sentenced to a whole-life prison term.

Todd Mitchell used his position as a police officer to attack the 33-year-old during routine house-to-house inquiries pertaining to an unconnected burglary in the same street.

During the sentencing, the judge described the crimes committed by Mitchell as 'sickening, tragic and devastating for all of his victims'.

Mitchell was already serving two life sentences for the assault and attempted rape of a 27-year-old woman in June last year and a further historic rape on another victim in 2003, which resulted in an unplanned pregnancy. He also pleaded guilty to two counts of perverting the course of justice.

The Old Bailey sentencing hearing heard how Mitchell had used a deceased colleague's police-issue warrant card to conceal his identity when gaining entry to the home of his most recent victim and had used coercive tactics to prevent himself from being apprehended. They also heard how the offence against Ms Nicholls involved a 20-year cover-up, during which time another man was wrongly convicted for Mitchell's crimes.

Addressing reporters outside the Old Bailey following his sentencing, Chief of Police Jo Constantin said she recognised the damage done by Mitchell, who had brought shame on his profession. Describing him as a 'coward hiding behind a badge', she said his crimes were 'a betrayal of his colleagues as well as his victims'. Ms Constantin said she believed there may be more victims and urged others to come forward.

The judge told 47-year-old Mitchell: 'Notwithstanding your guilty pleas, I have seen no evidence of genuine contrition on your part. You are a serving police officer who not only allowed the wrong man to go to prison but actively obstructed the investigation and tampered with the evidence to ensure that this was the outcome. You recently attempted to silence a key witness in the case by carrying out a similar attack on her, which no doubt would have ended in her rape and death had she not been rescued by Ms Shotton and Mr Raker.' Eve Shotton and Iwan Raker are legal representatives of the wrongly convicted man.

The Stranger on the Stairs

The majority of offenders convicted of a single count of murder are given a life sentence with a minimum term. A whole-life order is reserved for a small minority of the very worst offenders for whom life will mean the rest of their lives.

Lord Justice Higbee said the seriousness of the case made it 'exceptional' and that he was using his discretion to make a whole-life order.

This means that Mitchell will never be released.

Epilogue

Eve and Joe walk hand in hand along the bridleway that leads to the tiny village they have fallen in love in with, towards the house they have fallen in love with. It's a fabulous three-bedroomed property on a large plot, with two separate barns that are ripe for conversion, Joe says. One will be his workshop, the other a separate annexe for his mum, who has already sold her house in Woking and moved into 21 Norham Gardens, where she has temporarily replaced Joe as caretaker. Chas is abroad again for a few months, and so Dorothy will stay there until the annexe is ready for her to move into.

The house itself needs work, too, and isn't quite as Eve and Joe would like it, but it already feels like home to Eve. The kitchen is much like the one at 21 Norham Gardens – imperfect but somehow warm and familiar. There is a study for Eve and a lovely sunroom overlooking the garden, and the sitting room has a charming open fireplace, perfect for the cosy evenings she and Joe share together, now that the nights have drawn in.

But today there is plenty of daylight left after their walk up the track to the next village, where there is an eighteenth-century house with beautiful gardens and a tea shop. They have spent a nice hour or two walking, drinking tea and eating cake. Now they are on their way back and they are discussing their plans for the following day. They need to be at the airport by eleven, so they will be getting an early night.

Inside the house, Eve slips up the stairs to take one last look at her wedding dress before she folds it carefully and puts it in her suitcase. She and Joe will be getting married on the beach in Mexico in two days' time – just the two of them. She knows Sascha will be upset at missing out, as will Mackenzie, but this is the way she and Joe want it to be.

On the way back down, she pops her head into the room that will be her study when she returns. She has decided to stop teaching and work from home for the charity TFJ instead. She will fundraise and work on cases and divide her time between this and helping Joe with the renovations. She feels a wave of excitement wash through her every time she thinks about it.

She looks in on Joe, who is making dinner in the kitchen. She studies his face. She is conscious all the time of the damage that has been done to him. People don't see it immediately, but it's there and she knows he may never mend completely. Later, they will lie in bed and talk for a while, heads together, or maybe he will want to be silent. Whatever he chooses, Eve stays nearby. He likes her to be there in the house somewhere and she recognises his need for her presence as what it is. It is the fear of losing what he has, all over again.

Eve knows that this is the way trauma works. She knows

THE STRANGER ON THE STAIRS

that we expect what happened yesterday to happen tomorrow. She doesn't know how many more tomorrows it will take and whether there will ever be enough of them to reverse twenty years of hurt. But she doesn't mind. She really doesn't. She has everything she needs.

Author's Note

The Stranger on the Stairs is not a true story, but it was inspired by true events. I took my inspiration from one real-life case in particular and found echoes in several more. Disclosure failures are the biggest cause of miscarriage of justice in the UK, and over the past twenty-two years since I qualified as a criminal defence solicitor, I have repeatedly experienced the same frustrations that Sarah does. The system is not set up to support the many lawyers and innocence projects who care, and, in fact, it took the ITV dramatisation of one recent miscarriage of justice (check out *Mr Bates vs The Post Office* if you haven't done so already) to ignite public outrage and get justice for its victims. But the victims of this scandal are by no means the only ones.

As I write, the CCRC is being overhauled after an investigation was launched into its failings. I hope that a new era will begin that will allow better access to justice for those who have been wrongfully convicted. This won't, however, address the root cause of most wrongful convictions, which is that defence lawyers don't have the same resources at their disposal, nor do they have the same investigatory powers that the police and statutory bodies (such as the CCRC) possess but can choose not to use. This inequality of arms is acknowledged, and as such, prosecution lawyers are supposed to 'play nice' and share any information that is not of use to them and which might help the defence, for instance a witness statement or piece of forensic evidence that points away from the defendant. The problem is that the police and CPS themselves are the arbiters of what should or shouldn't be disclosed, and the disclosure rules in the UK make it extremely hard for lawyers to get access to all the evidence that exists in order to make their own judgement about what might be helpful.

No single police force is intended to be depicted in *The Stranger on the Stairs*; the issues raised are national ones and inefficiency in the UK criminal justice system is endemic. The problems are in large part due to twenty years of funding cuts; however, defence lawyers undergo an additional layer of difficulties for the reasons I've mentioned.

I haven't yet got Toby Jones lined up for a TV adaptation, but my aim in this and in all my books is to bring these kinds of issues to light, and also to show the good work that many defence lawyers are doing. As those who have heard me speak at events will know, I do not feel that we are well represented on TV or, indeed, in the press. That said, something like 13.5 million people tuned in to watch *Mr Bates*, and the reaction shows that people really do care. I am propelled on and encouraged by this, and this brings me to the people who cared enough to help me bring this story to life . . .

Acknowledgements

Thanks as ever to my editor, Selina Walker, and to the wonderful team at Century. As I said to you in the summer, Selina, you really do have the crème de la crème of brilliant people working alongside you and I know they will all be named on the next pages, but suffice to say you are all amazing and incredibly talented. To my agent, Judith Murray, and the team at Greene and Heaton – a big thank you, too, for all you do!

To the experts . . . A massive thank you to Sam Dulieu of the Future Justice Project for the hugely helpful conversation about the CCRC and Court of Appeal, and for all the good work you are doing. To my colleague and boss James Turner at Tuckers Solicitors and to my former colleague Tim Brown for your expert knowledge of the law and for the helpful discussions about child and vulnerable witnesses. To Clare Reynolds, who specialises in prison law at Tuckers, and to Nicky Padfield, Emeritus Professor of Criminal and Penal Justice at the University of Cambridge, for answering my questions about life licence conditions, parole and recalls to prison. Clare,

Acknowledgements

you were so great at answering my multitude of questions as I wrote. Thank you so much. Huge thanks to forensics experts Nigel Cook and Orla Sower for answering my questions about DNA and crime scenes and for being so interesting to talk to. Also to fellow author and former police detective and commander Graham Bartlett for help with this too. As always, I believe everything that happens in this story to be factually and procedurally accurate, but any remaining errors are mine and not theirs.

I am hugely grateful as always to my small team of early readers – Ian Astbury, Simon Kingston and Tara Kaby – for helping me to see what is working and what isn't. Thanks also to Amy Eastham, Karen Draisey and to fellow writers and friends Helen Solomon, Tim Logan and Lisa Howells, who all gave me some niche nuggets of advice about certain aspects of the story.

A shout-out to Pete at 2 North Parade produce store, Oxford. Pete is the only character in this story who is real – and so, of course, he doesn't know Joe or Eve.

Thank you to my friend Stef Hughes for the Stefanisms and for getting me into criminal defence work in the first place. I have a strong belief that people come into our lives at the right time for the right reason, and little did I know when we met in 1996 – two legal secretaries temping at the same law firm in Swansea – that as well as making a lovely new friend, meeting you was going to be the catalyst for the path I am now on.

To you all – the fabulous readers, bookstagrammers, booksellers, librarians and fellow authors who have given me such warm and enthusiastic reviews and quotes, and who have made

Acknowledgements

my day so many times over with a post, story or message on social media: you rock!

Thank you to my lovely family and friends for being so enthusiastic and for telling all their friends about my books and for buying them as presents and for cheering me on.

And last but by no means least, I couldn't have written this book without the support of my husband, Mark.

Bringing a book from manuscript to what you are reading is a team effort, and Penguin Random House would like to thank everyone at Century who helped to publish *The Stranger on the Stairs*.

PUBLISHER
Selina Walker

EDITORIAL
Joanna Taylor
Mary Karayel
Caroline Johnson
Sally Sargeant

DESIGN
Glenn O'Neill

PRODUCTION
Helen Wynn-Smith

INVENTORY
Lizzy Moyes

UK SALES
Alice Gomer
Emily Harvey
Kirsten Greenwood
Phoenix Curland
Rhian Steer

INTERNATIONAL SALES
Caroline Newbury
Sophie Agnew

PUBLICITY
Lily Capewell

MARKETING
Lucy Hall

AUDIO
James Keyte
Meredith Benson

Discover more from *Sunday Times* bestselling author Ruth Mancini

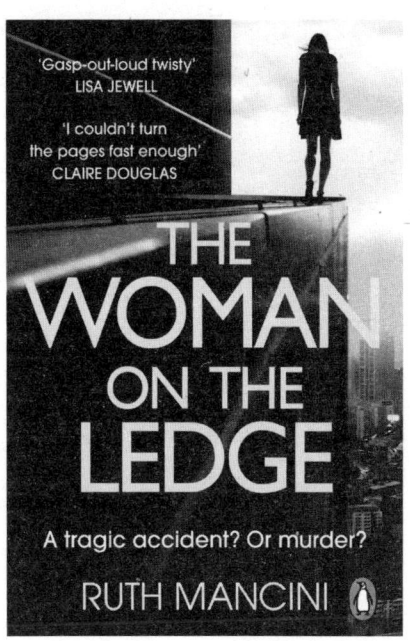

'Jaw-dropping. Absolutely outstanding'
Andrea Mara

A woman plunges to her death from a London bank's rooftop.

You're arrested for her murder, but you swear you tried to save her.

The police don't believe you. Even your lawyer has doubts.

You're hiding something – but who are you protecting, and why?

'Smart, twisty and propulsive'
Harriet Tyce

Lauren escapes to a Spanish seaside town, hoping to leave her past behind.

Hope's perfect life shatters when her baby, Sam, disappears.

Then a woman in Spain is found with a child matching Sam's description.

But Lauren is insisting Sam is her baby.

One child. Two mothers. And a past that won't let them go.